CLAIM TO FAME

CLAIM TO FAME

William H. Appelman

Carroll & Graf Publishers, Inc.
New York

Copyright © 1993 by William H. Appelman

All rights reserved

First Carroll & Graf edition 1993

Carroll & Graf Publishers, Inc.
260 Fifth Avenue
New York, NY 10001

Library of Congress Cataloging-in-Publication Data

Appelman, William H.
    Claim to fame / William H. Appelman. — 1st Carroll & Graf ed.
       p.   cm.
    ISBN 0-88184-935-9 : $19.95
    1. Hollywood (Los Angeles, Calif.)—Fiction. I. Title.
PS3551.P5575C57   1993
813'.54—dc20   92-47586
                                                   CIP

Manufactured in the United States of America

This book is for R.V.

Like Prometheus, they will chain you to a rock, where the memory of your own greatness will gnaw at you.
—Napoleon

Chapter One

Hollywood

The motel appeared to be air-brushed against the slick neon and night sky. On either side, low buildings housing porn shops, storefront churches serving as soup kitchens, clothing and collectibles-of-the-future shops paneled the wide boulevard. Lewis Rosenthal maneuvered the seesawing slab of his large black car off the road onto the badly pitted lot and pulled up to the small office.

Miraculously a large majestic palm tree, well out of proportion to the row of units, thrived just outside the entrance, its bark sadly displaying the autographs of Hollywood losers. Lewis looked up at its crown swaying wildly like a cluster of plumes, inviting the vaporous rain to film his face. Behind him, car wheels shrieked at each other, blotting out equally strident human sounds. He put his fingers around the vial in his pocket and entered.

The desk clerk appeared to be reading the same newspaper each time Rosenthal had come to the motel. The man's eyes seemed stitched together as he peered between the crusty lids, his eyebrows flickering infinitesimally in recognition. Without looking, he reached behind him and produced the key to cabin

9

nine, grinning at Lewis in acknowledgment of his act, as though it were a trick.

"Thanks," Lewis muttered, flattening a hundred-dollar bill on the counter. "I'll leave the key in the door when I'm finished."

The man produced a toothpick from inside his mouth and began manipulating it over the stubble around his lips. "We changed the movies," he said as Lewis walked out. "Have a good evening."

The door to cabin nine opened at his touch before Lewis could insert the key. He saw the familiar bareness, the stained chenille bedspread, the blond-wood headboard and matching dresser, the frameless mirror above it. In spite of the damp chill outside, the room was stifling with a vaguely unpleasant smell.

He walked to the far end, containing a counter with an inset sink, two small bars of soap, and a pair of paper-covered plastic glasses. He took one and placed it on the night table. Within minutes he was standing alongside the bed in his shorts, struggling with the tax stamp on the neck of the scotch bottle he'd brought in his case. The sight of himself fidgeting with it played back to him in the mirror.

He sat on the edge of the bed, which felt like a cardboard box filled with newspaper, and looked down at the black rotary phone. He reached for the fat, scarred wallet in his pants and removed a slip of paper identified by the initials S.H. Then he dialed.

"Hi, this is Chip." The voice was pleasant, although the words sounded scripted.

"It's Lewis."

"Lew . . . oh, hi, how's it going?"

Lewis shut his eyes, pursed his lips, and shook his head.

"Lewis . . . ?"

"Yes, I'm here; how's it going with you?"

"Swell. Anything you'd like to talk about?"

Again Lewis shook his head. "I'm feeling very inadequate. Very inadequate. I'm feeling I must take responsibility for all my mistakes . . ."

"Really."

"And see to it that I don't make any more."

"And how do you propose to do that?"

Lewis's eyes squeezed closed. "How do you think?" Silence, then Lewis heard what sounded like a muted sigh at the other end.

"How many times have we had this conversation, Lewis?"

"I don't know. Don't you keep records?"

"Yes. Give me a second." Lewis waited, looking up at a textured print of a busy Parisian intersection above the bed. The street was wet and reflected the colorful long dresses of turn-of-the-century women smiling and bustling about under dome-shaped umbrellas. "This is your sixth urgent call in three weeks." A chuckle punctuated the statement.

"Is that unusual?"

"There's no usual. Sometimes someone calls once and we never hear from him again. That could mean anything; either we lost him or we helped. Sometimes people just want attention, but you can't take chances. As far as we're concerned, they're always serious."

"And do I seem serious to you, really?"

"What happened today? Where are you calling from?" Suddenly the voice was officious.

"Same place: my home away from home." Lewis put his legs up on the chenille. "What happened? I messed up; what else is new?"

"Now, now. You're getting sanctimonious."

Lewis looked in the earpiece. The young man's choice of words struck him as inappropriate. Not rude; simply inaccurate. "I'm sorry. I fucked up."

"Come on. Think, man. Maybe you're just being tough on yourself."

"If not me, who else?" Again the muted sigh. "I'm sorry. Again, you're right. I am sanctimonious. Maybe I should just take two aspirins and go to sleep."

"Keep talking. By the way, what kind of pills *do* you have on you?"

"On me? Nothing. In fact, I'm lying here in all my fat hairy glory. It's quite a sight."

There was a stifled sneeze at the other end. Without thinking, Lewis's hand drew the soiled spread over his groin.

"You don't feel comfortable with your body?" the telephone asked with a nasal inflection.

"There, you've made me smile. That's a good one; comfortable with my body? It's a mess."

"Is that your opinion or did someone tell you that?"

"It's something I figured out all by myself. About the time I started growing tits and my stomach melted into a rhino's ass." He shook his head as he remembered his mother doing when he was very young and she was impatient with him. "But my body is not really the problem."

"Of course not. Your sense of inadequacy is a lot more complicated."

Lewis looked at the receiver indignantly. "Is that a warranted comment?"

"Lewis, let's stop pussyfooting around. Anyone who wants to kill himself regularly isn't feeling too great about himself."

Touché. The man had made an inarguable point. "You know, my friend, this place I'm calling from, I think it would drive a lot of people to suicidal thoughts."

"Is that why you're there? To put yourself in the mood? From what you've already told me, you're rich. You could go out in style at the Bel-Air or the Regent Wilshire. Why the melodrama?"

"I like the blinking neon. Blood red. It sets just the right tone."

"Are you in the movie industry?"

"What makes you ask?"

"Your sense of location . . ."

"Well, maybe I am a movie people. That covers a lot of territory," he added coyly.

"Look, don't tell me if you don't want to. But it kind of limits what I can do for you."

"I understand." He squirmed underneath the bedspread. "You're right. I'm connected with motion pictures."

"That makes a whole new ballgame. There are at least seven thousand, eight hundred and seventy two really good reasons daily why people in entertainment would want to kill themselves."

Lewis smiled; he could hear the interest in the young voice growing. "Success and failure; there are two."

"Right."

"And indifference, three."

"Correct. What's yours?"

"Hold on a second." Lewis jumped up from the bed and ran to the unit under the window. He spun the dial around until he heard a mechanical click and cool air began blowing in with a whoosh. "Sorry. It was getting warm in here. My reasons? The first five thousand."

"You're pulling my chain again."

"You brought up the seven thou. . . . Failure. I've recently experienced a major failure." Lewis wondered at the pause; was he punching up *fuck up* on his computer?

"Sorry, I couldn't find my cigarettes. You ever listen to that asshole on the radio who does movie reviews? Classical station? He sounds like he's someone's idiot nephew. But he has an opinion. Anybody can say anything he likes about someone's vessel of blood, sweat, and tears. You make art, you're a sitting duck. You know that." As if to give Chip a semblance of omniscience, a chord of thunder sounded in close proximity to the motel. "Wow, stereo! It sounds like it's just overhead. Where abouts are you?"

Lewis smiled and unscrewed the cap to the Chivas bottle. "In a thunderstorm." He tore off the crepe-paper cover and filled the plastic tumbler.

"West Hollywood?"

"You're prying."

"I'm supposed to; that's why you called me."

The time for bantering had passed, Lewis thought. The darkness of his vision, his view of the future, the past, descended upon him like a cowl. "I called because I want to kill myself, but I'm afraid." He'd made it sound so simple, so innocent.

"Why?"

There was a taunting quality in the man's question. "Why am I afraid?"

"Yes."

Lewis felt confused. "Because I don't know what's on the other end."

"You'll just have to cross to find out, won't you? No easy answers."

"Are you encouraging me?" Lewis felt a bolt of fear pierce him, now to the accompaniment of lightning. He saw himself in the mirror opposite; he looked like a paunchy mole. "I said, are you encouraging me?"

"Listen, man. We've talked, what five, six times? I still don't have any picture of what's going on. How serious you are. Maybe you just get your rocks off talking to strangers about death. But you're not sharing anything, like what's happening to you."

Lewis knew there was truth to the accusation. "It's all disappearing, slipping through my fingers. It's like being in a dream: first they come and take down the walls, then they move out the furniture. You feel an ominous wind blowing around you. Then they take your clothes, your teeth, they begin taking licks at your body with heavy straps . . ." He swallowed the scotch. "Is that enough?"

"Who are they? Why are they doing this?"

He swallowed again. *"They* are who grabbed the scepter this week. They are the people with the shortest memory. And the longest. They are merciless. They are who your parents were protecting you from. But then you realize there really was no one to protect your parents."

This time the sigh was undisguised. "Look. People who kill themselves don't talk in riddles. I don't think you're serious, and a lot of people are. I think you should leave this hotline open for them. I think you're a jerkoff that has no intention of snuffing yourself." He let the thought hang.

"Is that what you think?" The words came out surprisingly constricted. He squeezed his features in the fleshy palm of his hand. "Then I trust I must excuse myself for taking up your time. I will let you pursue your noble mission with people who truly deserve it, depend on your wisdom for life. I, the jerkoff, will not bother you . . ."

"Hold on. Okay, I apologize. Is that an accent I hear?"

"Is it? Only when I'm patronized. Yes, of course it's an accent. Are you deaf?"

"Sorry."

"Look, young man, I think I've taken up enough of your time. Sleep peacefully. I promise not to do myself any harm, all right? Does that make you feel better? Mission accomplished?"

"Okay, I'm a jackass; I'm supposed to make you feel better."

"I do. Absolutely. The weight of failure falls lightly from my shoulders. The terrible injustices I've done those I've loved and cared about very deeply will mend, eventually. I have, as you say, been pulling your chain."

"What kind of accent do you have? Is it German?"

"German? It must be the alcohol."

"Throw it out." The telephone voice became commanding.

"Throw . . . my scotch? No, I'm afraid I really couldn't."

"Listen. You're not thinking straight, you can't when you drink. Pour it out and get some sleep."

"Hmnnn. That sounds very inviting, sleep. How long do you think I would sleep? Ten minutes? Half hour? Even if I close the charming rubberized curtains and black out the lovely electrical fireworks outside, I doubt I could go an hour."

"Whoa, you really art directed your exit. Sounds like the Paradiso on Sunset. Or the Fantastic Flamingo off Santa Monica, both first-class dumps, very romantic for the big fade-out."

The young man's accuracy kept Lewis at bay. "What other advice do you have for me?" He could hear voices in the background, then his correspondent returned.

"None. Look, why don't I come see you. Talk it out once and for all. The truth is, I really want to help." Again Lewis could hear voices in the background. "You're at the Paradiso, am I right?"

Lewis wondered if he could hear him pour the scotch. "I did it to my wife. I've ruined her."

"Would I know your wife? Is she famous?"

"Yes."

"But you're not going to tell me."

"Is it necessary?" The rain was pelting the window now, for the moment obscuring the laborious sound of the air conditioner.

"The more I know, the more I can help."

For the first time, Lewis distrusted the voice. "I think I should respect her privacy. I feel I've left her exposed enough."

"Is that why you don't want to tell me who you are?"

"That's correct." The silence felt uncomfortable to Lewis.

"Well, I guess we're at a standoff. Call me back if you need me."

Lewis felt the echo of abandonment he had felt at the studio swell in him. "I'm sorry I'm not being cooperative. Actually, I'm being as cooperative as I can." He reached for the plastic glass, which had developed a hairline crack. "You do this on a voluntary basis, is that correct?"

"Two nights a week."

"Why?"

"Why? Most of us have to live with shit, deal in shit, eat it, most of our lives. It's nice to spend some time doing something clean, to think about someone other than yourself."

"I think you're right, that would be very nice."

"Your wife wouldn't be a movie star, would she?"

Lewis felt himself tense again. "You're determined, aren't you? I'm afraid I'll have to end this conversation."

"Wait!" Lewis heard the unguarded urgency in his voice. "I don't want to make this worse. You feel you're responsible for your wife's failure . . ."

"We've been through this."

"I know. I'm just trying to nail it."

"For who, you or me?"

"Fuck you."

The voice was so level, he wasn't sure he understood the words correctly. "What did you say?"

"I said, fuck you. If you fucked up somebody else's life, career, you deserve to suffer. How did you fuck it up? You were after something for you and you pissed on your wife in the process. That's how it happened, isn't it? And what's worse, in your scummy little mind you're trying to blame her for what's happening to you. What you did to yourself. You know, given this scenario, you might be right. Maybe she is better off without you. Maybe your plan, which I really doubt you have the courage for, is correct. Maybe you ought to do it . . ."

"Do it," Lewis said quietly, "kill myself." He looked down at his short hairy legs against the soiled chenille. "Will you help?"

A pause, then, "Yes."

"How?"

"I'll make it easy. I've had lots of experience. I know all the ways people go about it. I know which ones are best."

"You do?" Lewis felt helpless, exhausted. "I don't think I'm ready."

"Coward." There was vehemence in his voice. "What are you

waiting for? To bury her? Find a new victim? Screw someone else?"

"You're making me confused. Maybe it's the alcohol." Lewis felt stupid trying to make excuses for the young man. "You can't be saying this."

"Why not? Because you don't want to hear it?"

"Because your job is to save people, not commit them to death."

"Maybe I am saving someone, maybe I'm saving your wife. Maybe she knows what a cheesy little coward you are and she'd be grateful for what I'm doing. Do it, for Christ's sake!"

Lewis's fingers felt swollen as he reached for the bottle, shaking the telephone from his hand as he did. "Do it! Do it, asshole!" the voice screamed through the receiver. Lewis poured as the yelling became indecipherable; then he brought the phone back to his ear. ". . . You won't, you pussy coward." The young man sounded out of breath. Lewis sipped and listened to his breathing. "Are you all right?" he asked finally. The young man was breathing heavily through his nose.

"I'm all right," he said, trying to slow his heaving. "What about you?"

"It's psychology, of course, the most obvious sort. You want me to disagree with you. Be my usual perverse self. That's right, isn't it?"

"Well, you'd better figure it out." He was still breathing heavily, the voice hushed to a strong whisper.

Lewis slid the phone onto its cradle and stood, feeling the unsteadiness imposed by the alcohol. He balanced himself by keeping his leg in contact with the bed as he moved to the chair where he'd piled his clothes. He reached into the pocket of his coat jacket and took out a small brown envelope, its contents hard against his fingers. Then he brought it to the phone and placed it beside him as he made one more phone call.

When the motel manager did not find the key in the door as Lewis Rosenthal had promised, he let himself into the room. There was no shock in seeing the lifeless body sprawled on the bed. The manager lived with the feeling that there was always the possibility of this sort of thing at the Paradiso, almost as inevitable as the stained sheets.

Because it was not the first time he'd come upon one of his clientele in unusual circumstances, he'd learned that it could be useful to do his own private investigation before calling the police.

In spite of his perfunctory search, it did not take him long to come up with a half-expected find. His gray face twisted in a disdainful smile as he removed a brown envelope from between the mattress and box spring and inspected its contents. All that was necessary now was a little more detective work on his part, and figuring out how he could best capitalize on it, before he would summon the police.

Chapter Two

The scent of catastrophe mixes with hibiscus in the perfumed paths behind the Beverly Hills Hotel. Noses sniff the air like hyperventilating sharks. The powerful sneer, their entrails contracted with fear that one day it will be their turn.

The readers of supermarket tabloids sleep benignly, smiles on their faces, their sixth sense telling them that soon they will be feeding on a fresh luscious crop of scandal, taking pleasure in the tragedies that befall those they thought impervious by dint of wealth or fame. For them it is vindication, redemption from their own underused, muscleless lives, as though someone's fall lifts them in its wake. Smug pleasure plays across their mouths and souls as they covet the inexplicable, intoxicating abstraction of success but lack the will to win it.

In a suite at the Regent Wilshire, decorated in a way that never denies its hotel origins, Nora Howard sits and receives a stream of reporters prioritized and processed, alone or in small groups. Anesthetized by circumstances, she must, from time to time, remind herself of why it is all happening. Everything has been arranged for her, from the flowers to the makeup and hair artists to the underlying politics of her appearance. She is here to face reporters and tell them everything she knows and thinks and feels about the death of her husband, Lewis Rosenthal. She

19

does not clearly understand, nor has she asked, why her grief
must be made public. She does not want to know that deals
have been cut with certain tabloids that will exchange flattering
color photographs of her with her name trumpeted in thirty-
two-point type for the most intimate recollections of life with
her late husband. She has been styled demurely, her hair drawn
tightly over her scalp and wedged into an intricate bun. They
have told her to say as little as possible, to nod in agreement,
accept condolences, and weep freely when the mood strikes.
Her handlers have been augmented by P.R. people from the
studio who want nothing more than to disassociate themselves
from her and have sent their minions in to do damage control.

Nora watches as nuts and dried fruits are discreetly offered
from a variety of Oriental-looking bowls. The phones have been
arranged to buzz softly and they are whisked off their cradles
quickly, answered with hushed voices speaking rapid explana-
tions or instructions in short spurts. Nora looks at the dozens of
floral arrangements around the room and has no idea who sent
them, or if they were sent rather than orchestrated. The line of
good taste is almost crossed with the relentlessly saccharine
taped music spewing throughout the room like nerve gas.

Television people have been allowed in first, hosts and host-
esses of syndicated entertainment programs. The synthetic-
looking, brightly painted interviewers approach her followed by
others carrying video cameras and boom mikes probing the air
around her. Lenses focus in on her quivering lips and moist
eyes, go for inserts of her tightly fisted hand clutching a balled
handkerchief. The softer the voices, the more seductive the attitude, the more insidious the questions that spill over her.

In between forays of reporters, the hair and makeup team fly
in for touch-ups. Lights have been carefully arranged, a white
reflecting card lay near her feet, discreetly raised at appropriate
moments to wash out lines in her face. She wonders how she is
to register grief with an unsullied complexion.

Nora has allowed herself to become public prey because she
wants the contact with people. She has wanted to fall into the
maw of attention, concern, curiosity, whatever they would offer
her; compassion, she knew, was not even a consideration. There
would be plenty of time for being alone.

The woman sitting opposite her now has glittering blond hair that billows about her head as if forced up by tiny air jets in her skull. Her face is thickly coated with makeup that doesn't quite camouflage the little blond hairs tufting her jowls and upper lip. Her eyes and mouth are painted in primary colors and she repeatedly tosses her head back as though experiencing a persistent sea breeze. Her tongue darts out periodically, moistening her lips, and her eyes implore the air, searching for a signal to begin. She has said nothing to Nora beyond an initial hello and apparently has no intention of striking up any rapport before a camera is ready to record it. Instead, she nervously tips the clipboard on her lap, furtively glancing down, as though cheating on an exam. Finally she gets the signal she is waiting for and springs to life.

"Nora Howard, this is very difficult for me, almost painful, as it must be for all our viewers, to ask you to share your thoughts and feelings on the tragic loss of your beloved husband, Lewis. Before we get into the tragedy itself, can you tell our viewers how you met?" Her eyes go immediately to the clipboard as if to check the truthfulness of Nora's response.

"We met through friends, a small dinner party," Nora begins. She surprises herself with the calm, even tone of her voice. She catches a glimpse of her face in an etched Venetian mirror and is startled by how much like an almost young, chilly Lana Turner she looks. "Lewis was charming. He had the table riveted from the moment he sat down. I thought to myself, There's a man who's endlessly fascinating because he doesn't know it. Not too serious, not trying to be funny, just, I thought, extraordinary."

The interviewer keeps her puffy blond head in her notes as if she hadn't heard a word. "And when did things get, well, more romantic?" she says, snapping her attention to Nora. Her blond frosty hair is rivaled by a wide set of very white, very large teeth.

"We started dating a lot. Three or four times a week. We had long dinners at quiet restaurants. We did a great deal of talking." The crew and equipment form a fence around them.

"Can you tell us what you talked about?"

Nora is surprised the young woman is actually listening. "Food, wine. His travels, things he wanted to show me. There was almost no mention of my career." At that moment Nora realizes she is sounding like an actress. "I mean, that part of my life. It's very unusual for someone in show business to be treated like a real person. Lewis seemed to do it naturally."

"Is that what attracted you? He wasn't someone playing up to a movie star?"

"I just appreciated being treated like a reasonably intelligent human being." Nora could hear resentment in her own voice; apparently the interviewer did not.

"And how long ago was that?"

"About twenty years ago."

"And you were married about as long. Now, didn't Lewis become your manager almost from the start, even though, according to what you just said, he didn't appear to have much interest in your career?"

"Lewis was a very smart, very adaptable man. He knew our chances of staying together were better if we built something together. We decided my career would provide common ground."

"And build you did. We have some clips we'd like to show our viewers. Some of your most famous roles, lines you spoke that have become part of the language, scenes we all tried to imitate in our youth. Let's refresh our audience's memory of the work you and your husband put together before his unfortunate and untimely death." She looks sadly into the camera and freezes, waiting for the red light to go out. When she hears her own narration under the film appearing on the monitor, she stands abruptly and walks away from Nora without a glance. "I don't know why we couldn't edit the fucking thing later and get the hell out of here," she says to no one in particular.

Nora tries to watch the monitor, reflecting lights making it difficult. She hears her voice, a montage of her voices and those of her leading men. She catches glimpses of herself in outfits that look more than slightly dated. Then her face reappears live and she is caught unaware, watching herself intently; the contrast in not flattering. The blond reporter has slipped back into her seat, her face even glossier than before. She has been primed and primped for camera, Nora left to fade into her own reflections.

"Thank you, thank you," the blonde says with startling earnestness. "Thank you for all the memorable moments you and Lewis have brought us over the years. Culminating for many of us only last year with, no doubt, your biggest success, *Amazing Angels*. The picture no studio would touch." She turns to the camera slyly. "The one the Hollywood hotshots said would be laughed out of the theater; the kind they predicted people would never go to see anymore. But Lewis persisted and, God knows how, brought it to the screen as you both envisioned, in all its three-hour glory. And as Hollywood waited for the death knell to toll, it flabbergasted Tinsel Town by ringing up some of the biggest, hottest numbers the industry had seen in years." Nora follows her gaze and sees, having abandoned her notes, she is reading from a cue card. Slowly the woman turns back to her and speaks with great solemnity. "Eight Academy nominations, six actual Oscars. A triumph. You and Lewis are at the top of your game, leaders of the pack. What was it like, those moments of glory?"

"It felt very comfortable. It's a nice feeling, doing what you believe in and having it work out. I don't think we felt so much vindicated as happy others were sharing something we cared about very much."

Now a look of fright comes into the reporter's eyes. "And then it all disappears," she says ominously. "The applause is replaced by ridicule. The resounding triumph replaced by the loud thud of a box-office bust. Your next picture, your most recent and your last with Lewis, turns into box-office poison. No one comes. Why? What effect did this have on your marriage?"

Nora blinks, taken back by the disparate questions. "Why did it flop? I suppose we miscalculated somewhere along the way. Maybe in the execution; I really don't know why. What astonished me was the reaction, the decisiveness of it. I thought, well, we blew that one, on to the next. But that's not how this town sees things anymore. As I learned, it's all big business now. If a film flops today, you could be driving a major corporation into bankruptcy. It was quite startling."

Again the haunted look in the interviewer's face. "For Lewis it must have been devastating."

Now Nora sees him as he looked in the motel room, the police around his body, a fat, naked, middle-aged man hanging over the side of a lumpy bed, men with cameras igniting flashes. "I . . . I thought he was handling it, as usual, very well. I had no idea . . ." She allows her gaze and voice to drift off into the distance.

"Tell me what went through your mind that awful night when you got the call from the police." Her voice cuts through, filling the silent room like a screech. Nora, disbelieving, stares blankly, but the woman persists. "What went through your mind when you were taken to the motel?"

"How sad it was," Nora says quietly. "How very sad. My husband was a gentleman of the old school, more European than American."

The reporter flicks through her notes. "Yugoslavian, wasn't he?"

"Lewis considered himself a Serb." The reporter looks at her blankly. Nora thinks that perhaps she has distracted her. But she is wrong.

"The motel where they found him is only a few miles from where you live. But the worlds they represent could not be more different." She is speaking to the camera now. "You make the trek from the pampered, fairy-tale world of Beverly Hills, a police escort clearing the way through the wet night. There's little traffic on a Sunset Boulevard lined with the great mansions and ghosts of early Hollywood. Is that where reality sets in for you? Did you even hear the sirens? See the flashing lights? Feel the rain? When did the realization that you were part of a tragedy hit you?"

"It's a tragedy for everybody when they lose someone."

"But you must have known yours would be spelled out in headlines, flashed across TV screens. How does it feel to have your life split apart? Exposed?"

Nora looks at her strangely. "I've been used to living certain parts of my life publicly for quite some time. I accept it."

"Yes, but this had to be different. This was the sort of time when we all want to retreat into ourselves, find our strength; but you were forced to bear it publicly."

"I identified Lewis and he was taken away. I believe an autopsy was performed and then he was taken to a funeral home, just like anyone else."

"And can you tell us what was in that autopsy report?" The woman looks at Nora with distress, as though they are both searching their souls for the penultimate disclosure.

"It stated that my husband committed suicide. That he killed himself." Nora looks at the interviewer to see if she is pleased. The woman remains silent. "That is a very difficult thing for someone to live with, when someone you love does away with himself. It's very difficult not to blame yourself." Nora pauses. "I would have done anything, anything in my power, to have stopped him. Nothing means anything compared to the loss. I wish I had had the opportunity to tell him."

"Do you think your career had something to do with Lewis's death?"

"His *suicide.* Yes I do."

The interviewer moves in earnestly. "Your last picture was, by any measure, a disaster of enormous proportions. Are you saying *that's* what led Lewis to kill himself?"

"The industry can be very unforgiving. And I think Lewis was even more unforgiving of himself." Nora glares at the woman, trying to tell her with her eyes that the interview is over. For once the woman backs down, turns to the camera, and begins a string of commiserations ending with her sincerest wishes for Nora's bright and happy future.

Equipment is disassembled and the crews pack and leave. Other journalists, of lesser station, are shunted in and out singly or in small groups. Nora has told her story so many times, it has lost its emotion. By five in the afternoon, at her direction, photographs are prohibited; she knows what strain and fatigue can do to her face. Then she is left alone with a young British reporter. A small, plastic, ineffective-looking tape recorder is placed on a lacquered coffee table in front of the nubby tan sofa on which they sit.

"Tired?" he asks her with a smile and a certain degree of concern.

"Yes, I am," she says warily.

"I shouldn't be surprised." The warmth rises in his voice.

The friendly tone makes her more alert; she is aware that the more offhand the question, the more vulnerable the answer. "Well, it's almost over. What can I tell you that I haven't revealed to the world twenty times over already?" He smiles gently, no words forthcoming. "Perhaps you ought to shut off the tape if we're going to sit here smiling pleasantly at each other."

"If it makes you more comfortable." His hand reaches out casually and slides a button. "Would you care for a drink?"

"Yes, thank you," she says, pointing to a trayful of bottles on a cabinet. "Gin and tonic."

He rises awkwardly and she realizes he is one of the few reporters dressed in suit and tie. As he pours, she thinks how his clothing is more suited to chillier climates. "Thanks," she says, slipping the cool glass from his bony fingers. He settles back with a tumbler of amber liquid with one small cube of ice.

"Whose idea was this?" he asks her.

"What?"

"This circus."

She jerks her head down, uncomfortable. "I was advised it was best to simply tell my story, that there would be speculation. That honesty pays."

"In a publicity bonanza." His perfunctory smile displays yellowish teeth.

"I'm an actress, Mr.—"

"Wainwright."

"Publicity is one way I ply my trade."

"Aren't some things out of bounds, or isn't death one of them?" he asks.

"I've come to realize *life* is fair game."

"I see. Okay, then, let's play. Did your husband give you any last-minute warning he was about to do what he did?"

"No. In truth, it took me totally by surprise."

"Then, did he communicate with you *after* the fact, so to speak?"

Nora feels herself tense. "I'm not sure I follow. I haven't been to any séances, if that's what you mean."

"That's *not* what I mean. Did he leave you a note? A *suicide* note, I believe it's called." He swirls his ice cube in the glass. Seated with his back to the window, his features are indiscernible in the low light.

"No, there was no note." She flinches at his question.

"Of course not, what could he say? Except how much he loves you and how sorry he was for your last film's dismal showing. Isn't that odd, that someone would kill himself over box-office receipts?" He removes his glass from his mouth to reveal a smile. "I'm sorry, that came out rather crass. Isn't it a shame he hadn't discussed it with you. I'm certain you could have talked him out of it."

"That's something I'd rather not think about, Mr. Wainwright."

"Yes." He lifts the empty glass as if in a toast. "May I?"

"Of course."

"How about yourself?" He stands, peering into her untouched glass.

"I'm fine, thank you."

"It's around you were both working on a comeback," he says from the makeshift bar. "Isn't that a horrid expression? I mean, you've barely been away. Practically just off your biggest triumph. Then a flop and you're dead meat." He approaches the sofa. "Such a strange town, so unforgiving. They really do relish fattening up their little calves to turn into carrion. And the fans stand around chanting, throw another star to the lions." He sits in the corner away from her. "But who are the lions? If the truth be told, they're the fear and loathing and envy in all of us. You and your husband are just the latest to satisfy our appetites." He takes a big undisguised gulp. "It's too bad your husband had to die for such rubbish." He places the glass down with a solid thud and reaches for the tape machine. Nora eyes the equipment with fleeting fear. "Well, haven't got much of a story, have I? Not to worry, I'll simply piece one together from all the nonsense my colleagues write about you. And I promise I shall be kind." He smiles at her like a schoolboy. "Wasn't your husband just about to do a deal with Kimmelmann before Kimmelmann was dumped?"

She stares at him, knowing that she can never relax as long as there is a single reporter in her presence. "My husband was talking to a lot of people. It's not as though he was selling tickets for the return voyage of the *Titanic.*"

The Englishman snorts. "Of course not. I would say you're still a viable commodity. But this suicide thing, there's something creepy about it. Almost infects you through osmosis. Something tawdry about it, pathetic."

"I'm feeling very tired, Mr. Wainwright. I don't think I have any more insight left for your readers. I'm very sorry."

English formality shoots through him like a rod. "So sorry myself. Can't imagine why I'm going on this way. Just my own

morbid meanderings. What do I really know of Hollywood anyway? I bet there's lots and lots you could teach me. Bet you
know where tons of skeletons are hidden, if you'll pardon the
allusion. Like what happened to Kimmelmann. Or more importantly, about his replacement. Wouldn't Steven Wald get the
nod for most formidable player in the industry these days?" He
smiles at her charmingly. "Well, wouldn't he?"

"I'm an actress, Mr. Wainwright. I try not to get involved with
the politics of the business. I'm not interested in it and I'm not
good at it."

"Right. Do you think it would be too pushy if I grubbed
another drink off you?" His smarmy expression is undisguised.
"Especially as your people seem to have abandoned you." The
aloneness must reflect in her face and he grabs the moment.
"Would you consider Steven Wald a friend of yours?"

"Isn't that something you should ask him?"

"I'm asking you." Casually he picks himself up and ambles to
the bar. "Friend or foe, what do you think?"

Nora hesitates, then, "Friend."

"Aaah, how nice for you." He adds more ice cubes to his
drink this time and they clink in the silent room as he returns to
the sofa. "Things happen so fast here. They say New York is
supposed to be so energized that it leaves us lethargic Brits in
the dust. But I haven't seen that. Not lately anyway. Only the
muggers appear to have a buzz about them. But these Hollywood guys are fast. Wald jumps studios as Kimmelmann's being
led out the back door by his schlong. Reigns of any sort fasci-
nate me, probably because I'm British." He guffaws coarsely.
"So delicate, so precarious, the tumble can happen so suddenly.
We see it all around us, but we're never quite prepared, are we?
It's like chemistry really: a couple of circumstances, quite benign unto themselves, happening in conjunction with each other
. . . And everything changes."

Nora is not listening to him. The sound of his voice is like
darting birds pecking at her cranium.

"You and your husband were part of Kimmelmann's legacy,
including your deal on the Bradford book. The project that was
suppose to be your big comeback. Word is that Wald's red-
lighted the project. All of Kimmelmann's green lights are at

least orange, but your deal is dead. Is that what you'd call a friend?"

Nora says nothing; she feels fright and at the same time loathing for his unctuous presence.

"Wald's rejection, that would be a ripping good reason for your husband to . . ."

Suddenly there is a slam and she looks up. The door to the suite has opened and shut, allowing in her P.R. people.

"I'm sorry, darling, we've been on the phone. They're all so interested in you, all so sorry . . . Tony, you scoundrel; what are you doing here? We thought you'd packed and gone off with the others. Nora, sweetheart, can you forgive us for leaving you alone with this monster? Has he been asking horrible questions? He usually does. I hope you haven't told him anything."

As the P.R. man continues cheerfully berating his colleague, Nora's glance goes to the Englishman's tape recorder. She sees through the scratched plastic window that the tiny wheels are still turning.

After spending the night in the suite, Nora Howard dressed in what she'd worn the day before and left the hotel. Along Rodeo Drive, expensive cars cruised by slowly. On the immaculate sidewalks, unrushed, graceful young bodies sauntered past erect, finely tailored older ones with tight faces and peering, birdlike eyes.

At the corner of Camden, she saw the familiar shape of Danny D, a hairdresser of great popularity among the women of Beverly Hills. He was taking long strides in gray-skinned cowboy boots, his blond shiny hair pulled back and tied in a ponytail. His black silk shirt was buttoned at throat and wrists and tucked smoothly into high-waisted billowy black trousers. In his hand he carried a small white bag.

"Danny," she called to him. He stopped and adjusted his sunglasses as he looked at her. "Hi . . ." She drew her own glasses from her face.

"Sweetie, it's *you*. What are you doing here?" His arms went out to encircle her.

"Strolling," she said for want of a better explanation.

"Strolling?" he repeated, turning his head askew as he looked at her skeptically. "Come to the shop, I'll share my coffee," he said, holding up the white bag that looked tiny in his hand. "Honey, I can't believe it's really you. The one thing I love about Bev Hills is that everything's got at least one back door. So-o-o-o handy." His free hand dipped into a deep pants pocket and brought out a large set of keys. "Eeeny, meeny, miney . . . moe should do the trick." He pushed open the door and stretched his long body against the wall, allowing her to pass in front of him. "You got my flowers?" he asked as they reached his office. She nodded, slowly taking off her glasses and undoing the kerchief she'd placed over her hair. "Oh, your head doesn't look so bad; I couldn't imagine what was going on under there." He plucked at her hair with his long fingers. "When hair is cut right, it can go through any kind of shit." Suddenly his eyes widened and he leaned toward her. "I can't believe what you've been through, a box-office turkey and Lewis." His speech became stifled as tears filled his eyes and he shook his head. She reached out and gave him her hand. "I'm so sorry, Nora. I'm so fucking sorry, I don't know what to say."

"I know," she said, nodding as his head continued to shake from side to side. "I don't know what to think either." She forced a smile onto her face. "At this point, my advice to anyone would be don't get out of bed, pull the covers over you, and keep a food taster handy. When life wants to sling it to you . . ."

He took her hands, cupped them to his mouth, and kissed her fingers gently. "The referee's barely counted two; you'll be up long before he's finished." He turned his wet eyes upward and bit his lip. "It's so fucking unfair. I just can't believe it."

"Well, it only took me thirty years to get it all and a whole thirty days to lose it."

He peered at her warily. "Lewis left you gelt, no? Tell me *that,* at least, is not a problem."

"That at least is not a problem," she said softly.

"Thank God for small favors." He lowered his voice. "But still, I don't think it's such a good idea for you to be seen out shopping . . ."

Her smile almost became a laugh. "That's not exactly what I was doing. It's stupid, but I didn't want to go home."

"I know exactly what you're saying," he said with total confidence. "You don't know how much loss I've had in my life. For one thing, forty pounds over the last year." He pressed his stomach with the flat of his hand and smiled impishly. "Then there was the Triumph convertible I, you should excuse the expression, *lost* to a young friend. Not to mention three wretched *affaires de coeur* I've had this year. Believe me, I know about heartache. Being crimper *du jour* doesn't mean I don't know it can all go flat tomorrow. That's the joyous thing about happiness; you don't have to worry about its maintenance and upkeep for ever and ever. It has a way of picking up and taking care of itself, with or without you."

Nora poked the white bag he placed between them. "You said something about . . ."

"Of course. I just have to bore you to death before I give away anything. Lucky for you I was in a two-cup funk this morning." He ripped open the bag and removed the pair of containers. "Oh my God!" He inhaled loudly, placing his palm on his chest. "Imagine this! A genuine grade A movie star's lips are about to touch my coffee. If only the boys back in Des Moines could see this. I think I'll have the cup ironed and framed, with a little plaque that says, Nora Howard's lips touched here."

She tore open the packet of sweetener, poured and stirred.

"You know, doll, if you need someone to go to the films with or a not-too-classy dinner party, I want you to know, disreputable and unpresentable as I am, I'm always available. In fact, that may be my single greatest virtue."

Nora lowered her cup. "That's sweet."

"Sweet, shit. I'm a star fucker. I lo-o-v-e to go out with the rich and famous. And I can promise you, as long as I'm around, a curl will never go astray. How many men can make *that* statement?" His brows dipped in a mock frown. "Too many, as so many women, much to their chagrin, have discovered. Isn't this coffee divine? Imported all the way from Little Santa Monica Boulevard a half block away. Have you seen what works in that little coffee shop lately? I'll tell you one thing, they're not all out pumping gas in Santa Fe or San Jose or whatever." Suddenly his face dissolved into wide-eyed innocence. "Why?"

"Why? Why'd the picture flop? Why'd Lewis . . ." She straightened in her chair and sipped coffee.

"Kill himself . . ." he finished absently.

She stared at him, as though searching for comprehension. Then she turned away.

"What?" he asked, suddenly alert.

Her head made small flicking motions, shaking away whatever thoughts she was having.

"Natural causes?" He watched her immobile face. "What's left?" he asked almost inaudibly.

Her answer was in her expression.

Danny sighed and slumped in his chair, like a puppet gone slack. "Nora, sweetheart, my darling beauty. The one thing I've always given you credit for is knowing when they turn off the camera. Unlike half the down-filled heads out here, you know reality. I will also allow that you've been under maximum emotional stress lately and are entitled, if anyone ever was, to fantasize. But . . . murder?" He made a face that suggested he'd tasted something disagreeable. "Honey, sweetheart, without opening old wounds, the book that Lewis optioned from that fabulously crinkly New England hunk? I heard Wald was squeezing his balls on that one. That's on top of the most notable turkey of the year. I don't mean to be harsh, but the man had motives."

Nora closed her eyes. "I'm not pinning medals on his grave, but Lewis was unbelievably tenacious. And nothing brought it out like a no."

Danny appeared to be moaning silently. "You're going to make yourself miserable if you believe there's something out there responsible for your pain." He hunched his shoulders. "It's just too horrible to contemplate." An urgency overtook his concern. "What are you going to do about it?"

She heard herself sighing deeply, the sound mingling sadness with frustration. "I don't know," she said simply.

"Good. If in doubt, don't." He took her hand. "Lewis is dead. It's horrible. But what difference does it make how? It's not going to bring him back, knowing every last detail." He sat up quickly, his eyes shrewd and knowing. "If you take your doubts to the police, to anybody, the whole town is going to know. If it's not funny or decadent, they don't want to see dirty laundry. They'll sniff their handkerchiefs and turn the other way. Death isn't anyone's favorite topic." He allowed his dimples to emerge

slowly. "Give it some time. If there's something fishy, it'll surface, believe me."

She watched him studying her face, inventorying the damage.
"All right, I believe you," she said, wondering how long it would
take.

Chapter Three

New England

Michael Russell liked almost everything about America. The country made him feel like an adored pied piper in a nation of worshipful children. In England, where he'd emigrated in his teens from Poland, he felt like a gerbil, condemned to spin forever on his exercise wheel. He would always be the grocer's son, even if he owned every supermarket chain in the British Isles.

While he had been received by the upper class, even courted, to put an historic interior right or restore a wing to a neglected relic of their glory days, he knew he would eventually be dismissed with a thank-you-so-very-much as they disappeared down the chilly corridors of privilege.

But in America! Here he was openly admired, joyously, eagerly coveted! It was a country where accomplishment was appreciated, where a fluke of genes did not put you on a pedestal. He adored America; here *he* was the aristocracy and the lazy inheritors of *someone else's* accomplishments the commoners. In gratitude, he'd set out not only to dazzle the Americans by his wealth-building prowess, but to share it with them. Any man who wanted to work twice as hard as his neighbor found nirvana working for him. Anyone who didn't share his predilection for seventeen-hour workdays and seven-day work weeks found himself in trouble.

He'd discovered long ago that he had a gift for sizing people up. The tales about his ability in this area had credited him with coming to judgment in ten seconds; an exaggeration perhaps, but not far off the mark. It was with this God-given and frequently exercised homing device that he had come to choose Steven Wald to run the movie studio he had recently bought. The key had been Wald's understanding that he was not some star-fucking foreigner looking to schtup every siliconed actress in Hollywood. The man understood that the studio was simply one piece of a complex puzzle Russell was assembling. He published books, he published magazines, he published newspapers, he owned TV and radio stations, and he was forever looking into the possibilities of new media. The studio was meant to plug into his elaborate corporate apparatus. How canny, he thought to himself, how close it was, controlling such an empire, to having the influence of a president or king; better, the influence of a president or king *maker,* which was perhaps more powerful, certainly more autonomous.

There had been no question in his mind that Wald was the pluperfect man for the job, with one teeny tiny reservation: he didn't like him. There was something cold and inhuman about him. Not the sort of business ruthlessness that he was surrounded with, indeed, practiced himself. But a soullessness, which he found chilling.

Michael Russell walked to a twelve-on-twelve paned window and looked out at his Connecticut estate. The house, part of a hundred-acre complex that included a riding rink, a stable for a dozen Arabians, three tennis courts, indoor and outdoor lap pools, among other amenities, looked as though it had been built soon after the town of Crofton had been founded in 1771. In fact, the entire compound had gone up in under a year; by the second, the plantings appeared to have existed for generations. It represented the sort of instant gratification that he adored and which, to his delight, America was pleased to afford.

A large man, he held his morning teacup delicately in his

fingertips, his back turned to his wife, her voice barely penetrating the computerlike machinations of his mind.

The Crofton house had given Aida Russell a temporary raison d'être, for in her own way she was as ambitious as her husband. Her current preoccupation with things mahogany and chintz did not bother him at all; he knew her to have impeccable taste and judgment, and to be a shrewd shopper as well.

"Then it's settled, the library will be red and white, glazed, of course. I don't think it matters that it will look like thousands of other libraries, with botanical and sporting prints. There *must* be reasons people of taste make them all come out like that."

"There must, indeed," he said, actually agreeing with her logic. Besides, it was not a room he planned on spending much time in. He had seen to it that he would have a private study: spare, functional, undecorated, filled with fax machines and computers. "I think you're doing a marvelous job, darling. I've never been happier any other place in my life."

"That's very sweet of you, dear." She smiled to herself, knowing that among his former residences, Auschwitz loomed most dominant. "Quite a handful, though."

He turned his full attention to her. "Let someone else run it. You go out and find . . ."

She dabbed her lips with her napkin. "As a matter of fact, I'm thinking of getting involved with the Hartwood Playhouse. It's not twenty miles north of here. I thought, if it's all right with you, I might sit on the board. It's simply chock-a-block with the right sorts." She smiled unkindly at the thought. "It's been around for fifty years, which apparently is an eternity here." She looked at him slyly. "What do you think?"

"By all means, as long as you've assured me it's filled with the right sort." He smiled back at her.

"I'm curious to see if the *new* Englanders are anything like the *old* Englanders."

"I should hope not!" He'd always known he possessed about himself something elephantine. If one was to do a wicked caricature of him, he knew he would look like a floating parade balloon with small pointy feet and hands. His eyes were all lids and looked like slanted crescents. His large nose drooped bulbously and his mouth was thin and mean. All in all, he often thought, it was just as well he had acquired a great deal of money.

His wife, on the other hand, looked like a thoroughbred. Handsome, if not beautiful; expensively dressed but hardly a billboard of what was in fashion. She was extremely knowledgeable about politics and business, the result of spending several hours daily reading newspapers.

Here again his instinct and acumen about people had proven accurate. She supplemented his weaknesses, social and diplomatic, with considerable charm. And displayed over the years deep understanding and loyalty toward him, two not insignificant attributes. As she was saying something to do with Palladian in regard to the library, he noticed out of the corner of his crescent eye one of the telephone lines flashing. A second later, there was a knock on the door and the appearance of their houseman, Julian.

"Mr. Wald on two for you."

Russell swung enthusiastically for the telephone. "Good day, Steven. How are you?" He had made it a point to sound avuncular to the executive.

"I'm perfect. Yourself?" The voice was low, controlled, with the ever present possibility of sarcasm.

"Fitting quite comfortably into the New England life-style." He was careful to pronounce the area as two separate words. "How are things in Mogul Land?" He'd begun calling Hollywood by that name simply because the first word sounded to him like Mongol.

"I had three directors and a line producer for breakfast. Now that I'm wound up, I'm ready to rip the hearts out of a couple of writers and disembowel a gaggle of agents."

"That's my boy. But is there anything unusual happening?"

"I got out of that Kimmelmann deal with Rosenthal and his wife."

"That shouldn't have been too difficult; didn't I read he just died?"

"Not that simple. But not to worry."

"I haven't since you took over." What it was he didn't like about the man became even clearer in his mind.

"I wouldn't have bothered you with it, except for one thing." He paused.

"Am I supposed to ask with bated breath what that is?"

"The property they had. I see something in it for us. Not the way Rosenthal conceived it, not with his widow. Not even as a film."

Russell was beginning to feel uncomfortably out of his element, and he sensed the studio chief knew it. "What then? Mini-series?" he threw in.

"No. Series series. You know what it's about?"

"I'm afraid I don't. Should I?"

"Possibly. It's about where you live."

"I'm afraid I'm not following." His wife was making a succession of questioning, disgruntled faces at him for reasons he couldn't fathom.

"New England. What time and circumstances have done to that bastion of pride and principle."

"And prejudice, if I'm not mistaken."

"It uses the area as a microcosm. Really the disintegration of America, the pollution of it, the abuse. Setting the stage for a revolution, a backlash."

"Provocative. But is anyone going to tune in to see themselves fall apart?"

"I think so. The writer was smart enough to season it with potboiler stuff. The usual: family dysfunction, sex, money, crooked politics; the tried and true."

"So . . ."

Ennui sneaked into Wald's voice. "So, you can look at it as a nighttime soap or as politically correct drama." He was clearly working at being patient.

"That's not what I asked. I meant, Why haven't you bought it?"

"I want to talk to the author. Which is why I'm calling. He lives in your neck of the woods. I thought I'd fly in, go over some stuff with you, and arrange to meet him."

"Sounds enterprising. By all means. When would you like to come?" He turned his head to see his wife's scowling face.

"I'll have to get back to you."

"By all means. We'll arrange a lovely inn for you." He smiled benignly at Aida.

"Thanks."

"Bye, then."

Wald's voice, hardly varying from a monotone, was the sort of voice, Russell thought, perfectly suited to a killer.

Ben Bradford admired the way the Partridgefield postmistress contained herself as she looked at his package.

"You can send this book rate, you know," she said with some authority and careful indifference.

When he advised her he wanted it to arrive as soon as possible, she very quickly said the words *Beverly Hills, California* and began index fingering to a page in her book. He wondered what, if anything, the words conjured up for her.

"This'd be fastest," she said, turning a small pad to him revealing the numbers she'd written on it. Clearly, in her mind, nothing short of an inheritance notice could be worth the figure.

"Really? That much?" he said, to reassure her that despite being a successful author he shared her views. Then he made a show of reluctance and paid. She pasted a metered tape on the brown envelope and pounded it with a postmark rubber stamp. He felt a thrust in his chest, as in the early days when sending off a manuscript heralded a quiet adventure. As she placed the envelope carefully on a pile, with due respect for its premium shipping rate, she repeated the words *Beverly Hills* and looked at him with the barest hint of a smile. "Thank you very much," he said and left slightly embarrassed, as if he'd been showing off.

Outside the post office, spring was dispersing its eternal rain. For Bradford, the somber gray-and-brown days came and went with a depressing sameness, interspersed with equally somber and numbing nights.

It was curious, he thought, that the fortunes of his novel, recently headed for major-motion-picturedom, now destined for remainderdom, had not bothered him. Perhaps because he hadn't believed it would happen in the first place.

The project had gone from a piquant, flattering phone call from Lewis Rosenthal to the quasi reality of a treatment. Rosenthal had spared him the embarrassment of asking what one looked like by sending him a pile. Then gently editing his efforts with confidence-building enthusiasm. When he'd satisfied the producer, the wait had been punctuated with encouraging bulletins, big names and huge numbers dropped. Then the biggest news of all: Rosenthal's death.

He'd flown west for Rosenthal's funeral, partly out of a sense of business obligation, partly out of curiosity. He'd been taken aback by the sight of big stars acting like real people, their faces drawn, their bodies flagging.

The crowd around Nora Howard had dissipated quickly, perhaps, he thought for no reason in particular, forever. For a time he had wondered whether she actually knew he was present. Only toward the end, after the final eulogies, had she made a point of coming to him, touching his hands with her black gloves, and saying something so softly he hadn't caught her words. He'd leaned down and kissed her veiled cheek, also uttering something probably inaudible. And then she'd turned, distracted, unsure of where to go in the dwindling crowd.

Now, Nora Howard had called to say what he'd always suspected would happen: the dream had melted. He'd immediately thought with embarrassment of the local papers, having devoted so much time and space to what had seemed his meteoric rise to celebrity. Now would come the retraction, another Hollywood tale gone awry. Except that it hadn't quite ended, and this accounted for the pleasure he was feeling in spite of the news she'd given him.

She'd spoken to him openly, telling him not only what he needed to know about their project, but eventually about herself. He'd wondered if speaking to him, a writer isolated in a New England farmhouse, hadn't made her drop the artifice of an actress. Instead she had talked to him as one lonely person to another.

Almost reflexively he'd told her that he was having a play produced at the Hartwood, that she might think about coming east and appearing in it. His offer had come out without thought, although he knew the Hartwood people would be most accepting of a movie star in their midst and on their stage. Nora, of course, had declined to commit herself. But he recognized something in her voice that made him believe, whether or not she was aware of it, that she would.

The play he'd sent her, *The Limner,* was his compensation for the years of writing journeyman magazine articles, sweating out his now-not-to-become-a-major-motion-picture novel, but most of all, writing it had become consolation for losing his wife to a quick, chilling pancreatic cancer death.

Because she'd wanted no treatment, her remaining six months became preparation, readying him for the inevitable weight of memory and hollowness of loss. They'd spent the beginning of that time in New York City, seeing every show and dining at every serious restaurant. Then they'd gone to London and Paris to do more of the same. Their lists ended with the expiration of her energy.

The rain had stopped, leaving the chill of a damp April in the air. Instead of returning home, he drove the perimeter of a large valley, past overflowing culverts, winter-yellowed lawns, and the first tinges of new green on the trees. Looking at their anticipatory gesture, he felt the pulse in his chest quicken as he allowed himself to contemplate the confluence of events that might bring himself and Nora Howard together.

Aida Russell knew well her role in life; she would always be an outsider. It didn't matter that her husband had been OBE'd or that he would soon, as rumored, be knighted. She knew the recognition signified no more than a commendation from a chamber of commerce for bringing home the pounds.

On the other hand, their instant home and the Old World grace she had imparted to it were looked upon appreciatively in the States. The very mystery of its creation had intrigued the local gentry, who could not have been more pleased with the outcome. Thus it was without much surprise that Aida received the news that the wife of a former governor was on the phone. She thanked Julian and took the call in her morning room.

"Mrs. Shannon? This is Aida Russell."

"Hello! I don't believe I've had the pleasure of meeting you, but I'd like to make up for my misfortune by inviting you and your husband to a party I'm giving in honor of the Hartwood Playhouse people. I understand you're recently on the board."

The statement floated like a question awaiting an answer.

"Yes, I am, to my delight."

"Ours, too. We love new blood."

Aida wondered whether there wasn't a hint of sarcasm in her voice.

"The Governor and I have been looking after our wonderful

theater for lo these many, many years, practically since the days of LeGallienne. It's very dear to our hearts. I imagine with your husband's show-business connections you should be able to make quite a mark."

"Well, they're *his* connections. And I suspect he leaves things show business to those who understand it better than he."

"That sounds very shrewd. Leave things to the experts; that's what I've always done. When Dick was spending all that time up in the state capital, I decided to start up my own little enterprise, as you probably know. Left it to the experts, just kept an eye out to see they stayed out of trouble, didn't have to worry about finances, that sort of thing. Just let them do the job right."

Aida knew that the Governor's wife had merchandised much of New England's lore and heritage the way Andrew Lloyd Webber did his musicals: quilts, honey, preserves, furniture, pillows, weather vanes, curtains, glass, pottery, and everything commercialistic under the New England sun had been turned into a gingham-and-lace conglomerate.

"Never lose the homemade touch, I tell them. That's what we're selling, not *things*. Send the little ones off to school and make a little extra money in your kitchens. *Those* are my experts, those who still know how to sew like their mothers did."

Aida had passed her barrackslike factories; she wondered whether the woman had recited her home-and-hearth fantasies so many times she'd come to believe them.

"Anyway, it keeps me busy, and out of trouble, as Dick says. Seems people just can't get enough reminders of a simpler time, when practicality counted and excellence was expected."

Aida realized she was sounding like her own catalogues.

"It's kept my family together, too. Gainfully employed. Nothing like keeping the generations close to home, don't you think? Do you have any children, Mrs. Russell?"

Aida noted that the singsong recitation of her homilies had congealed into a hard-edged question.

"We have a son, who looks after Michael's publishing interests, another in London. And a daughter in California."

"What does she do?"

Aida thought the question impertinently direct, but remembered that was part of the American conversational style. "A mother and a writer, children's books, which, by coincidence, her father publishes."

"That's exactly what I was talking about; keep it all in the family. Anyway, I think you've gotten on board for one of our more exciting seasons. Ben Bradford, our wonderful friend and neighbor and the author of last year's biggest best-seller, about all of us, of course, has written just a wonderful play. Needless to say, Ben will be coming to our party, and what I would call a good cross section of our happy little community. May I count on you and your husband joining us? On the sixteenth?

"I'm sure that would be fine, but I'll have to check with Michael."

"Well, you just remind him what's the use of being big and powerful if you can't do as you please. And I certainly hope it pleases you both to come. I'll send a formal invitation, of course, but I felt I wanted to get to know you a little bit on the phone."

"It was very kind of you to call. I certainly hope we're able to make it."

"You *must* make it. It's the perfect opportunity to meet everyone under what I hope will be very pleasant, sociable circumstances. I'll enclose a little map so you'll be able to find us. And, of course, there'll be little party favors, the newest things from my catalogue."

"You're making my mouth water, I can hardly wait." Aida looked at the seventy-five-thousand-dollar gilt Chippendale mirror that had recently been sent from London. "I love those darling little napkins you make, the ones with the duck borders and gingham centers."

"You do! I'll send you a gross. They're among my favorites, too. It's all so exciting. Selling my little bibs and aprons seems so mundane when the season rolls around. I sometimes think that in some other life I was on the stage myself, the reason why I relate to it so well."

"Perhaps you were."

"Well, I'm not so sure you'll think so when you see me. Unless I came in a totally different package. Anyway, put the party down in ink immediately. And I'll just jot down about those napkins for you." Her speech slowed as she'd apparently begun writing the note to herself. Suddenly Aida heard a half swoon, half gush over the phone. "You won't believe what just walked into the room. One of my beautiful little granddaughters wearing an advance model of our little Early American dresses for toddlers. She looks like an absolute angel. I think they're going to sell very well. Speaking of dress, just wear the sort of thing women do to the garden parties your queen throws." She held the phone away from her mouth. "Yes, angel, Granny will be with you in just a second. Well, Aida, I've taken up more than enough of your time. See you on the sixteenth, then."

"You're very kind. Good-bye."

Aida knew it was the sort of invitation Michael coveted. He genuinely enjoyed meeting new people, trying to win them over. As for herself, she would smile pleasantly at everyone, appearing slightly enigmatic to mask her fear of meeting strangers. It didn't matter that in recent years she wore the most expensive gown or the best jewels in the room. Neither the millimeter of her pearls nor the depths of her charitable generosity could make her feel anything less than an alien.

Chapter Four

Hollywood

Chip Walker awoke with the same queasiness he'd been experiencing since the evening of Lewis Rosenthal's death. His nights, now that he wasn't spending them at the suicide-prevention hotline, had been filled with the symptoms of a sick man: sweats, nausea, chills. Had the days not been perfectly normal, he might have entertained the notion that he was really ill. But by the time he'd dress and reach the studio, he was feeling his normal self.

He enjoyed the feel of the lot with its hangarlike stages, cottagelike offices, and hierarchically arranged parking spaces. Yet, even after working there for several months, Chip still felt furtive walking around.

The big event of his morning had been riding with Wald's assistant, following the big cheese, who drove his own hot sports car. Wald was flying to the Springs for whatever reason and when he'd arrived at the airport, he'd gotten out of his car and left it at the curb; it was customary for someone in a car behind to drive it back to the studio or his home. The first time Chip had witnessed the stunt, he'd laughed at the imperious gesture. But for Kevin, Wald's aide, it was just another piece of crap he had to take. Naturally Chip had wound up driving the studio car while Kevin got to take the Aston Martin. It was then he realized how really little there was standing between his going from a Ford to an Aston Martin; only one jackoff of a flake called Kevin.

Now the sun was bouncing off metal walls, drenching the lot in heat. Only mad dogs, Englishmen, and himself, Chip thought. He'd never seen the Englishman that owned the place, only read about him, heard stories, but as far as he knew, he hadn't set foot on the lot since Chip had begun working there. Class, he thought, paying a couple of billion dollars for something you never went to see. Either the sun or the thought of such wealth began making him dizzy, and he realized he hadn't eaten since breakfast.

Back inside the office complex, walking down the corridor to Wald's office, he could hear Kevin's voice. Or rather his high, trill of a laugh. "No!" he kept repeating between bouts of uproarious whoops of appreciation. As Chip approached his desk, he saw that Kevin had changed into shorts and a tennis shirt, his limbs and face tanned an even honey color. "If you let me off this frigging phone, I can make it out to the beach in an hour," Kevin shrieked. Chip watched as he rolled his eyes for his benefit, using his fingers to pantomime the chattering mouth at the other end. "Enough already. Thank God I don't have a car phone." Kevin was tapping edges of folders on his desk, straightening papers, slipping things into his file drawer. "All right, Delores, in two seconds I'm hanging up on you." Chip wondered how this hyperkinetic fount of gibes had wound up personal assistant to the Big Guy. "I'll be there, gods of the freeway permitting, in an hour," he said and put down the phone. "Hooky time," he said, smiling at Chip. "It's quality not quantity, right? Did my chores for the Colossus and I'm off. Cover me on the odd chance . . ." He let the thought float. "And have a nice day." He blew Chip a kiss across a horizontal palm and exited.

When he had gone, Chip walked to Kevin's desk and began absently pulling open drawers. He wondered whether whatever Kevin did was beyond him. The problem being he wasn't sure what that was, other than making Wald's appointments, taking his dogs to the vet, and collecting his abandoned cars. Even that wasn't bad, getting to fantasize in an Aston Martin every now and then. The thought had given him the start of an erection.

After he estimated Kevin to be out of the building, he moved to the door of Wald's office, almost certain that it would be locked. Slowly, as if he were acting on one of the sound stages, he twisted the knob. The latch sprang open. The space inside was vast. Wald's desk, monstrously large, appeared to float in the enormous room. Huge paintings, no more than swatches of color, hung from thin brass rods along the ceiling. Equally abstract chunks of bronze on lucite pedestals were spaced like islands about the room. Low, creamy leather chairs the size of loveseats faced the desk like pews to an altar.

Wald's thronelike chair was covered in a spotless nubby white fabric. As Chip sat in it, he noticed several panels of buttons built into the desk controlling God knew what kind of electronic apparatus. Even the phone looked like a piece of flight equipment.

On Chip's right, one drawer was stuck open because of the protruding edge of a black leather book. He quickly reached for it. The idea of a telephone book with handwritten names and numbers struck him, in this office, as primitive. He held the book in his hand without looking at it and squeezed, as if some of the magic contained within would disperse into his grasp. Once again he felt light-headed, almost swooning at his proximity to importance. Each name, he was sure, represented a fairy tale.

He was startled at what he thought was a sound from the outer office. Depending on who caught him, being at Wald's desk could mean his job. He jumped out of the chair and peeked outside. Probably a fax machine. He closed himself in again. The telephone book was still in his hand. As he returned to the desk, this time with the casual swagger of familiarity, he opened it to **R.** It was no surprise that Lewis Rosenthal's number stared up at him. He dialed.

"Hello?"

It threw him that she had picked the phone up herself on the second ring. "Hello? Hello?"

He knew she would hang up if he didn't speak quickly. "Mrs. Rosenthal?"

"Yes?"

"I was a friend of your husband. How're you doing?"

"Who is this?"

He looked down at the phone book. "My name is Robert. But you wouldn't know me anyway."

"I knew all my husband's friends. How did you get my number?"

"I've just told you, I was a friend of your husband. How is it that you're picking up your own phone?"

"Everyone's out."

"Everyone?" He was truly surprised. He imagined her house to be vast, filled with dozens of Mexicans running around in crisp white jackets.

"What is it you want?"

"To give my condolences."

"That's very kind of you." Then, as an afterthought, she added, "Was there anything else?"

"Would you be interested in how he died?"

"What do you mean?"

"You don't think he really killed himself, do you? We both know what a physical coward he was."

"Who is this? What are you saying?"

"That Lewis was too pussy to kill himself. Sorry, that was crude. Are you still with me?" He heard a noise at her end, like something dropping. "Fine. You don't have to say anything if you don't want to. I like talking to a movie star and having her listen back." He pushed himself away from the desk and placed his feet on it. "Well, Nora, I could give you all the gory details or we can skip to the bottom line. Right. I'll spare you the details. Lewis was assisted in his decision to leave this world. It's not that he hadn't thought about it, or didn't want to. You could say he had mixed feelings." Now he heard nothing at the other end. "Perhaps you know why. He talked about you a great deal. He was very proud of you. He felt very responsible for you. I mean in the sense that he made you what you are today. When things started to suck, he felt responsible for that, too. You know what I mean? Lewis was one of those guys who carried the worries of the world on his shoulders. I mean, like, the *world*. So you don't have to go around blaming yourself. He was very confused and very unhappy. Let's just say he got a friendly nudge. How's that? Not a bad way to put it, right? You might not see it now, but one day you'll agree, it was really the kindest thing for someone to do."

"Give me your number, I'd like to call you back."

He smiled to himself. "What's the matter, Nora? Nature calls? Anyway, I'm afraid I can't do that, give you my number. I'm at a friend's and I'll be moving on. Just wanted to touch base. And wish you luck. Made any plans for the future? If there's anything I can do to help . . ."

He heard her click off quietly. He smiled again and put down the phone. If his friends could see him now. In the catbird seat. In control. On the A team. All his youth, he had heard he was a loser. That his eyes, which he later discovered were beautiful, looked like a cow's. He hadn't questioned the verbal abuse. Or the punches. In fact, he'd learned to take it all. Silently and stoically. It was all he could do, never giving his father the satisfaction of showing he'd been hurt. Pain became absolution, something that happened to the physical part of him. It stung, felt warm, triggered tears that he'd suppressed with all his might. Which, as it turned out, was considerable. That was childhood. It had always seemed the strangest thing to him, the notion of family. Something you saw on television or in other people's houses. His parents were simply two adults fate had entrusted him to. And he to them represented nothing more than perpetual disappointment.

It was amazing what getting out from under their regret, their rage, their forlorn disappointment had done for him. He was actually making it, impressing people, feeling appreciative stares, approval. And now that he'd had a taste of it, he wasn't going to stop. There was so much room for him to maneuver, so much higher he could go. It was like a wonderful game, one in which he could make up the rules as he went along. There was no one to stop him, no one to say no, to insinuate he wasn't good enough to play. No one he couldn't be. He knew—he'd already tried it. His life was like gliding, he was taking matters into his own hands, coasting on the currents of what was happening around him, picking up a tail wind; he was flying by the seat of his pants. Hello down there! Fuck you!

Chapter Five

Beverly Hills

Coleen Copeland stretched out on the long white sofa, feeling like a spy behind enemy lines; it wasn't Nora's home she was infiltrating, it was Hollywood. She moved her sturdy body about on the smooth fabric, parodying what Harlow would have done with such a prop.

Before her self-imposed retirement, she'd been a vastly acclaimed theater star, occasionally wafting onto large and small screens when the offers were too outrageous to refuse. In her prime, she'd attacked the stage with a power that scared even herself, breathing fire and luminosity into plays of the period and forging reputations for their authors, her accomplishments proving more lasting than those of her playwrights.

"Aren't I something?" She stared owlish eyes at Nora. "Not only do I invite myself out for a visit, I'm emptying your bar faster than I unpacked." She stood and moved past Nora, touching her shoulder affectionately.

"I'm delighted you're here."

"See if you feel that way in two days." Coleen poured for both of them.

Nora enjoyed listening to her honey-soaked, throaty voice. A magnificent instrument on stage, in private her voice was like an adagietto for cello. They'd met years before on a TV mini-series; Coleen, who was maybe ten years older, playing her imperious mother. The first day she'd appeared on the set, done up as a rich dowager in black velvet and diamonds, she'd said, I always wondered what I'd look like embalmed. The crew had laughed and warmed to her instantly. Later, in the one scene that necessitated any real acting, a scene in which she heard of the death of Nora's character, she'd kept everyone silenced a full thirty seconds after the director had called cut. Then she'd broken character and gone into a bawdy Irish folk song, leading them all out to the nearest bar.

"I can't believe I'm saying it, but I'm almost happy to be here. You know how long I've been holed up in dumb, frigid Partridgefield?"

Nora shook her head smiling, accepting the drink from her friend.

"Three fucking years. You know why?" Her eyes were wet with a devilish glint. "No place else to go! I'm not even sure I'm wanted there, but they pretend. 'Must be kind, the old dear was famous once.' Except for my daughter, she doesn't pretend anymore. At first it was, Mother, you must stay with us, rest up, then you'll work again. Except I didn't, want to work anymore. More fun drinking than killing yourself on the stage every night. Believe me, you shake a lot less from the DTs than you do from stage fright. Anyway, when my daughter and my adorable son-in-law saw I had no intention of returning to the goddamn stage or the goddamn screen or even play the boob tube, they very politely suggested I find a place of my own. Which I did, a condo where I don't have to lift a finger or kiss mother nature's ass. But, God, it's boring! People thought I was crazy giving up glitz and glamour to live among the quaint and retarded."

"Are you?"

She swallowed half her glass. "I told you, art sucks. Makes warts inside your brain." She looked at Nora sweetly. "No, not art. Art's not the culprit. Show business, that's the traitor. Look." She held her hand out and stared at it. "See? Steady as a rock. You know what turned me off the business? I was getting plenty of work, so it's not like sour grapes. It was that they were expecting so much. Too much. I was becoming like this holy acting icon. At the height of my art, leaves no acting stone unturned, that's what they said. You'd have thought I never had to go to the toilet, for God's sake." Disgust filled her face as she swung her empty glass in her rock-steady had. "No, there was more. All about me, I began to see fear in the eyes of my colleagues. Fear of growing old, fear that the next facelift or new toupee was going to look ridiculous, fear that you're becoming stale and shopworn and unsalable. I said to myself, What's wrong with you, are you too stupid to realize the danger you're in? There I am, acting my head off, loving it, getting these fabulous reviews, too dumb to know that it could all disappear tomorrow." She checked Nora's glass, saw it was full, and returned to the bar. "But I wasn't as stupid as I looked. I got out before they could get me. Left them wondering before they could start pissing on their Coleen Copeland dolls. I got plenty of money and nothing much to spend it on back east. You should taste the food—turkey gumbo, tom turkey with stuffing, mashed potatoes, mashed potatoes, mashed potatoes. It all tastes like it came out of the same Elmer's glue bottle."

Nora watched her friend return to the sofa and deflate into the middle-aged woman she was. "You've come to see if I need help. That's nice."

"Bullshit! I didn't come to rescue you. I just felt like a tour of movie star homes." She leaned toward Nora, bunching her thick cheeks into a smile. "You're more like my family than my family. We are family. Every two-bit tap dancer and every peroxide broad that ever swung her tits in front of a camera, we're all family. God, we are wonderful. I must be getting old. I used to see a lousy performance and think, Where'd that broad come from? Send her back to running a sewing machine. Or I'd see some kid that looked like a Greek god, who had no idea words were supposed to mean something. Guys like that I thought should be used in laboratory experiments. Not anymore. Now I look at them and say, Honey, God bless you. God bless your guts. God protect your innocence. You're too young or stupid or gorgeous to know that the jackals are just waiting to eat you alive. Old makes you mellow. Or maybe it's the booze."

Nora watched the actress sadden. When she'd called, Nora realized how curious it was the way actors could pick up where they'd left off a year or a decade earlier, like their lives were on hold while they were working. Or was it the other way around, that work was their lives and everything in between was filler? Nora remembered how much Lewis respected Coleen, which made her feel that much closer to her.

The older actress sat up straight at the edge of the sofa. "Now, that sentimental crap aside, I also have an ulterior motive for being here. I've been commissioned by Ben Bradford to talk you into doing his goddamn play. And if I can't talk you into it, I'm to wrap you around my neck and carry you onto the plane." She paused and stared at Nora. "Which I hope I have to do, because for that I get a bonus. By the way, is the play any good?" She stared at Nora innocently.

"Haven't you read it?"

"Of course not. You expect I prefer to eat myself up alive? Not me. Stay out of harm's way. If I read it, I'm certain I'd want to do the part. Then watch out, it would be scratch-out-your-eyes time. No sir. No temptation, no regret. Is it good?"

"I think so. I have no idea what audiences will think, but . . ."

"Fuck 'em, who cares? Feel, yes, we get paid to make them feel. But I'm very sorry, I'm just not interested in their intellectual opinions. When they've retched up their guts and souls as many times as I have, they can tell me what they think. Until then, I don't give a rat's ass."

"You've heard what it's about?"

"Oh, sure, this Early American deaf-dumb portrait painter who knocks up this Early American chick. Only he never screwed around with her, and the mother, you, is trying to save him from being hanged by the gentle townsfolk so she can get in his pants herself. Isn't that the general idea?"

Nora felt delight at the actress's presence. "It's a very good play. Question A is, Can I do it? B, Should I? And, C, What for?"

Coleen looked at her indignant. "Pul-eeze, spare me this modesty shit. Of course you can. Why? For fun. C, to have a real job instead of this film manure." She looked forlornly into her empty glass. "Plus it wouldn't hurt for you to drop the sturm und drang around here for a while." She turned shy. "Much as I hate to admit it, Partridgefield is so fucking beautiful this time of year you won't fucking believe it. And I can't begin to tell you all the famous broads that have trod the boards of the Hartwood. It's like a classy thing to do. Plus I want to spend more time with you. And I sure as hell ain't going to spend much more time in Lala Land. Visit a couple of old sellouts I know and back to being abused by my daughter." She looked at Nora quietly and earnestly. "Do you want to talk about it?"

"Lewis?" She stared at the older actress. "Sometimes, I still feel like it never happened. That he's in the next room working. Even at night, if I reach out and spread my hand over the mattress, I think maybe he's gone to the bathroom." She gave in to tears.

Coleen sat next to her, arm around Nora's shoulder. "Honey, honey, honey, I'm sorry I started you off. I didn't mean for you to have bad feelings. I just meant if you wanted to talk about it."

Nora drew herself up, her face placid, almost remote. "You know why I delude myself? Not because he's dead and I'm alone. I'm afraid of how he died."

"Pills," Coleen said softly. "They don't hurt. He just drifted away."

Nora searched the actress's face and shook her head slowly. "No."

Her voice was so low, Coleen barely heard it. "No?" she echoed her.

"I don't think that's how it happened."

"You mean, like he had a heart attack or something? What *do* you mean, that's not how it happened?"

Nora shrugged as if she'd lost the ability to speak.

"Hold on a second . . ." Coleen appeared to be struggling with the idea. She shook her head "You've got doubts and you're just sitting here suffering with them?"

"What am I supposed to do? Tell the tabloids I think my husband was murdered? The police have already said suicide." She shrugged again. "How did Lewis get to that motel? *Why* did he go there? Who was he involved with and why would they want to . . . ?" She lifted her glass and drank in earnest. "How could I be so unaware of so much of my husband's life? You see what a can of worms it turns into? And would it bring him back?" Nora felt her heart cramp and tears return.

"Oh, Jesus. Look, Nora. For sure you've got to do this play.

You keep sitting here, you're going to drive yourself crazy. Listen to me, these heebie-jeebies, these goblins whispering in your ear, it's normal. It's all part of grief. Honey, you've really got to get yourself away from all this. Jeez, I had no idea. I came out to help Ben land himself a fancy leading lady and I wind up practically saving a life."

Coleen buried her nose in her glass as Nora thought about the phone call, wondering what other demons might be lying in wait for her here, and thinking there might be more truth in Coleen's prediction of her going mad than she realized.

"Has the eagle landed?" Kevin asked Chip, his face red from exertion. He'd entered the warren of cubicles near Wald's office breathing hard, but had slowed his pace to appear casual. "Eagle" had become their code word for Wald.

"Nope. You're cool."

"Last night was a heavy date night," he confided cheerfully as he arranged papers on his desk. Then he held two fingers up to Chip. "Imagine that, in these trying times, two dates."

Chip looked at him with concern. "Don't you get scared, fucking around like that?"

He shook his head knowingly. "Caution, caution, caution. I know every safe-sex trick in the book; in fact, I could write my own."

Chip allowed him a smile. "That's good, that you're not inhibited."

Kevin raised his brows and looked at him slyly. "Inhibited? Moi? You must be joking. I want what I want when I want it." He snapped his fingers. "And if I don't get it, I take it," he said with drama.

"That's a great attitude. Does it apply to work, too?"

"Work? Not really. I'm happy looking after the bald eagle; beyond that I don't have much in the way of ambition."

"Really. This is Hollywood. I thought everyone had a fire in their belly."

"I do, I do, but not for work," he said vampishly. "If I ain't tried it, the body can't do it."

"Wow," Chip said with admiration, "maybe you *ought* to write a book."

"I have considered it. But it would have to be illustrated. I couldn't begin to describe some of the things I've done."

Chip nodded. "I'm impressed. And none the worse for wear, are you?."

Kevin looked smug. "Absolutely not. Healthy as a horse."

"Good for you." Good for me, too, Chip thought, realizing that his little chat with Kevin had given him an idea.

Steven Wald enjoyed sailing down the halls, past the desks of acolytes and sycophants, poking his impressive head unannounced into offices, plucking papers off desks, some even while being read, throwing out questions, absorbing compliments. Instinctively he ran the studio as if he were a feudal lord, taking his droits de seigneur, at all times defending his territory, making sure his authority reigned absolutely unquestioned.

Then there were times he practiced disarmament, like stopping at someone's desk, usually someone in a relatively menial position, and doing nothing but engage in small talk. It was in one of those expressions of enlightened despotism that he appeared at the small cubicle belonging to Chip Walker.

"It's nice to see that not everyone runs out at lunchtime to touch up their tans." He cocked his head toward Kevin's desk and smiled like a bemused but understanding parent. "How come you're not out there with the rest?"

Walker appeared to blush. "I kind of enjoy reading through these." He patted a stack of scripts on his desk.

"Find anything interesting?"

Chip held his flush. "Maybe." His manner grew braver. "How many pages does it take before you know whether something's good or bad?"

Wald grinned down at him. "Pages? I don't have to read a word. I simply put my hand on top of the title page and I know." His eyes squinted in an attempted smile as he looked back at Kevin's desk. "Good for you. All he cares about is who's in it and what they're going to wear."

Chip shook his head slightly in a modest attempt to disagree.

"You don't think so?" Wald asked. "Am I missing something?"

Chip appeared hesitant. "I think maybe he's preoccupied with other things."

Wald looked at him curiously. "Like what?"

The young man shrugged. "Personal stuff."

"His two hour lunches should take care of that." Walker seemed hesitant. "Not to mention his nights. Does he think I don't know what time he gets in?" Wald smiled. "I really don't care as long as he makes sure the masseur arrives at my house on time and the restaurant is holding the best fucking table in the house for me; that sort of thing he does very well." He allowed himself to dwell in his bonhomie.

"I'm glad you're so understanding," Chip said solemnly.

The conversation, which to Wald was so much mental chewing gum, suddenly made his antenna rise. He let his smile fade and nodded back. "I hope things are working out." he said reflectively. "With Kevin's personal stuff." Wald watched the man's face with interest.

"I don't think he spends all his lunchtimes sunning." There was an undercurrent of protectiveness in his words.

Wald signaled agreement with his eyes and continued staring at Walker.

"He doesn't really talk about it . . ." He tested Wald with his gaze. Then he smiled, as though banishing his doubts. "I imagine he goes to see his doctors."

Wald felt his brows tighten, a creepiness spread across the back of his neck. "What for?" Suddenly the color in Chip's face drained. "I mean, he takes such great care of himself, all those vitamins he pops, why the hypochondria?"

Walker appeared to retreat, his expression blank. "Right."

"He does take care of himself, doesn't he?" Wald asked, trying to retrieve his knowing tone.

"Of course he does." Chip looked at him as though sorting something out, then with resignation. "Those aren't vitamins, they're medicine." He said the words as if the thought was so self-evident, he couldn't understand anyone not getting it. Then fear entered his eyes. "He hasn't told you?"

Wald conveyed nothing.

Chip looked away. "He's fine, Mr. Wald. I . . . I tend to make assumptions.

Wald turned and started for his office. Then he looked back. "Don't worry about it, Chip." He smiled. "And tell Kevin not to spend so much time working on his tan. It's not good for him."

*   *   *

Steven Wald enjoyed driving himself around town. Even
when stuck on freeways, he relished the idea of being alone,
thinking, flashing on solutions. On the way to Malibu, the violet
sunset ahead of him was so perfect, he found himself staring at
it as though he were at a drive-in. He opened the windows,
allowing the cool breezes to tease his face, relaxing him further.
Then he thought of Kevin.

In his own little perverse way, he was actually quite fond of
him. Which was why the thought of Kevin catching the plague
had actually passed through his mind on more than one occasion. There'd been times Kevin was so loose around him, he'd
casually alluded to his escapades in ways Wald found quite
funny. For one brief moment, he'd actually contemplated the
idea of a sitcom built around Kevin's life-style. But the fact that
he himself was nonplussed by such behavior did not eliminate
the fear engendered by hearing the news about him.

Along with regret, there were practical ramifications. What if
the poor fucker wanted to keep on working? Knowing Kevin,
he'd show up on his last legs if he thought Madonna was going
to breeze through the office. Was it selfish of Wald to want to
spare himself the—what?—discomfort, embarrassment, the
need to compromise on the man's ability to perform? Where
did self-interest end and common sense start? Since when was
enlightenment meant to get in the way of efficiency?

Fortunately these were not questions he had to answer. His
assistant had said nothing to him; there were, technically, no
ethical issues to face. He could make the call with a clear con-
science. Except for Walker. Would *he* say anything, the only
possible link between innocence and deceit? Wald doubted it. It
was Hollywood, and everyone dreamed about their own sunset
to drive into, just as he was doing now.

The days after his brief conversation with the eagle, Chip
arrived at the studio with considerable enthusiasm. Of all the
scenarios he'd proudly alluded to with Wald, the one he'd con-
cocted himself held the most interest for him. He'd get to the
office early and wait for the key players to arrive. Once everyone was in place, all he had to do was sit back and wait for the
plot to thicken.

For his part, the studio head began to act distant, if not out-right rude. Puzzlement was all over Kevin's face every time he'd make some aborted attempt to communicate with his boss. Mercifully his confusion soon ended. Wald apparently called the Human Resources Department and told them to manufacture some reason to get rid of his assistant. Kevin only knew he was out, cutbacks, he'd been told; he was given a generous severance, first-rate references, and told to clear out his desk and be gone that afternoon.

In his stupor, he'd confided to Chip that he hadn't the vaguest idea what he'd done wrong, or how he'd antagonized his boss. He didn't believe a word of the story that had been told to him, but he knew there was no point trying to refute it. He'd lost Wald's trust, in spite of his loyalty. Chip had commiserated, even suggesting archly that Wald lived in a closet within a closet within a closet, implying that perhaps *that* had something to do with the unfair decision.

Kevin had not even finished packing when Chip called Human Resources asking to be considered for the job. As circumstance would have it, that was precisely what the personnel director claimed to have had in mind.

As for Chip, he sifted through a mental index of personalities he'd developed and stored away over the years. He'd shown a subtle instinct for confronting people with the person they'd wanted him to be. As you desire me, Chip thought.

The Resources guy he knew he could play like a fiddle. The only hump to get over was the business of age. Chip had originally put down his correct date of birth. Now he was faced with reconciling his twenty-something face with his thirty-something age and filling in the disparity with the substance to justify the new position. As it happened, the gentleman from Resources seemed to lose track of the conversation while smiling foolishly into Chip's ridiculously blue eyes.

His interview with Wald had been a curious affair. The man had suddenly turned shy, avoiding his gaze, as though Chip knew the real reason for Kevin's dismissal. Chip himself struck a polite attitude, unanxious, without a trace of the obsequiousness he'd seen Kevin exhibit. His stated willingness to work the sort of hours Kevin abhorred, and Wald's uncharacteristic mellowness, made him feel he had the job before he'd left

Wald's office. The only surprise was the generosity of the raise that Resources had engineered for him.

Almost as soon as Chip Walker started working for him, Wald's gut told him he'd made a mistake. There had been many Kevins and many Chips around him over the years; he understood them without even having to think about it. Some simply enjoyed inhaling the heavy scent of power, loved seeing the infrastructure on which all the tinsel hung. Others wanted to taste the business for themselves, salivating to be part of it. Some were harmless, some less so, like Chip.

He'd come through the personnel grilling with flying colors. Not in town long enough to become jaded, with the sort of level-headedness the Midwest apparently had a lock on. But Steven had seen through the department's report the minute he'd come into his office for a face-to-face interview. Looking at him directly, he could see it in his mouth, the little twist in the corners; but it was most apparent in the eyes. How could he have missed it before? Chip had looked straight at him, through him, the way good film actors did with a camera. There was no fear in his eyes, no admiration now, no respect. They seemed to want to gouge out as much of him as they could, to understand what had put him on top, swallow up anything that would work for him. The look was not uncommon in town. It belonged to the secret coven of the rich and successful, also the overthrown and defeated. He had seen the look still ignited, even when the game was lost, in the fallen, still snarling, like an animal chewing at its leg to get out of a trap.

The idea of Walker having even remote knowledge of why he'd gotten rid of Kevin bothered him. It was only a question of time before Chip would have to follow the career path of his predecessor.

He lifted the phone. "Chip, we're going east. Make us arrive on the fourteenth. You game?" He adopted a jocular, almost paternal attitude toward him.

"Great. Would you believe I've never been?"

Wald wasn't entirely sure he spoke the truth. "I put the details in my calendar. Check it and make the arrangements. The New York office knows the car I want. And get a gift for the

Russells." He scrunched his fistlike face into a smile; in a distant mirror he saw his large bald head looming like a helmet.

"You got it," the young man said softly, his voice taking on an odd seductiveness.

Wald disconnected him and dialed the New England writer directly. "Is this Ben Bradford?"

"Uh-huh. Who's this?"

Wald had calculated that he'd be waking the man, but the voice sounded strong and alert; already gruff. "Steven Wald." He announced it like a gavel striking a wood block.

"Ah, yes, the gentleman who pulled the plug on my book."

"That's why I'm calling. To clarify." A tone of conciliation had come into his voice.

"I heard it's dead."

"The original deal. By the way, I'd suggest you get a new agent, one who opens his mouth." Wald continued. "Yours is a pussy. But that's not my problem. I want to discuss another project with you, based on your book."

"Call my pussy agent."

"No thanks. I'm calling you."

"Another project? An animated feature, no doubt."

"That's very funny." Wald reminded himself that Hollywood people never laugh, they simply declare their intentions.

"I'm busy with a play right now. I don't think I'd have time for anything else."

"Who says this instant? I just want to talk with you."

Bradford hesitated. "Talk."

"Not on the phone. I want to come see you."

"No kidding."

"No kidding, but before you have your pool dug, you should know I was coming anyway."

"I'll put my ego back on life support. When?"

"Fourteenth."

"I'm in the middle of rehearsals."

"What happened to the Protestant work ethic? We'll meet after. Or before. You might even like what I have to say."

"Really? For how long will you mean it?"

"Listen, buddy. It was Kimmelmann who promised you a picture, not me. I'm just the guy who stopped it. Give me credit for not throwing out the baby with the bathwater. We don't all think as fucked up as Rosenthal, if that's your benchmark."

"Sorry, I can't."

"What? Forget Rosenthal? He was a loser. Apparently he agreed with me. He killed himself."

"I don't think we're going to be able to do any business together, Mr. Wald."

"Hold it. Let's put our opinions of Rosenthal aside. We're talking about your book."

"You're rewriting history, Mr. Wald. Turning my book into a film had everything to do with him."

"I'm not Thomas Aquinas, Mr. Bradford. I'm not going to get into a discussion with you. The fact is, he's dead."

"You make it sound like an accommodation."

"Why is it I always get a headache talking to authors?"

"Because we're so superficial compared to the heavy thinkers you usually deal with."

"Mr. Bradford." Wald lowered his voice. "Would you give me two hours to discuss your book?" Wald envisoned the writer: a red plaid flannel bathrobe, a yellow dog following him, walking to a hanging cabinet and pulling out a quart of vodka. So begins the day of the northeastern author.

"One."

"I'll call you."

"Yeah."

They both hung up. Wald knew the East well, having lived and worked there. Which was why he found the dazzling, sun-baked, bird-of-paradise, hibiscus-bright shallowness of L.A. so appealing. Nothing complicated, just the simple ritual of young smooth limbs that paid homage to the sun being paid homage by fat white wrinkled types. Here everything was casual, languid, upbeat; the smiles all punctuated by large white teeth; the taut golden faces framed by helmets of gold hair. Here he lived in a neighborhood of palaces, each one unabashedly trying to outdo its neighbors. None of that false reserve, smug under-statement the East prided itself on. Excess on top of excess, youth elbowed out by younger. The sort of financial treachery not even attempted on the curbs of Wall Street. A piranha paradise. The thought made him smile, then think of Chip. Perhaps he could lose the young man in the East; he would make calls and see. Or perhaps left to his own devices, he would set his sights on something else. Fat chance. Here he was working elbow to ass with Mr. Power, about to snooze across the country with him in a private jet. He buzzed the assistant. "Where am I lunching and with whom?"

"Hall Carter, director. In your conference room."

"I want to go out. Tell him to meet me on the steps and tell someone to get my car."

"Right. Anything else?"

"Yeah, stop trying to be so fucking perfect."

Chapter Six

New England

Nora Howard, in tanktop, shorts, headband, and hand weights, was enjoying her morning jog around Partridgefield. In truth, she enjoyed the double takes, the cars swerving slightly or slowing when they realized they'd just passed a Movie Star.

What had been towering skeletons just days before were becoming green shapes. Soon the gaps and crevices between the trees would be obliterated. She compared the ranging free-form exuberance of the landscape to the manicured tropical formality of Beverly Hills where everything, including people, looked like topiaries.

Her running shoes made rasping sounds on the gravel along the side of the road. She inhaled deeply, the air heady with the sense of sanctuary, and felt the spots of sweat on her jersey catch the breeze. And then it struck her, for no apparent reason, that today would be the day she would listen to the tape.

The fact that it existed at all was something Nora hadn't wanted to deal with. She thought of the simian gestures of the night manager from the Paradiso, his furtive looks, how he'd slipped her a note the night she'd gone to identify Lewis's body. It said she should call regarding something belonging to her husband. He had wanted only two hundred dollars for the tape, despite his protestations that he was taking a big chance by not turning it over to the police. She'd never doubted the authenticity of his find, or the notion that Lewis had made it specifically for her. Nor had she been quite ready to bring herself to listen to it.

Now Nora found herself disoriented, unsure of where she was or which direction she was headed. She poked her head about as if trying to catch a scent in the air. The muscles in her legs were starting to ache. A car passed, the driver craning his smiling head out the window, saluting her with an upthrust thumb. She smiled back, raising her weight in a half-mast wave. The small blue pickup pulled over.

"You're a long way from Hollywood." The driver was young, pleasant looking.

"Hi. I'm lost."

"Where were you headed?"

"Nowhere in particular. Except now I'd like to get back to where I came from."

"The theater?"

She shook her head, wondering how much damage the perspiration and the bright sun were doing to her movie-star image. "I'm staying with the Shannons. Do you have any idea where that is from here?"

"Sure. You're not far."

"That's good news. Want to point me in the right direction?"

"Easiest thing would be to go back about half a mile and take a right. Keep going a quarter mile or so and it'll be on your left. Actually, the easiest thing would be to get in and I'll drive you there. Then I can tell everyone how I picked up this movie star hitching, which no one will believe."

"Why don't I just sign an affidavit that you did and run back by myself?"

"Nice of you, but I can't say it if it's not true. My name's Tim D'Amato, in case you want to tell someone about the nice young man who stopped to help you."

She smiled. "Okay, Tim."

"You're staying with the Shannons?"

She nodded. "You know them."

A look of amusement passed quickly over his face. "Sort of."

He started up the engine. "I'm coming to see your play. Any good?"

She shrugged. "I think so."

"That's good enough. Good luck. Break a leg, isn't that it?"

"You got it." She smiled and waved as he pulled onto the road, then turned to follow his directions.

It was the Shannons' custom to invite any star of sufficient magnitude to stay in their guest cottage. Nancy had seen to it that it was replete with antiques, Oriental rugs, and little reminders of Mrs. S's booming business. Over the years, through additions from countless auctions Nancy Shannon had attended, the cottage had grown as luxe as a four-star European hotel suite. While it was far too grand for Mrs. S's own taste, it was her way of establishing her worldliness to anyone foolish enough to doubt it. When Nora returned to the cottage, it was clear someone from Mrs. S's staff had returned it to its pristine state. In the bedroom, she saw a note next to the telephone that read: "Dear Nora, Please join Dick and myself for cocktails and dinner. Around six. Love, Nancy." There was something Elizabethan, she thought, about being a player at the disposal of the lord and lady of the manor.

She moved silently across the waxen, wide-plank flooring to a large satchel and removed a brown envelope. Her heartbeat began to accelerate and she tried to calm it by holding the package against it.

Now, without allowing herself to think, she slipped the tape from its manila camouflage and took it to the elaborate audio system the Shannons had provided for their guests. Curiously, there was no hesitation as her finger went to the power button, a small red light acknowledging her gesture. Another button sent the jaw of the cassette player out, into which she deftly fed the plastic box. She snapped the compartment shut and pressed PLAY.

What she was not prepared for was the intimacy of Lewis's voice. It was as though his words were being thawed, their sound caressing, the accent unusually thick with urgency. As he addressed her she closed her eyes and sobbed.

"My darling Nora . . . what I'm going to tell you is both a confession and denial. So you will understand the whole truth, I must begin with a meeting between Mr. Wald and myself. I had not spoken to you about it because for me it was such a humiliating experience. I knew from the amount of time I had been kept waiting and the distracted way he received me that things would go badly. When I walked into what was Kimmelmann's old office I was struck by the amount of furniture that was *not* in it. It had taken on the appearance of an elegant bunker and Wald the gestapo caught among a mass of war plans. His remarkable blue-gray eyes seemed lit with a spark of malice that startled me.

"At first he didn't ask me to sit. It was only after I enquired with my eyes that he said to be seated. Then he told me what I'd suspected: our project was dead. But what he said was that *I* was dead. Not the project, which had possibilities. But he did not wish to discuss it with me because, he told me frankly, he had no trust in me. He was exercising a clause in our contract allowing the studio to pull the project if our development proved unsatisfactory. In essence, I had assigned the rights to them in return for money up front. He sneered at what a fool I was to sign such an agreement and how it showed my uselessness as a producer.

"Then he talked about you. He told me I was a Svengali in reverse, that I had been handed a piece of magic in you and had reduced it to tatters. That it was one of the more tragic wastes in a town full of tragic stories. Do you think this could be true, my darling?

"Since then, I have begun to find truth in his words. In our last debacle, it was I who insisted on calling all the shots; we saw to what stunning effect." She cringed at the rueful sound of his voice. "Which brings me to the purpose of this message. After listening to Wald, I thought a great deal about the possibility that you would be better off without me. I came to see it as an act of love, of selflessness, a way of making amends . . . But I cannot do it. Suicide. The word is so dramatic, poetic, isn't it? Perhaps there is still enough self-esteem left to believe that in some small ways you need me. That my loss would cause you pain, which is the very last thing I want to do. Or perhaps I am just a coward. Then there are selfish reasons: I love you and I do not want to leave you.

"But—isn't there always a but—for certain reasons, I believe

I'm in danger, the decision taken out of my hands . . . Even more ironically, perhaps I deserve to die."

Nora heard sounds she couldn't identify, until she realized they were coming from Lewis. Half whine, half shriek. Then a series of grunts that seemed to be the word no. She heard a scream and *no* raised to a shout, followed by what sounded like muffled conversation. Suddenly there was silence and Lewis's voice came back, calm, with its familiar touch of irony. "I am now free of paranoia. You've come to make sure. My days of fear and self-hatred are over. And in return, all I must do is die. . . ." He laughed his familiar caustic laugh. "So this is to be my little claim to fame . . ." His voice shattered in sobs. Then the noises on the tape became a mechanical hum.

Instead of tears, Nora felt a bitter, nauseating taste in her throat. She wanted to press a reverse button, begin again with the last time she had seen him, replot his and her own existence. In theater, in art, there was the flexibility of change. There was a way of pursuing truth; but life was immutable. When the curtain fell, it stayed down.

Hollywood

The day before they were to fly east, Wald surprised Chip by inviting him to lunch. The assistant was prepared; there was no point hovering near the pinnacle of so much power if you didn't have a plan to plug into it.

The parking attendant jumped at their arrival. "Perfect day, Mr. Wald. So good to see you again." The young man was Mexican, his smile oversize. *"Very* good," he emphasized.

"Lucy in the kitchen?" Wald asked with familiarity.

"Of course," the young man answered pridefully.

"Good." Wald indicated to Chip to precede him. The restaurant was dark, low-ceilinged, the walls plastered with bullfight posters and piñatas. Again Wald was graciously received and led to a large booth in the back. "Is okay, Mr. Wald?" He nodded and almost invisibly slipped the maître d' a folded bill. "Two margaritas," he told the man, who pocketed the money with equal stealth. "And tell Lucy we'll have my usual, twice." He looked at Chip. "It may not be great, but it's better than most. So how bad a pain in the ass am I?" he asked smoothly.

Chip laughed nervously. "No way. I think you're great." Wald looked at him archly. "I know that sounds kiss-ass, but it's true. I think it's great the way you cut right through the bull."

"Yeah? What else do you like about me?"

"That you go right to the good stuff, like you have a built-in divining rod."

"I do. What else?"

"You've got no time for fools; you're not big on schmooze like most guys out here."

"So far," Wald interrupted, his voice low and hoarse, "I'm like fifteen other studio guys, maybe ten. If you think that's all it takes to go to the head of the class, you better watch more carefully."

Chip felt himself blushing as the waiter brought their drinks and disappeared.

"Cheers," Wald said lightly.

Chip reached out his glass too late to touch Wald's.

"What I mostly do is work hard. And think. Look at the facts and decide. See how simple it is? I don't buy this pussy gut stuff. Just look at the facts." He took a sip of the tequila.

Chip nodded slowly, as if recording the thought in his mind. "Were you always in show business?"

"In entertainment. Show business is for people who want to take off their clothes and exhibit themselves. Entertainment is a business. I came out of marketing. I take whatever product the artists come up with and try to make it look like it tastes good. Give it a handle people can understand. No magic about it. Just read the numbers Sunday night, weekend attendance figures, like a report card. Half the dorks who make movies have no idea what they're making or who they're making it for. And those who do, make films that look like they're pasted together from audience opinion cards." He took another swallow. "Did I say something you didn't understand?"

Chip took his first sip and shook his head no.

"You're from where, Des Moines? What exactly did you come out here to do?"

Hustle, Chip thought. He'd almost forgotten he'd told him Des Moines. He wasn't even sure where it was. One day he'd have to get a pocket computer to keep his stories straight. "I like movies." Then, embarrassed, he added, "Who doesn't?"

"I like movies, who doesn't?" Wald imitated. What do you like about them? Jacking off in the back? Watching what the women wear? Getting off on strange stuff busting out of people's guts?"

Chip looked at him with contrition. "I know it sounded dumb. I could hear as I was saying it. I'd like to produce."

"Good. You've just given yourself a lot of latitude. Like there are those who do, those who teach, then somewhere at the bottom, just after the critics, are those who *produce*. Good, I like that." His fingers flashed up in a V ordering another pair of drinks.

"In fact, I have a project in mind right now." Chip recognized how stupid it sounded, the thought confirmed by the twisted grimace on Wald's face.

"A project?" he mimicked by attenuating the words. "This may turn out to be a very fortuitous lunch for me. Or weren't you thinking of coming to us with it?" He shook his head. "You like Mexican food?"

"I guess you develop a taste for it out here."

"You develop a taste for a lot of things out here. How long have you been here?"

"Eight or nine months." Chip decided short answers were his best defense. And omissions. The big bald fart looked so smug, so omnipotent. There were stories he could tell the turd about himself that would grow hair on his ugly scalp.

"And here you are lunching with a studio head. Only in America."

Chip smiled sweetly.

"Tell me about your project? Is it wonderful?"

Chip was surprised at how fast his attitude melted; he also knew the freeze-up could be seconds away. "Well, it has to do with my extracurricular activities."

"Are you sure I'm supposed to know about those?" Wald teased.

"Actually, I'm kind of proud of it." Chip was still wary, but allowed a slightly sanctimonious note to creep into his voice. "An organization called WAYS."

Wald smiled. "At this point, there are more acronyms than words."

"We're At Your Side."

"Sounds like an escort service."

"It's a suicide hotline."

Wald scratched his jaw. "I'm impressed."

"You wouldn't believe how many people out here try to kill themselves."

"I don't doubt it. And for good reason, I would imagine."

Chip looked at him reprovingly. "In most cases, it's a terrible waste." He waited to see if Wald would disagree. "This town has built-in rejection. It's like, have a good day, you suck. It's all done so pleasantly that people start thinking if all these swell guys are telling me to kiss off, there must be something wrong with me. Soon they just feel like part of the scenery."

"They tear the scenery down after every show. And every bus brings a bumper crop of fresh, bright-eyed boys and girls with longer limbs, shinier hair, whiter teeth, and a more insidious willingness to please."

"Keeping the faith is hard," Chip said pleasantly.

"You think I'm cynical?"

"Perhaps a tad."

Wald smiled. "I bet you and your fucking hotline haven't seen half the basket cases I have. This town's a fucking mortuary of overthyroided, overambitious, overvain people who had it and blew it. Forget Mary Macintosh Apple, who can just get back on the bus and pick up her life where she left it. I'm talking serious burnouts. I'm not talking about blowing an audition. I mean blowing your family. I mean blowing a fifteen-million-dollar-a-year career by a couple of wrong choices. I'm talking about your real casualties, your Lewis Rosenthals. And you don't think seeing that pass before my life day in day out isn't enough to make me cynical?"

Chip, who had been listening attentively to everything Wald said, started at Rosenthal's name. "I get what you're saying. Give me another year before I go jaded."

"Really, smartass? I wonder if after you've seen enough people chopped into mincemeat you still think there's anything worth saving."

"I have to think there is."

"Okay, hotline man, fly through the phone waves every night and save those lives. Let me just tell you one thing. None of us is immune. Tomorrow I could be Russell's breakfast and Thursday Russell could get fed to the investment bankers and Tuesday the bankers can go to jail and get big black dongs shoved up their asses." Wald looked up and spotted the waiter approaching with a tray of dishes. "There, I just gave you a great appetite, right?" What a load of macho crap, Chip thought. Then the food, which looked like it was made of plastic and cardboard, was spread across the table family style. "Good appetite," the waiter said, eying the excess appreciatively.

"Eat," Wald ordered and began filling his plate. "So what does missionary work have to do with your project?"

Chip was trying to decide which food looked the most eatable. "Everything. Can you imagine the stories I hear? Things people wouldn't share with their mothers or lovers. Each case is a detective story; you have to figure out from what they say which are the red herrings and which clue is the key to their lives. Find out what took them to their abyss and use it as a flag to make them stop."

Wald continued eating as he spoke. "And this to you is entertainment?"

"Sure. Everyone wants to see someone worse off than themselves."

Wald stopped eating abruptly. "What did you think of Rosenthal?"

Chip tried not to break stride and continued loading his plate. "What do you mean, what did I think?"

"You're the suicide maven; what's your take on why he did it?"

Chip felt himself instantly decompress. "It's been in the papers. Like you were saying, things turned against him; he couldn't deal with it."

"You mean *I* turned against him. That's it? He must have had balls like BBs."

"I guess so."

Wald watched him struggle with the food. "Too bad he never

tried your hotline. Bet you could have brought him back from the abyss." Wald's eyes followed him like a cobra's, then he smiled. "You heard something about him, at the hotline. He was a client?"

"I couldn't say. All that stuff is confidential," Chip said with his mouth full.

"Not to me it's not. As long as you work for my office, nothing is confidential from me. What do you know about Rosenthal's death?"

Chip shook his head, chewing as if he had an indefinite amount of food in his mouth.

"I'll wait." Wald took a slug of tequila. "When you're finished digesting, you can give me the abridged version or the unabridged truth and save yourself time."

Chip started to cough, looking for a glass of water; what a dumb hard-on. Wald snapped his fingers and put his hand to his throat, summoning the waiter with two glasses and a pitcher. "Just leave it," he said.

"I hear he did call the hotline," Chip said finally. "Losing a client isn't something anyone brags about."

"Especially a hotshot like yourself. You didn't happen to speak with him on any occasion, did you?"

"Some of these people who call, they speak anonymously, in cryptograms. It's possible I spoke with Rosenthal and didn't know it."

"It's also possible that you did."

"Sometimes we find out more about the clients we lose in the paper than we get over the phone."

"And that's supposed to mean you did talk to Lewis but have nothing of interest to say about it."

"I'm not saying that."

"Listen, Mr. Development. I've got friends at police headquarters who could get me phone records, every call he made from that dippy little motel he picked to check out in. I could not only find out who he called, but when he spoke with them. I could piece together your life and his life and make it look like you were asshole buddies." He sipped the water now. "But why would I want to bother? Unless I decided you were holding something back on me. And why would you want to do that?

Unless you thought I was involved. Is that what you don't want to tell me?"

Chip put down the water and went for the margarita.

"Or is there more? Everyone knew I pulled his little project from him, so it's not like all of a sudden I become the heavy. You know something more about Rosenthal's death than you want to tell me." Steven leaned back. "Fair enough. You only work for me. I don't own you. I'm sure you have your reasons. I'd like to have thought your loyalty was such that you'd find it unnecessary to have secrets between us. Apparently we haven't reached that point. One wonders if we ever will." Wald reached for a tortilla and began mopping his plate. "This the first time you tried the wetback stuff?"

Chip nodded. "It's good. I think it's growing on me."

Wald looked up and snapped his fingers for the check. "Don't bother if it's for my benefit."

Chip Walker had put himself on automatic pilot. Roberta Welles, the young woman beneath him, whose breasts looked like miniature Frisbees, had relinquished her synchronized moans for erratic whimpering sounds. Expecting the change in her orgasmic orchestration to signal a more rapid thrusting on Chip's part, Roberta was disappointed to find his pneumatic pumping continued at the same robotic pace. Resigned, the crying sounds dissolved to low throaty grunts, once more taking their cue from his rhythm.

For all Chip cared, Bobbie might as well have been two pillows or a grapefruit. As the secretary to the director of Creative Services, she sat two desks away at the studio and served as his occasional luncheon partner. On impulse, he'd asked her to dinner, then if she cared to go home with him. She had accepted in both instances, then a third, when he'd asked if she cared to fuck. He'd been careful to indicate the perimeters of the last invitation, as he had no intention of allowing her to stay the night.

Much as some people were able to think best walking a beach or pacing a room, Chip found fornication the perfect mind opener. Once he'd put his body in gear, the peripheral sensations allowed his thoughts to ascend in flights of asymmetrical logic, making disjointed associations that sometimes took the form of revelations. So it was the night of his lunch with Steven Wald as he began plugging into the various repercussions.

It was apparent that Wald could care a rat's fart for anything Chip felt or cared about. As far as Wald was concerned, he was a supernumerary. Any advantages from working for the studio head would have to be gleaned by his own initiative. The man's style was despotic, rude, totally self-reliant. But what was most disconcerting about things learned during his Mexican lunch was that Wald had inadvertently associated him, however tenuously, with Rosenthal's death.

Of course, it had been his own fault. He was so anxious to impress Wald with his *development* material, he'd completely overlooked his links to Rosenthal. The question that remained was whether Wald would forget the matter or push further into it. Like checking with the police. Some career opportunity little Kevin's job had turned into.

Roberta had begun making different noises, sounding now more impatient than ecstatic. He had paid so little attention, he was unsure whether she had reached orgasm or not. He became attentive, even lowered his lips to her neck. Her groans curled into little throaty rattles. Suddenly they increased exponentially, becoming deeper, more guttural, fluttering rapidly like a moth near a sixty-watt bulb. His mind reluctantly gave up on Wald's possible modus operandi, even his own safety, and focused on the renewed sensitivity he was feeling and on fine-tuning his own reactions to be in perfect synch with those of Bobbie Welles. As though on a timer, both bodies detonated simultaneously.

Chapter Seven

New England

Around 10 A.M., the actors began assembling at the Hartwood Playhouse. They presented themselves at the large metal coffee urn, most catching their reflections in the mirrorlike column to make the necessary adjustments. To an actor, they spoke of the *The Limner* in tones normally associated with a newly discovered Mozart concerto, perhaps owing to the fact that Ben Bradford, author, was also Ben Bradford, director.

Ben had stopped at the Shannon estate to pick up Nora at the cottage, and their entrance turned the lethargic morning chatter into an appreciative wave of anticipation and highly perfected smiles.

The cast was a mixed lot: dedicated professionals dotted with a sprinkling of stars at various stages of their careers. None had reached Nora's heights, although several had come close.

Tony Newland had perhaps come closest. He was playing the part of Nora's husband, a not very choice role except for one major scene in which he was to break down upon discovering Nora's infatuation for the young limner. At the first run-through, he had dissolved his colleagues to tears even as his own hand shook holding on to the script. He was thin almost to

79

the point of illness, which set off his severely chiseled features
as though they were carved of translucent alabaster. His manner was formal and courtly, except for the pleading aspect of his
eyes, much like those of a puppy who is used to and fearful of
being kicked. It had been only seven seasons, maybe eight, since
Tony Newland had been nominated for both a Tony and an
Oscar in the same year; the latter actually falling within his
grasp. After that, those who followed his career admired the
caution he appeared to exercise before choosing his next role.
Several years later, it was obvious that he had no master plan
and the bright trajectory of his career had diminished to a soft,
if luminous, glow.

Ben and Nora approached him first. "Good morning, Tony,
I'm sorry you couldn't have dinner with us last night." Ben
patted the actor gently.

"Yes, well, I thought I'd explore a bit. I find one must be on
one's own to get to know a place. I tried going to the movies;
the first and last show was at seven. Can you imagine? Drove
around anyway; hardly saw a soul. I suppose it's a bit like Beverly Hills, no one on the streets." He smiled bravely, although
they all knew it was several years since he'd lived there.

Nora watched the little tic happening at the side of the actor's
eyes and mouth, his smiles beginning with a twitching action of
one cheek. "It is too bad you couldn't have joined us. Coleen
was full of spicy tales about everyone, even if she had to make
them up."

"There, well, you see? I'd have spoiled her fun. I'm sure she
had a shocker or two to tell about me."

"In fact, she didn't," Ben said as if dismayed. "Try as we did,
all we could get out of her were eyes lifted to the heavens and
hands crossed on her breasts as she sang your praises."

The actor held up his long tapered fingers and shook them
swiftly. "No, no, no, that's not possible. How could a genius like
her find anything good to say about me?"

"I think the two of you should get together and fight over
who worships the other more."

"I'm flabbergasted she even recalls my work."

Nora noticed his shortness of breath; she looked at his light
tan and wondered whether it wasn't makeup. "Come on, Tony,
actors shouldn't be modest, it spoils our image."

"Honestly, Tony," Ben said, feeling him flinch as he put his hand on his heavily padded shoulder, "tell me if you feel uncomfortable with anything. I trust your instincts." He left to join a small group at the coffee urn.

The actor turned to Nora with a look of urgency. "May I say something I haven't had the nerve to tell you but I feel I must?" She nodded almost imperceptively so he could continue. "I'm so grateful to Ben for giving me this part. I would have done anything to work with both of you. As you know, I've been coaching." His look told her the word said it all. "We used to be neighbors, remember? When was it, a year or two ago? Perhaps three. I had the series then. Little did I realize my *golden age* was coming to an end." Now that he had begun, he seemed unable to stop. "Broadway, Hollywood, and TV in ten years. Then nothing. It all dried up. Like that." He silently snapped his fingers. "Why? I wasn't on dope, I didn't drink; it just ended. I'd always thought it was just a terrible mistake, that my name kept getting misplaced or my answering machine was malfunctioning. I even began to think my agent was purposely sabotaging me. All she did was be the first to acknowledge what was happening by dumping me. What *had* happened? As far as I can tell I became dated merchandise. Like lipstick, I just faded away." The cheek twitched again and the smile reappeared. "Nora, my dear, I hate being such a bore, especially at this hour of the morning." He braved a smile. "I just want you to know how nice it is to be working again." He brought his hand up to touch her arm, but it brushed by like an air kiss. "I . . ." His voice became low and resonant. "I want you to know how sorry I was to hear about Lewis. It must be awful for you."

Nora nodded and smiled faintly.

"The poor man. What a difficult decision it must have been."

She allowed him time to continue the thought, but he said nothing. "Where are you living now?"

"I've moved to New York. A small flat on West Twenty-second. And in my Toyota; still can't get over my habit of jumping in a car and taking off. I keep it on the street; I don't bother replacing the radio anymore. A far cry from my Jag days." He smile broadly. "Well, what goes around comes around." He said the phrase as though unsure of its meaning. "One never knows where things shall lead. For me, regional theater, I should think.

I'm beyond the point of getting the big break and the thought of a comeback embarrasses me, admitting I've been away." He shrugged his shoulders. "I've already had my fair share anyway. I suppose it's time to leave the glory to others. Perhaps . . . perhaps Lewis had the right idea."

It was clear to her he'd been struggling with the thought. "Tony . . ." She gently touched his neck; he seemed so fragile.

"Who knows . . ." He made a small bowing gesture and walked away.

Billy Carroll, the actor playing the young artist, had arrived at rehearsals with his perpetually sleepy eyes at half mast, his pouty mouth looking particularly sullen. Audrey Dalton sat in the front row of the theater watching his befuddlement as he tried to negotiate two cups of coffee. "Sweetheart, is there any tea up there?" she called to him as he lifted the paper cups from the table. The actor looked back over his shoulder, then to her and shrugged. "Never mind, coffee will be fine, I suppose." She watched the way his young body, dressed in tight jeans and a loose T-shirt, negotiated the wooden steps down from the stage. "Thank you, darling," she said, using both hands to take the paper cup from his grasp.

"Sure."

"Sleep well?"

He smiled at her shyly. When he'd left her room she'd been pretending to sleep, her fluttering false eyelashes giving lie to the performance. It was out of kindness that he never remained to see her in the morning.

"I did," she said with a mock catlike stretch. "Oo-o-h, I slept marvelously."

"You must have, you look wonderful."

"More, more, more," she said coquettishly.

"Very few people can be glamorous twenty-four hours a day." Or want to, he thought.

"Yes?"

"Like you, darling." He'd not gotten over marveling at her resilience. After a flashy start in the fifties, she'd spent decades slogging around the world after work, then been scraped from the sludge of Cinècitta C films to regain notoriety as the queen of wickedness on a nighttime soap, or serial drama as she called it.

"Oh, that's so sweet." She put two fingers in his long floating curly hair. "Has our star arrived yet?" she asked facetiously.

His eyes shot sideways, indicating where Nora was sitting, talking to Ben.

"Oh, good. It's so wonderful to watch her unfold her art." Her vaguely British accent added a tartness to the words. "She's fast reaching the stage where the only thing left is one of those I-took-off-my-make-up-so-you-can-see-I'm-really-acting sort of parts. Which, of course, I don't knock; they've resuscitated many a career." Her hand played languidly over the soft bouncing waves of her wig. "Next thing you know you're showing your tits and giving simulated blow jobs on screen. That's *really* acting." She brought the cup to her shiny scarlet lips. "Oh, that's yummy. You know just how mother likes it."

Billy took a slug of his coffee.

"I've worked with her before, you know; not as anyone would notice. She supported me once. Supported me is being kind; she had four or five scenes at most. The rest were left on the proverbial cutting-room floor. It's such a rough business, I really don't know how I've survived as well as I have." She could see the young actor was getting bored. "You, my young friend, have a long, brilliant career ahead of you. All you need are a few contacts which, of course, I can take care of. You've got it all, the looks, the talent, the ego. Terribly important, the ego. Without it you're nothing; look at Tony. He's got the smell of fear about him. The long pauses, the empty eyes; he'd dead. Professionally and spiritually. Terrible thing, failure. Well, we don't have to worry about that, do we?" She gave a playful tug to his chin. "Have you heard the rumor about Lewis?" she asked almost as an afterthought.

"Nora's husband?"

She nodded patiently. "Recently deceased, yes. I heard she was livid with him, blamed him for fucking up her last picture. That she was about to throw him out of the house. That's how he found his end in that grubby little motel where salesmen go for . . . Wasn't that a sad way to go?"

"I suppose. I guess he just wanted to get out of everyone's way."

"Oh, you're such a sweet boy, putting a smile on everything. I don't think it was so considerate, just sleazy."

He relinquished the point to her. "Anyway, she seems quite upset by it."

"Quite upset, my ass. Certain people, certain people who *know*, say she pushed him into it, the suicide. Personally, I think he deserved it. Treated women like shit. Pardon me, *merde*. He toyed with women. Made promises that seemed quite convincing. But they all disappeared when that little piece of *merde* got what he wanted."

"That's a pretty awful thing to say."

"Yes, my young friend, life is sometimes awful. And it in turn makes us do awful things to survive." He looked at her heavily made-up face. Even in the dim light of the theater, she looked like a waxen replica of her former self. "These days one rotten move can kill you. As it did Lewis. At your age, you could survive two, three, even four disasters. Gawd knows I've had my share. But today, with everything so accelerated, you must do anything you can to change your spots when you're in trouble. Why do you think I'm here in this place playing a mother? Because the public gets excited only when it doesn't know what to expect." She looked at him coyly, pursing her lips. "Fortunately, I'm very adaptable, don't you think?"

"Uh-huh," he said as pleasantly as he could. He wondered how seriously she took herself. Or if she allowed herself any self-reflection. Then he thought about what was left after one went beyond camp.

She slipped her arm through his and rested her head on his shoulder. "Anyway, I think I'm going to love theater. So much more real, none of that superficial TV nonsense. I'm so bored with all that, so tiresome. The only reason I put up with it was for the money. But how many jewels can you wear and still be in good taste? Mine are stuck away in safe deposit boxes because of those dreadful insurance companies."

The actor looked at Ben, hoping he'd soon bring an end to the morning's pleasantries and begin rehearsals. Leaning against him, Audrey's thick hair all but obscured his face. At first he hadn't realized she wore wigs, not until someone pointed out the various lengths of her hair at different times of day. He'd begun to feel sorry for her, until he figured out there was essentially nothing at her core to be concerned for, that she was in constant retreat from whatever it was that had been herself. He was unsure how he'd let himself be acquired by the fading artifact; he only knew she gave the best head he'd ever had.

Veronica Lindhurst, an actress of considerable age and reputation, looked about the company, an eclectic mix of apprehensive but enthusiastic beginners, bored old hacks, the dislocated, and those like herself, there to act simply because it was important and necessary.

For her, acting was synonymous with Ibsen, Chekhov, and Shakespeare. It was about working with great directors and actors. The theater was one's reason for living; life outside something one did to get back to it. The world was a place for pleasantries, eating and sleeping, getting from job to job. But one became meaningfully alive only on the stage. It felt as safe and secure, as full of pomp and peacefulness, as the Catholic church. But, just as people had once briefly declared God to be dead, the theater as she knew it had indeed passed on, and the terribly sad part was there were few like herself to actually mourn it.

For her, summer theater still held more substance, more possibility, than the other venues she'd been forced to sample. Recently she'd been told by her agent to get on a plane. She'd flown to Hollywood and been put up at a hotel with mini-suites instead of rooms. A car had been provided, driven by a brash if likable young man, his cap set rakishly on his glorious bed of blond hair, his eyes the color of old-fashioned turquoise swimming pools, who had told her she was like an alien goddess in a heathen garden of plastic palms. The metaphor had confused and disturbed her until she was brought into a large conference room where she was invited to join a group of people to discuss a proposed TV pilot. After ten minutes of intent listening, her mind began to convulse and the young driver's description seemed as clear as a child's storybook. Soon she found herself fixating on the peculiar clothing worn around the table and the intense posturing. From it all she gathered she was being asked to play a stern grandmother, forbidding but vulnerable, remote but reachable, cold but human; she even found herself making notes when the conversation turned to her role.

That night, back in her hotel room cum mini-apartment, she read the script they'd given her. She had exactly three lines: 'What are you doing down there?'; 'Where are my glasses?'; 'Will you all go home so I can get some sleep?'

She gathered the three questions were meant to be comedic, that her character or caricature was meant to be a likable curmudgeon. She reached for her notes: remote but reachable, cold but human. From Galsworthy to this, she thought and began to cry.

The next morning, when the agreeable young man came by to take her to the studio where the pilot was being shot, she was waiting for him in the lobby with her bags packed.

"That bad?" he'd asked without need of explanation. "I wouldn't, if I were you," he added, picking up her bag and walking to the elevator. "I hope you forgot to check out."

In fact, she had. She followed him up to her rooms and waited as he returned the suitcase to her bedroom.

"Got your script?" he asked as he held the door open for her. She nodded and walked past him. Then, as they waited for the elevator, he whispered, "Do you know what tens of thousands of actors in this town would give to audition for this piece of shit, let alone have a line to say? It's all part of the same thing, isn't it? Heavy-duty stage work, serious films, cartoons, burlesque, and this crap, in descending order. You say your words and you take your money." She'd smiled at him, somehow believing him, and allowed him to drive her to the studio.

On the sound stage, as she waited among the gaffers to say her three lines, her limbs had felt weighted down. The director had introduced her with great fanfare to the cast and crew, reciting her history sketchily, as though the words had no real meaning for him. Then she was asked to say a few words about herself, update everyone, as it were. She'd felt no connection with these people, as foreign to her as if she were addressing a shop of machinists.

Who would have thought, she muttered to herself, watching the inanity being enacted ten yards away. Soon after, she'd retreated east to find an offer to work at the Hartwood.

Now, watching her colleagues playing out their various agendas, she questioned, as she had done on very few occasions, why her devotion to the theater had been so unquestioning. And as she looked at Nora, she remembered that the producer of the pilot had been the actress's husband. Dear God, she hoped, let the theater, in its infinite capacity to redeem, give this woman solace and hope.

Ben looked among the assembled players hoping the time would soon come when he could talk to the characters he'd written and not this assortment of assembled egos.

"Ben!"

It was someone administratively connected with the Hartwood whose function, Ben thought, was to spy and report back to the trustees.

"Ben! . . ." He appeared to be catching his breath from the short trip down the aisle. "Mrs. S wants to know if it would be all right for her to address the cast; she's got something real special to tell them." He accented his words with a conspiratorial wink and smiled.

"I guess. When does she want to come?"

"Now."

In the back of the theater, the door opened. A smallish, pale blond man leaned forward like a discus thrower to hold it as a tightly permed blue-haired woman walked by him. Her face was a pleasant mask of fine-featured whiteness and her short, slightly stocky body moved with graceful bearing.

"Ben," she said softly and descended toward him. "I hope I'm not interrupting." Her eyes flicked quickly and intently around the theater. "No, I see I'm not." She looked at him with school-marmish sternness. "I should think mornings are difficult for actors; I suppose most of them are night owls."

Ben ignored her logic.

"As you've probably heard," she continued, "it's been my custom to say a few words to each cast during the start of rehearsals. I imagine I'm one of the few people left who can still bring a sense of continuity and tradition to the Hartwood. Which I intend to keep doing as long as I'm able. Beside, I have a little treat I want to tell them about." Her attitude suggested she was about to speak to a group of children, announcing an overnight campout.

Ben leaned against the top of the seat behind him. "Ladies and gentlemen. Please. May I have your attention?"

The laughter and rumble of conversation faded.

"Thank you. As you can see, we have a very special visitor. Someone who, for all intents and purposes, *is* the Hartwood."

Appreciative nods and sounds from the crew mingled with the crinkled-browed confusion of some cast members.

"Mrs. Shannon, who's raised more dollars and done more to keep this theater going than anyone save, perhaps, Mr. Shannon." He paused for comprehending titters. "She's come today to give us her benediction, if you will. And perhaps a little something more, if I'm correct."

"You are indeed." Her projection filled the theater into the balcony. "First, let me thank Ben for allowing me to distract all of you from the concentration your art demands. But I've come to welcome you, not just to the Hartwood, but to our entire community. Many of us just hibernate all winter until the time all of you come up and bring to us your art and your magic. As you know, this area is renowned for the brilliance of its fall foliage. But I can assure you, it pales next to the magnificent colors each of you bring to our lives through the exercise of your profession.

"As you also know, this theater has hosted . . ."—she paused to dutifully survey the room—"a multitude of actors and actresses, some of legendary proportions. From the Stickneys to the LeGalliennes to the Hepburns to the Nora Howards." She stopped again to look appreciatively at the actress she'd just elevated. "You might say there has been so much magic in this hall that the walls tingle with it. I think you, as actors, can't help but be touched and influenced by those who have played here before you. And perhaps it's one of the reasons that each season this theater seems to bring out the best in the people who appear here. That, and such talented people as Ben Bradford, who's not only a major talent but a local one as well.

"Obviously it's not my intent to take too much of your valuable time away from rehearsals, but I did want to mention that my husband, who couldn't be here this morning, feels at least as strongly as I do about the importance of your work here and the perpetuation of the Hartwood tradition."

Ben and other locals knew instinctively why the Governor

had not accompanied his wife. A vodka toast at dawn to the day followed by a vodka-accompanied breakfast would have resulted in his traditional midmorning nap.

"Nonetheless, you are still going to meet him, and that's the special treat Ben alluded to. Saturday a week we're having a party to get the season off the ground. Besides the Governor I want you all to meet many wonderful members of our community who work so hard and so diligently behind the scenes so that you can all go forth and act your hearts out. We're also going to have two extra special guests, from Hollywood and as far as London. Mr. Michael Russell, who the papers always seem to refer to as the media tycoon, will be joining us as well as Mr. Steven Wald, the head of his motion picture studio. Can you imagine how mind boggling such a heady guest list is for such simple country folks as ourselves?" Mrs. S placed her hands on the pearls at her throat and blushed on cue. "As if it weren't intimidating enough having the likes of stars like Miss Howard, Miss Dalton, and the rest of you around to remind us how provincial we all are." She squeezed her eyes together and bowed her head as if in grateful prayer. "Anyway, we'll see if we can muddle through without bumping into the trays of canapés or spilling drinks on ourselves. My husband and I do hope you can join us. We so look forward to getting to know our actors each season. May I express the wishes of both of us for an exciting and successful season. Good luck, God bless, and thank you."

"And thank you, Mrs. S." Ben began clapping, leading to general applause. "I know we're all looking forward to celebrating the new season at your party and appreciate your words of encouragement. Now I'm afraid it's time I start leading our merry little band of players through their paces. Thank you so much for dropping by, Nancy."

"Thank *you*, Ben, for allowing me to speak. 'Bye everybody."

Once more, the door opened for her and she departed, blue head held high, sensible shoes firmly in touch with the ground.

Chip was surprised to discover how cheerful Wald was on the flight east. The studio head had commandeered one of the more commodious if garish among Russell's corporate jets. It included a facsimile of a mirrored bedroom as well as a faux-marble shower. Steven had made a show of coaching Chip on the variety of splendid wines aboard as well as displaying the compartments brimming with adult games, video cassettes, and sexual aids. Since their departure he'd played the perfect host, and Chip wondered why.

"What do you think?" Wald asked as he sat up on the bed leaning against the headboard, his legs stretched in front of him.

"Beats Greyhound," Chip said.

"There is something to be said for vulgarity," Wald continued, looking about. "People shouldn't knock it until they've tried it. Now, where we're going, it's a bit different. You've never been, right?" Wald's smile melted into a sneer at Chip's nod. "Well, we're going to buzz through New York. You might want to take a Circle Line tour. Catch the Statue of Liberty, the Empire State Building, and you've got it covered."

Chip passed on his sarcasm. "Have you ever lived there?"

"Oh, I did a lot of living there. Before I became an Angelino. Actually, I'm more a bicoastal." He gave Chip his nasty grin. "Take your pleasure at both ends, so to speak. Especially when you can bicoastal like this." He gestured about the cabin and pushed the buzzer on the headboard. "Drink?" A houseman-steward appeared immediately. "What'll you have?" Wald asked his aid courteously.

"Beer."

"Montrachet," Wald spit out and clasped his hands behind his head. "Who's watching the hotline while you're gone?"

"There are plenty of volunteers."

The attendant brought the drinks. Wald sipped and looked at Chip queerly. "I wonder if Rosenthal died in the saddle and they simply painted it over and said it was suicide. I can see that. What do you think? Possible the suicide crap is a cover-up?"

"Possible. I doubt it. Everything I learned at WAYS and read about Lewis Rosenthal says victim to me, fits the profile perfectly."

Wald sipped contently. "Life works in such mysterious ways. You know, his widow just happens to be treading the boards in the town we're headed for. Isn't that a remarkable coincidence?"

"She's doing a play by the guy you want to speak to."

Wald couldn't remember if he'd told him or he'd figured it out. "Precisely. You're doing your homework." He smiled at him.

Chip smiled back. "I even read his book. I think it's got a lot of possibilities."

"Something you'd like to develop?" The smile turned mean. "Want me to green-light it for you?" He held Wald's stare. "It's nice to know you agree with me. Gives me confidence. Remind me to send flowers to the widow Rosenthal. I think that would be a thoughtful gesture, don't you? 'Hollywood's loss is the theater's gain,' something like that."

Chip scribbled a note.

"Now you remind me of Kevin. He wrote everything down, but he couldn't think. Just did what he was told. Did it well, too," Wald said reflectively. "Wonder how much longer he has left?"

Chip inspected his face for concern; his question appeared to be an idle one. Wald shook his head slowly as he put down the empty wineglass. ". . . Come along like buses, the dumb fucks." He shook his head harder. "Why do they have to go and kill themselves?" Now there seemed genuine concern in his voice. "If Kevin were here, I wouldn't be sitting with an empty glass."

"Sorry." Chip looked about for a buzzer as Wald reached up and pressed the one on the headboard. "Don't worry, I got it. Kevin always did know how to push buttons," he added absently. "When the attendant appeared, Wald's eyes simply brushed the empty glass. "Another beer, Chip?"

"No thanks, I'm fine."

"He's fine," Wald repeated to the steward. "Did you know my assistant was a WAYS suicide expert? Rather an antisuicide expert. A kind of Brother Teresa among those who want to escape this vale of tears."

The attendant smiled politely at Chip and left with the empty glass.

"Is it something people do impulsively, or do they think about it for a long, long time?" Wald made the question sound rhetorical, but he sat waiting for an answer.

"Mostly, it's well thought out."

"I would think so." He stared at his stocking feet. "I would think so. They say no one's a hero to his valet; I wonder if anyone's ever a success to himself?" His stare floated to Chip. "Sorry if I'm boring you. Being in one place for any length of time makes me philosophical. That's why I like to keep moving." He swung off the bed, giving Chip a look of disgust. "I don't want to be disturbed," he said, walking into the forward cabin and slamming the door behind him.

Nora sat on the patio of the Shannon cottage sipping mineral water. Her hosts had become accustomed enough to her presence to allow her some privacy.

The countryside had greened and the Shannons' apparently endless lawn spread emerald to meet it. When the phone rang, she looked at it with incredulity that someone was thoughtless enough to disturb her bliss.

"This is Nora," she said, uncertain whether it might be the Shannons buzzing through from the main house.

"Is it?"

The voice immediately made an electrical path down her back.

"How are you?" he asked.

The familiar tone seemed mocking; it wasn't the first time she'd heard that edge.

"How are you enjoying New England?"

"Who is this? Who do you want to speak to?"

"You, Nora. I'm a fan, remember?"

She did.

"I can't wait to see you on the boards. It's a clean slate. Different coast, different medium, different marital status. Wow. So much change for one little woman. Boy, you must be tough."

"I . . . I don't want to have this conversation."

"Then why don't you hang up? No, wait. Only kidding. I want to talk to you. See how you're doing. Whether or not you're enjoying your widowhood."

"Why are you being so cruel?"

"Am I? I guess it's my nature. But how many fans do you have who would travel three thousand miles to see you on the stage?"

"Are you getting pleasure out of toying with me?"

"That depends; do you enjoy being toyed with? How are you enjoying the country? Beautiful, isn't it? So pastoral. Bucolic. I mean, cows and everything. I think it's great."

"What do you want?"

"Just checking in, seeing how the Shannons are treating you. How are rehearsals going?"

"They're going very well."

"Excellent. Ben Bradford's a very talented man, don't you think? Very talented. The word is out Steven Wald wants to get hold of his book, the one you and Lewis were going to make into a picture. Don't you find that interesting?"

"It's an interesting book. Ben is very talented."

"For sure. The question is, is he ambitious as well?"

Her heart beat fell out of synch. "What do you mean?"

"Coy doesn't suit you. Wald. He's coming here to talk with your friend Ben, isn't he?"

"Where did you read that?"

"Read it? I *know* it."

"You follow the business very closely."

"Don't *you* find show business fascinating? I mean, the people it attracts, a varied and interesting group. Like *your* little company, for instance. I bet each one has a story. And dying to tell it."

"I suppose so."

"I suppose so. Really, give me a little more credit. Don't try to blow me off with inanities. I might have something very interesting to tell you."

She sipped her drink and waited for him to continue.

"Ah-hah! Finally I've got your attention. Good. Your friend Ben, how much do you trust him?"

The question surprised her. "A great deal."

"Bull. He's like all the others, all you other showbiz types. Out for himself. Inside the belly of every actor or writer or director is a colossal tapeworm called ego. Absolutely insatiable. Every time it smells fame or success or money it goes into a feeding frenzy."

"What does that have to do with Ben?"

"You think he's any different? It's like saying someone's shit doesn't stink."

"What's your point?"

"It's not my point, it's yours, really. At least it should be. You think it's just a coincidence that his book bounced from your husband to the hottest guy in Gollywood?"

Nora finished her glass of water, wishing it contained wine instead. "I'm not sure I follow you."

"Really? I give you credit for being two steps ahead of me. So far, if you'll forgive the crudeness, who stands to benefit most from your husband's death? Not you, certainly; rug's been pulled right out from under. Not even Wald; he could've red-lighted the project with or without your husband around. Just peek about you. Who's got this big studio honcho winging in special for a little tête-à-tête? Why it's that lean, mean, and tweedy New England-y author. After you and your husband had fallen from grace, he couldn't very well have just packed up his marbles and gone to the other side, could he? Not after all you and Lewie-baby had done for him." She didn't respond. "Poor baby. It's hard hearing things you don't want to know. How closely did Ben and your husband work together?"

"He stayed with us."

"Fair to say they got pretty close? Male bonding and all that?"

Again, she let him hang in silence.

"You think the author in Ben could have triggered Lewis to kill himself? Given him the reasons, the means, the encouragement; maybe even used his nice New England-y bedside manner to help him?"

Still Nora said nothing.

"Just a thought. Perhaps when your long country walks make you contemplative, the notion might be something for you to chew on. Good old solicitous Ben. There with a helping hand when you needed one. So terribly thoughtful."

Now she could no longer restrain herself. "You have a very scummy mind, you little coward. My husband killed himself. Don't you find it disgusting trying to turn me against someone who's tried to help me? I don't for one second believe what you're saying."

"Isn't that too bad. What more can I say, then? Break a leg?"

She hung up, as he probably expected she would. A chilling breeze lent an ominous character to the darkening landscape around her. She began thinking how unforgiving it must be in winter. How helpless one could be against nature. And how tough and resilient one had to become to adapt to it. She wondered how tough and resilient Ben *had* become.

Chapter Eight

When Coleen Copeland realized her dress was close to Mrs. S's in hue, her heart sank. At that moment it dawned on her the aquamarine she'd chosen for the party was the color for gracefully aging old ladies. The thought that she and Mrs. S had *anything* in common let alone a fashion statement horrified her. After the initial shock, however, she was able to pacify herself that her own dress was considerably more contemporary than Mrs. S's, which looked like something the Queen Mother would be happy to wear.

The party, spilling out from the enormous Shannon living room through its three sets of french doors to the large flagstone terrace beyond, was bigger than Coleen had expected. The various contingents hadn't yet separated, social dilution requiring more time and alcohol. The actors gravitated to and stayed with other actors, the social and affluent and the political set mingled among their own, and the rest watched nervously. A path of smiles broke out as Coleen made her way to the bar. Several elderly gentlemen in agitated grumbling conversation, one of whom was Dick Shannon, stepped back graciously to make room for her.

"My, don't we look handsome tonight, Governor."

"And don't you look radiant."

"Just watch me after a couple of *vodka martinis.*" She hit the words as a cue for the bartender. "I'll send off sparks like a supernova."

The governor let loose a guttural chuckle. "Mrs. S certainly knows how to throw a party," he said, looking about his home.

"She sure does. Bet she was a great help when you were in the Governor's Mansion."

"I can't begin to tell you. She can talk to just about anyone about just about anything. I myself prefer talking to a crowd. Never felt comfortable with this one-on-one stuff."

No kidding, she thought as she watched his eyes yielding to the temptation of those around them. "I don't know, you've never had much trouble communicating with me, Governor." She allowed a lascivious overtone to her voice.

"Well, you're easy to talk to. Any woman as worldly wise and intelligent as yourself makes conversation an easy and gentle pleasure. Of course, most people aren't like that. Usually just trying to sell you something. Or, when I was a politician, trying to *buy* you."

His companions, who had remained mute, laughed.

"Same when I was in show business. And forty pounds lighter," she said. The bartender leaned forward with her drink. "Remember, every time you see this tired, fleshy old face coming out of the crowd, it means vodka martini," she told him.

"Tell me," Shannon said, taking her elbow and guiding her a few feet away from the others. "This actress friend of Ben's, Nora Howard, is she a friend of yours?"

"Oh, you know how all we actresses know each other. We make it a point so we can gossip behind each other's backs."

"What do you say behind hers?" he asked mirthlessly.

Coleen frowned. "I was only teasing, Governor. She's a dear old friend. I've never heard a bad thing said about her."

He looked down gravely. "Well, I myself have always admired her presence on the silver screen. Fact, I didn't know till Ben told me she was coming to our theater that she did stage work."

"Then you're in for a pleasant surprise."

"Good. Be sure and introduce me when she arrives." He looked at her conspiratorially. "The truth is, some of those actor types make me uncomfortable. They talk to you like you're a camera."

"You're just mixing with the wrong actors."

"I'm afraid so." He played with the empty glass in his hand. "Your friend, Miss Howard, she's a recent widow, I believe."

Coleen nodded slowly.

"Suicide, I hear."

"That's what we all heard."

He raised his eyebrows and studied her. "You say that with some question in your voice."

"Did I? I hadn't intended to. It just came as such a surprise and shock."

Without turning around, he extended his arm behind him and snapped his fingers. Immediately the bartender appeared with an amber-colored refill. "Thank you, son." He downed half the glass with a practiced toss. "Why would anyone want to go and do such a thing?"

"We all have our dark moments, don't we?" She fixed his stare.

"Yes, I suppose. But I can't honestly say I've ever seriously contemplated ending it all."

"Well, why should you? A man of your accomplishments. Then there's Nancy and all this . . ." She made a flourish with her hand.

"Oh, you don't have to remind me how lucky I am. Thank God for that every day. And publicly on Sundays. That's why it's so inconceivable to me that a person could do such a thing."

"Well I'm sure if he had it to do over again, he wouldn't have," she said matter-of-factly.

"Really? How do you know?"

"Well, I can't be sure. It's just my thing about all suicides. That if they had a good night's sleep, they'd change their minds."

"That strikes me as a very sad thought. I mean, if you're right, it's very sad. But worst of all . . ." He leaned forward to take her into his confidence. "It strikes me as highly ungodly. A sacrilege. But, of course, one shouldn't visit the sins of the husband unto the wife."

Again she noticed the empty glass in his hand.

"Well, this is a party: eat, drink, and be merry. And here I'm depressing you. I should be ashamed of myself."

"Never mind, Governor. You're just a sensitive, inquiring

man dealing with the unfamiliar. Do you think you can do that snapping trick again?"

She held her own empty glass up to his confused face, wondering how in God's name she was able to live with her own hypocrisy.

After considerable conversation, it was agreed that Tony Newland would accompany Ben and Nora to the party. He'd argued with them, separately and together, that it was not in his nature to make small talk with a lot of strangers. But the actress and the playwright had gone to some lengths to persuade him that owing to his work he wouldn't be a stranger to them. Begrudgingly, he relented. Now, feeling as conspicuous as the Tin Man, he'd regretted his decision the moment he'd walked in the door.

For one thing, Ben and Nora had been wrong. What were presumably the townspeople had looked up vaguely as he'd entered, then turned away quickly with lack of interest. If indeed they'd come to see people from the mysterious world of show business, he'd proved a disappointment. Occasionally he caught the flicker of semirecognition, a knit or raised eyebrow, but the spark never gained enough momentum to be considered acknowledgment, let alone appreciation or even curiosity. He thought back to the golden days, and how warming they had been. Stardom was like a womb, one could float in the soothing fluids of success, be nourished by the offers, the flatteries. Then he was aborted. In a blinding rush, he was in the harsh, noisy, blinding world of reality, alone, swimming in the detritus.

It was then his hand had begun shaking, and still hadn't stopped. Also when he'd started losing weight, even height, he thought, although he suspected that wasn't really possible. It was then when the world's indifference set in. What did it matter that he'd once been famous; he was no longer.

"Tony," Nora whispered to him, "I can tell by the look in your eye you're thinking about bolting. Don't. Give it a chance."

He nodded meekly, pleased with her concern. "I won't until I've had three conversations with three different people. I promise."

"Good. And don't be disappointed if you have a good time."

He smiled and squeezed her hand. "I promise."

Then he saw the thin, blond young man coming through the door. If he could have chosen anyone in the room to speak with, it would have been that young man. But he knew that he would never have that conversation. That the very idea of talking to the young man would attract the mocking stares he'd spent a good deal of his life trying to avoid. He became so distracted with the thought, he hardly noticed the large bald man who'd come in with him and who was attracting the attention of practically everyone in the room.

"Hello, I'm Nancy Shannon."

"Steve Wald."

"Yes, I know. And I'm so delighted to welcome you to our home."

"That's very kind."

"When Michael Russell called and asked if it was all right to bring you, I nearly fell off my chair. Imagine, having one of the most successful men in the entertainment world come to our little party. I was beside myself."

"There's absolutely no need for that. It's my pleasure."

"I won't even ask what brought you to Partridgefield."

He smiled at her as though they shared a secret, then craned his head toward the terrace. "Just spectacular. Your home is beautiful."

"Oh, that's so kind of you to say." At this point she noticed the young man who had caught Tony Newland's attention. "Hello, I'm Nancy Shannon."

"I'm sorry, Mrs. Shannon. This is my assistant, Chip Walker. I hope you don't mind."

"Of course not. You must be one of the best and brightest to work for such an important gentleman as Mr. Wald." She extended her hand to him.

"It certainly is a wonderful opportunity to learn."

"I'm sure."

She turned back to Steven. "Did the Russells come with you?"

"Yes indeed. I'm afraid Michael's gotten distracted by the view outside."

"How kind of him."

She said it, Wald thought, as though taking credit for the entirety of nature. "You know, Mr. Wald, in our own small way we're involved in show business, too. Theater, actually, if that still counts."

"It does indeed. As far as I'm concerned, the gap gets smaller and smaller."

"I'm so glad to hear you say that. Sometime I wonder if the stage isn't becoming archaic, given your hundred-million-dollar movies and those video cassettes."

"All part and parcel of the same thing," he said reassuringly.

"Then you'll come see *The Limner,* I hope."

"Absolutely."

Suddenly she turned to Chip. "And you, too, young man. You must come see the play, as well."

Wald watched the top of her blue head bob as she peered between the people around them.

"Perhaps I'd better look for the Russells. I hope they haven't gotten lost," she said gaily. "So delighted you could come. The bar's just over there," she said, her arm poking out behind her like a rudder as she moved toward the front door.

The power of the gentleman being greeted by Nancy Shannon was not lost on her son-in-law, Congressman Neil Sheedy. Although still in his early thirties, he was not at all uncomfortable with his own considerable accomplishments. Then there was his family, often spoken of as the First Family of Partridgefield. They'd lived and enjoyed much success in the area for two hundred years. When opportunities arose, the Sheedys had been among the first to embrace them. Which accounted for their opening several car dealerships just after the great war, the buying up of considerable acreage, now developed by those high-technology companies as plants and think tanks, and establishing themselves in politics, among other more mundane enterprises like opening the area's first video rental shop. This strain of ambition, however, had manifested itself in Neil Sheedy in ways that were at first hard to detect.

On the surface, he was relaxed, a man's man given to an inordinate amount of fishing, golf, and tennis. He had married Catherine Shannon at twenty-four and rapidly begat three offspring, all girls. His wife, who sang beautifully, often did so in church and at special fund-raising events.

What went mostly unspoken was the fact that Neil Sheedy hardly ever fell asleep before 3 A.M., and only then for a fitful three or four hours. This in spite of enjoying complete silence in a bedroom separate from his wife Catherine. While everyone who knew the family, which was virtually the entire town, remarked at the amazing resemblance between Neil and his daughters, the comments always brought a stab of sadness, even pain, to Catherine, as the children had been conceived through the ministrations of Neil's brother, Jim, her marriage having never been consummated. In spite of this, which occurred at Neil's urgings and his desire to erect the best possible façade, the three of them never spoke of the deception. In fact, Catherine Sheedy told everyone, and had come to believe, that hers was a marriage made in heaven. She'd never doubted her husband. She'd simply assumed the situation was caused by deficiencies in her own makeup and quietly regretted it.

Neil himself, who had never found soul searching either necessary or even seemly, also had never thought it necessary to explain his behavior, either to his wife or himself. Whatever impulses drove certain parts of his life were best left unexplored. He had come to look upon his own unique urgings as something separate and apart from himself, like the sorts of magazines displayed in plain brown wrappers that he was so politically opposed to.

Philip Steadman, a longtime friend and former teammate, approached him. "Enjoying the sideshow?" Steadman had long ago perfected the ability to add innuendo to even his simplest comments, a facility Neil enjoyed thoroughly, as his own demeanor consisted of a generalized bonhomie. "Do every year."

"I don't know where your mother-in-law finds them. Shouldn't say that; I do. Her hard-on, I mean Hartwood, Playhouse. Place reeks with them."

"That, as they say, is show business."

"That, as they say, is one business best to stay away from." He inspected Neil. "Catherine's looking real good these days. You must be doing something right, keeping her looking so happy." He elbowed his friend in the ribs. "Now look over there at Ellen." He indicated his tall, gaunt wife who was talking to a pair of similarly large-boned, unadorned women. "Know what they say about still water?" He looked at his friend anxiously. "Ain't true." Again he elbowed the congressman. "Heck, she's all right. Runs the house like a battleship and pays all the bills on time; what more could a man ask?"

Behind them they heard a woosh of conversation and a wave of shuffling as people shifted and angled themselves to watch Audrey Dalton, TV's queen of menace, make her entrance.

"Maybe a piece of that; that's what a man could ask for," Philip said to his friend, stretching his neck along with the others for a better look. "Tell me, buddy, you wouldn't want to try that out for size."

The actress had decided to go with levitated décolletage for the evening and was clearly enjoying moving her bosom regally through the room and watching the stares it collected.

"What do you say, Neil boy?"

"Ssssh!" The congressman looked around furtively. "No comment," he added, as though ending a press conference.

"Come on, don't tell me you wouldn't want to slurp around them, just for one night. One loo-o-o-ng night."

"Can't say I wouldn't consider it," Neil said with a shy smile and as softly as he could.

"That a boy. That's my buddy. Think we could get introduced, you being a congressman and all?"

"Probably. Then what?"

"Maybe I could just brush up against 'em. By accident, of course."

The congressman smiled and shook his head. "You just don't grow up, do you? That may be your most endearing quality."

"Endearing, my ass. Nothing endearing about me. Best thing you can say about me is that I know a good piece of ass when I see one. And that I usually want to take a bite out of it." He squinted and laughed appreciatively at himself. "Anybody else important around here beside the movie stars?"

"Just one of the world's biggest media conglomerate owners."

Steadman looked around cautiously. "Wouldn't be that large fellow with Mrs. S, would it?"

"Right on, buddy."

"And who's the bald guy with them?

"Runs the big guy's movie studio."

Steadman whistled softly. "Your mom-in-law's really packing in the biggies tonight." He made two scoring motions in the air. "I'm real impressed. Makes me feel humble to be breathing the same air as those bigshots."

"You might even get to shit in the same pot as one of them," Neil said quietly, to the delight of his friend. "Except I'd do it before, not after, if you know what I mean."

His friend worked to suppress his laughter. "Thought we weren't suppose to believe that crap, about catching stuff on toilet seats?"

"Well, you might want to reconsider far as this crowd is concerned." The congressman bowed his head as a large, glassy-eyed woman with a sharp beaklike nose passed. "How're you doing, Joanne?"

"Oh, just fine. Just fine. Like to get out and see what Nancy's rounded up for her annual do." The woman was trying to hold her glass steady by pushing it against her throat. "Nice crowd. Very nice crowd. Movie stars." She nodded, as though agreeing with herself. "Just as they say, they always look smaller when you see them in person. The screen blows them up. But in real life, they're just like you and me. Well, more like you than me, I suppose. You're a young fellow going places; I'm just an old lady who's never been." She swallowed what hadn't splashed out of her glass. "Except around the golf course a couple of thousand times."

"Nice talking to you," Neil called after her as she headed for the bar.

Steadman was eying Nora as Ben led her around the room, stopping ever so often to introduce her. "You can have the widow, Neil. She seems a little tamer than the one with the tits. Miss Boobs of 1970 is more my cup of tea. I've got an enormous capacity for big-boobed women, as long as they've got a capacity for what's big about me." He slapped his friend on the back. "If you get my drift." He allowed his laughter to continue, then brought it to an abrupt stop. "By the way, Neil. You *are* going to stop Mr. Feinstein from taking over the old Chartwell estate?"

The congressman had to stop and think to follow his thought. "Oh, *that* deal. Not to worry. Dead in the water. The selectmen can tie it up in enough red tape to keep it from happening in his lifetime."

"Atta boy." Once more his eyes teared, followed by laughter. "Would be real funny, though, if he started his kind of country club and kept *us* out, wouldn't it? Except he wouldn't want to keep anyone out, as long as they were paying customers. That type doesn't care where the bucks come from as long as they come. Fact, they care more about bucks comin' than comin' themselves." This time he dissolved himself in laughter, lowering his chin to the knot on his tie in an effort to stifle it.

Neil Sheedy remembered from their college days the difficulty his friend had containing himself even after one drink. It was a good thing for him, he thought, there was no such thing as date rape back then.

Steadman had contained himself enough to speak again. "You suppose he'd make everyone wear those little black beanies before they could come into his club?" Again the words got lost in a rush of laughter. "And make the men dance separate from the ladies." This time his body bent at the waist, as if he'd dropped something. "I'm sorry, I'm sorry," he said, choking. "Maybe you ought to let Feinstein go ahead with his plans. It might be worth it just for laughs."

"I think we'll be able to find a better use for the property."

"You bet we will," Steadman agreed, a semblance of sobriety returning. "Well, what do you say we mix. Star fuck, as the saying goes. Nice talking to you, old pal." He grabbed Neil around his shoulders. "Just like the old times."

The congressman watched his friend make a leering pass at the buxom actress who had joined the large bald movie head in conversation. Neither took notice. Then Neil's eyes fell on the young blond man who appeared to be in attendance to the movie mogul. The man caught his eye and smiled. Neil smiled back curtly and turned away. He often wondered if it were true, that men like himself had an uncanny ability to suss out others with their inclinations. There was something in the blond's grin, however, that told him that in this instance, that assumption might not apply.

Steven Wald was delighted to see Audrey Dalton. That he'd had something like an affair with her at the height of her popu-

larity had provided substantial grist for his legend-making pro-
paganda. Particularly after he'd reputedly tied her up one memorable night, and proved, as she later recalled, to be insatiable.
They'd remained friends over the years and here in the country
both instantly saw the opportunities their companionship could
once more provide.

"My flesh feels raw from the stares," she said to him, delicately tracing her finger over the porcelainlike texture of her
chest.

"It doesn't look like you've done too much to discourage it,"
he said pleasantly.

"It's part of my charity work," she said taking a deep breath.
"Just look at what the poor slobs have to schtup all year round;
they all look like bull dykes."

"Some people like 'em."

"I'll pass, thank you. Perhaps that explains why my career
isn't what it once was."

He watched the perfect mounds of her breasts rising and
falling with gentle precision. He'd heard she'd had them recently overhauled and felt slightly foolish being impressed with
the results. In fact, he was impressed with her entire body, and
appreciative of the effort and discipline it must have taken to
maintain it. It was a small, perfectly proportioned figure that
she had learned to wield with regal authority.

"This is all so fucking New England," she said, looking out
pleasantly at the view. "Boring, boring, boring. Look at it.
Where are the great jewelers? The couturiers? Restaurants rife
with caviar and blini? Where is civilization?" Her voice dipped
to a low mocking tone. "Don't think I'm jaded. I know nature is
perfectly lovely; birds, trees, deer, and all that. But what are you
supposed to do after you've filled your lungs with nice clean air?
Strolled the wooded paths? It all begins to blur very quickly."

"And here I thought you were about to lock yourself up in a
retreat."

"Hardly. Do you really think this is a career move for me,
treading the boards?" Her voice was a mocking growl.

"These days any job is a career move."

"But what about stars? There can't be an overabundance of
them?"

"You must be joking. Haven't you noticed? These days we

make stars in forty-eight hours and dispose of them in twelve. It's called marketing."

"I call it bullshit."

"Then why are your ratings tanking?" He did not even stop to consider his remark; he knew the reptilian thickness of her skin. "Because if we want another star, we can hatch it instantly."

She snuggled up to him. "That's very encouraging to hear." She ran her tongue over her permanently moistened lips. He wondered if she hadn't had them pumped up, too.

Her eyes grazed the room, catching lots of embarrassed stares, which she greeted with an impregnable smile. "We did spend a season of sin together, didn't we?"

"That memorable, was it?"

She remembered marveling at the fact that he'd had the nerve to show his little weenie to someone with her connections and chance it getting around town. As it happened, she hadn't told a soul. She knew one day he would be too powerful to fool around with and was not about to burn any prospective bridges. "Come on, darling. I'm just teasing you. I just meant people's taste change. We all change."

He looked down at her; suddenly her face had gone hollow, the eyes in thick rings of mascara glaring like those of a crazed raccoon.

"Do you remember me when I was beautiful? Really beautiful? When I didn't have to paint myself up like a drag queen to look like me? It's fleeting, isn't it? All of it." She squeezed his arm, and the dazzling porcelainwork of her dentistry shone through again. "Oh well, we all do what we can to make it through the long dark night of our lives."

He studied her face blatantly; she was right, she did look like a drag queen.

The man had the drawn look of someone the limner might have painted. Ben had known him more than twenty years, during which time he'd been living at the Asa Hamilton Home, an expensive refuge for wealthy alcoholics, people with minor mental impediments, and, more frequently in the past decade, druggies. While the therapeutic benefits of the home were questionable, its main advantage seemed to be the extraordinarily liberal policy that allowed its clients to roam freely during the day as long as they spent a certain amount of time in counseling, returned in the evenings, and paid, or had paid, their sizable monthly bills. It was into this cold, clinical environment that Charles Higgins had been given over by his family and had spent most of his life. He had little more to show for it than the bloodless, toothless look of one of his forefathers. Now, in his fifty-fifth year, having had no responsibilities or accomplishments in his lifetime, he wandered about Partridgefield as a disquieting remnant of what was once the Puritan ethic.

"How have things been going, Charles?" Ben asked gently.

"Oh, very well."

"That's nice to hear. Who brought you?"

"My cousin, Edie, I believe. We're somehow related to the Shannons and I get to come every year. To the shows, as well."

"Do you? You like theater?"

The man thought about it and shook his head contentedly, as if remembering a pleasant secret.

"They're doing a play of mine this year," Ben said.

His eyes clouded.

"It's about a nineteenth-century portrait painter; they were called limners." Ben let the thought settle on him. "This was before photography and they'd come around and paint you and your family, a record for the future."

Higgins nodded with assurance. "Yes, my family has some like that. Sad-looking people in the pictures."

Ben nodded.

"So sad. They look like they worked very hard and never laughed."

"You're right. But they must have laughed sometime."

"Do they in your play?"

Ben smiled at him. "Not really."

"It's a sad play?"

"A little."

Again the retreat in his eyes.

"But don't let that stop you from coming."

"I'll come because it's your play."

Ben wondered why his cousin brought him to a place filled with people drinking alcohol. "Did someone get you some soda?"

"I don't want anything. Just to be around people."

"But aren't you all day, at Hamilton's?"

His expression turned harsh. "But they're people like me."

"*I* enjoy being around you."

"You wouldn't if you had to spend all your time. What is your play about?"

"A man falsely accused of something. And without the means to fight back. How people take advantage of other people."

The older man thought for a moment, then said, "The part I like best about going to the theater is after the lights go out and before the curtain goes up. People get very quiet and you can't see anything. But for that moment you imagine what you're going to see. Then just as the curtain goes up, you hear yourself breathing and begin to feel something, like a hand brushing over the hair on your arm. Sometimes people cough, because they're nervous. Like they're going on a trip into the big black space around them. And then you see the lights and actors. I don't know how they can speak; I would be so nervous. My heart pounds for them. And then they say the first words and you begin to see where you're going. If it's a good play, they make you laugh and cry. And then at the end they all come together and hold hands and bow to you. I clap at them. Because I should be doing the thanking and bowing. Then I go back to Hamilton and think about the actors and the play in my bed. I even remember words they say and how they say them." He smiled at Ben a bit helplessly, as though he'd run out of words. Then Ben saw he had stopped because Nora had joined them. He remained silent, his smile frozen.

"Nora, I'd like you to meet my friend, Charles. Nora's an actress in my play."

Higgins nodded briskly but did not look at her. "Nice to meet you."

"Charles is a great fan of the Hartwood. And I think I persuaded him to come see *The Limner.*"

"That would be very nice," she said, instinctively squeezing his hand. "You must come back and tell me what you think."

"Oh, I can't. I have to go back to Hamilton's right after. But thank you for inviting me." He looked sheepish, unable to contain a smile. "I think I'll feel more comfortable with you on the stage than afterward. I don't have to talk when I'm watching. It makes me feel good to look and listen."

"It makes *me* feel good *having* people listen and watch."

He giggled, then cautiously extended his hand.

The Governor, who no one had taken seriously for twenty years, had been circling the room, stopping at small groups in which he could recognize a face to tell a joke. Because he had been repeating the same joke for the past half hour, he would sometimes begin in the middle, or even with the punchline. Most of the time, his listeners were unaware of the errors as his words had become so garbled, the once famous rhetorical flow dissipated in a squall of alcohol.

Having finished another disjointed recitation, he raised his trembling glass and held it before him like a lantern. As he turned in search of more familiar faces, he found himself looking into the face, then the bosom, of a famous TV actress.

"Oh my God, weren't you . . . ?" he asked, trying to recapture the mellifluous quality of his vocal range.

"That depends," Audrey said, tilting her head back and looking down the length of her nose at him. "Who do you think I used to be?"

"Was, is, and will always be that great femme fatale . . ."

"Well, you just think about it." She petted his cheek and began to turn.

He reached out and stopped her. "Excuse my manners, madam, but I don't believe I've introduced myself. I'm Dick Shannon, former governor of the state."

"Oh, how sweet. And I'm, or used to be, Audrey Dalton, former small-screen siren."

"My word, so you are! Imagine, Audrey Dalton in my own home. I'm overwhelmed."

"Yes, well you'll get over it, I'm sure. Do you think you could fetch me another drink, Governor?" She held her empty glass out to him.

"I can do better than that." He raised thick fingers in the air and snapped them, summoning a matronly woman in a black dress with white lace trim around her collar and cuffs. "Miss Dalton will be having a . . ."

"Scotch and water, please."

"And I'll be having the usual."

The woman took their empty glasses and disappeared as the governor stared appreciatively at the actress's breasts.

"I don't mind telling you, Audrey, you are what they call ageless."

"Am I?"

"Still a very attractive woman in my estimation."

"Really? Still?"

"Absolutely. Why, half the emaciated young things in this room can't hold a candle to you."

"How encouraging."

"Right. Guess they don't make 'em like they used to." He spoke with a show of confidentiality that allowed him to bring his head close to her chest.

"Your drinks," the uniformed woman said matter-of-factly.

"Of course," the governor responded, taking Audrey's first and handing it to her.

"Thank you so much. How long have you lived here?" she asked, looking about in an attempt to appear interested in what she considered a cloying mix of chintz roses, lace doilies, and overly carved Victorian furniture.

"Ages. Belonged to my father."

"How nice for you."

"I take that as a compliment coming from a woman of your worldly tastes." He squinted mischievously. "You wouldn't be appearing at our playhouse, would you?"

"That's right." She sang the words.

He closed his eyes and sniffed the air, coming closer to her as he did. "That's just lovely. Exactly what a woman should smell like."

"Me?" she asked coquettishly.

"None other." Suddenly he looked alarmed. "Has anyone bothered taking you about and showing you our lovely countryside?"

"Not exactly."

"I'll be darned. Then I insist. It would be my pleasure to do so."

She watched amused as his eyes kept darting off her breasts. "And will Mrs. Shannon be joining us? You know, so we could have a little girl talk," she said teasingly.

"Well, I hadn't thought . . . She's a very busy woman, you know. Has more damn charities and boards . . ." Again he leaned in conspiratorially. "I myself, after all those hectic years of being governor, love taking the time to relax, dally around and smell the roses, so to speak. Allows me to make up for all the things I missed as a young man." He looked at her knowingly. "Fortunately, I'm still young enough to sow a few seeds."

"How lucky for you."

He leaned farther in order to whisper in her ear. "As I hear tell it, lucky for the ladies, too, if I may appear to be a bit immodest."

She pulled away from him. "Do they volunteer the information or do you hand out questionnaires afterward?"

"Nothing as formal as that. Sort of unsolicited testimonials, you might say. Anytime you might be free, I'd love to have you smell the roses with me," he said, a leer spreading across his face.

"I'm so sorry, Governor. I feel a stuffy nose coming on."

"Shame. Well, good luck in your theatrical endeavors. Mrs. Shannon and I will be sure to come and cheer you on. Lovely having you here." He took a courtly step back and swung around to head for the bar.

Michael Russell had found it virtually impossible to expel his hostess from his side. Even Aida, who was used to being ignored, had begun to feel irritated. If Nancy Shannon was aware of either's discomfort, she did not show it. In actual fact, she found Russell quite blinding. It was not the physical makeup of the man; he was large to the point of being gross; and his slicked-back hair gave him the aspect of a penguin. It was his enormous success that she found riveting. She knew him to be of humble origins, although his carefully modulated British accent did much to obscure it. But his rise to a position of great wealth and global power she found intoxicating.

In almost every way he was the opposite of Dick Shannon. Her husband, in spite of holding high elective office, had always been nothing more than a well-meaning, cheerful bumbler of limited mental capacity. His rise had been facilitated by family connections, money, and a considerable number of political receivables held by his father, who *was* a man of distinct accomplishment.

Dick's good luck and innate charm had served him extraordinarily well until alcohol had confounded the former and turned the latter into self-parody. Russell, on the other hand, was who she would have liked to be, religion aside, had she been a man. And now she found herself mentally deifying him, this immortal, in her own home.

"What a wonderful place you have here," Russell said, making an effort to drag his heavy-lidded eyes across the room. "So English."

Nancy's jaw dropped and froze. "Mr. Russell," she said in suppressed reverential tones, "that's exactly what I set out to capture. Dick and I have been to so many stately homes in your magnificent country, and while we know Barrington Manor can't hold a candle to any one of them, it was their essence we tried to capture."

"Well, I think you've succeeded admirably."

"It's a lovely party," Aida volunteered, "such a wonderful mix of people."

"Why, thank you." Nancy positioned herself more intimately with the couple. "They are so colorful, show people. In the beginning, when I first started working with the Hartwood, I wasn't particularly fond of them. I found them almost coarse. I still think so when I see them around food; they act as though they'll never see any again. And I often detect a certain insincerity in their manner, all the make-believe kissing and telling each other how marvelous they are. But then I realized what wouldn't be genuine in normal people is perfectly natural to them. Don't you think so? Well, we have a flock of them here tonight. They are terribly amusing at parties—it's like another stage for them."

Russell's attention went to the guests. "I see you've even imported a movie star or two for us."

"Oh yes. Nora is staying with us, you know. In the guest cottage. She's terribly sweet. I haven't heard her say very much about her late husband. I guess they get used to slipping in and out of emotions very quickly. The other one, Audrey, is a real vampy type, isn't she?" She looked at Aida knowingly, then back to Michael. "You wouldn't care to see the rest of the house, would you?"

"The ha'penny tour, then; my feet get so tired so quickly these days," he said, reddening at the thought.

"Just the highlights, I promise." She laced her arm through his and smiled again at Aida. "Let me show you the family room we've put in downstairs. We built it for the grandchildren, really. They, of course, are the *real* joys of our lives. Do you have any?" she asked as she proudly escorted the dignitaries in a conspicuous path down the center of the room.

Chip Walker, in spite of his fondness for show business, had never really been star struck. He'd met enough of them in his brief time in L.A. to verify his inherent belief that their shit stank as much as his and that their requirements always exceeded their accomplishments. In fact, he found the most intriguing part of celebrity to be the sense of superiority he felt over those paying the price of it. But there was one actor in the room who intrigued him, and that was because she was no longer in the business.

He had become a fan of Coleen Copeland as a boy for reasons he could never explain. Then, as a young man, he'd become fascinated with her ability to penetrate a character with a tap of her finger, a blink, an intonation so deadly accurate and illuminating, it appeared to be the work of a sorceress. It was a facility he'd tried acquiring himself. And now she was standing in the very same room, apparently thinking about who she would chat up next. Chip decided to make the decision for her.

"Ms. Copeland?"

Her saucer eyes widened, waiting for him to continue.

"I'm Chip Walker, Steve Wald's assistant."

Her eyes continued in their surprise mode. "He needs assistance, even at a party?"

Chip laughed. "I suppose he brought me along more as a perk. I'm off duty."

"Hard to tell with you Hollywood types just what you're up to." She continued her doe-ish gaze.

"I assure you."

"Shucks. I thought I was going to be rediscovered."

"You never left. I watch your movies on video all the time. You're, like, the best."

Her brown eyes examined his. "You sound almost genuine."

He smiled boyishly. "Why wouldn't I be?"

"I dunno. Why would you care about an old broad like me? Besides, film was never my thing."

"Can I get you another drink?" He reached for her glass, but she pulled it away.

"Her Eminence has people to do that."

She snapped her fingers in the air as the Governor had done. "Tell the nice lady what you're drinking."

Chip handed over his glass to the dour woman in black. "The same as my idol." The woman peered at them with displeasure.

"Now she'll tell everyone I'm an old lech for young men." Coleen shrugged. "They'll make up one thing or another anyway."

"Why do you live here?"

"New York's too fucking dangerous for a single lady and L.A. gives me the willies. If I could speak any foreign tongues, I'd probably move to Europe. And now I'm too old to learn. So that left Partridgefield."

The woman in black handed them fresh drinks like a reprimand.

"Thank you, ma'am," Coleen said as she strode off.

"Why aren't you appearing in this new play?"

She looked at him cautiously. "I'm re-tir-r-red. Which means I don't act anymore. Not even socially."

"Is it a good play?"

"You bet."

"So why entrust it to the washed-up widow?" He looked vaguely in Nora's direction.

Coleen was about to blast him with a wait-a-minute-buster but decided against it. "Why'd you say that?"

"I live in Hollywood where you can feel such things in the air. People send out these vibes when they walk into a room: I'm rising; I'm on top; I've had it. You can feel their karma like a temperature; cool, cooler, coolest, tepid, hot, hottest. From her you get frost bite." He spoke with Billy Budd–like innocence.

"And you're an expert in these matters?"

"I also know what I hear. Remember, I work for the man who, at the moment, there is none hotter than."

"You read his karma-temperature?"

"That and the trades. He wheels, deals, dices and minces, makes and tears asunder. Believe me, I know Nora is deader than a doornail."

Coleen was astonished by the confidence of the young man's pronouncements. "People go through stages. Careers wane and rise. She ain't through yet."

He seemed amused. "I admire your optimism. Or is it that you've lost touch with the business?"

"When you make up your mind you can kiss my ass." Now she made no effort to hide her contempt and turned to leave.

"Hold on. I didn't mean to offend you. I didn't realize she was a friend of yours."

She turned to him, her feeling once more in check. "Doesn't matter. You don't talk like that about a person who's had a career like hers."

"And her widowhood, do we make special allowances for that, too?"

Coleen was tempted to slap his face. "I think we've finished talking, Mr. Bigshot's Assistant."

Before she could turn again, he took her arm and held it tightly. "You'd be spiting yourself. I think I can tell you something you'd be very interested in knowing. I knew Lewis Rosenthal."

He had put so much implication in the words, she didn't bother trying to remove his hand. "Yeah? So what? A lot of people did. He must have been in and out of your big boss's office all the the time."

"That wasn't how I knew him." He could see from the expression on her face that he could release her arm without fear of losing her.

"Come on, you're not going to tell me he came on to you, are you?" Somehow her intent to mock didn't quite reflect itself in her voice.

"No, I'm not. You think that's the only way I would have known him?"

"Truth is, you don't look like you'd have had too much in common."

"Only life and death." He smiled as she took in the words.

"What's that supposed to mean?"

"I talked to Lewis about him killing himself many times."

"Oh, really? He confided in you? You're full of shit."

He shook his head and stared at her. "Not about this. I knew every intimate detail."

"How?"

Now he smiled. "You're starting to believe me?"

She nodded.

"I worked for a suicide prevention hotline. I took his first call by chance and talked him out of it. Then he began asking for me, every time he couldn't deal with things. But a funny thing happened. I began to realize he had no intention of ever going through with it."

"What are you talking about? He *did* kill himself."

"Did he?"

Suddenly she felt terribly sober; her bare arms had turned cold and she felt sweat forming in their sockets, thinking back to Nora's words. "You're suggesting he didn't?"

"I'm very sure of it."

As they looked at each other in silence, the dour woman in black took their empty glasses and replaced them with fresh drinks without saying a word.

"After a while," he continued, "I began to feel that each time he'd call he was using me. Even playing with me. Pretending he was going to take his own life, except what he was really doing was sucking out mine."

Her voice sounded disembodied when she finally spoke. "And what did you do about it?"

He saw how rigid she had become and smiled. "I didn't kill him, if that's what you're thinking."

"You just told me he didn't do it himself."

He nodded.

"But someone did, that's what you're saying."

He nodded again, still smiling.

"And you know who it is?"

"I have a pretty good idea."

"Why haven't you told the police?"

"Because I can't prove it."

To her own surprise, she hadn't touched her latest drink. Now she raised it to her lips and took a large swallow. "Why are you telling me this stuff? Because I'm your idol?"

Suddenly his expression turned intense. "Because it isn't easy living with it. And you always seemed the most real, the most honest person I ever saw."

She took a step back and screwed up her face. "You're not one of those nut cases that obsesses on a celebrity and does something wacky to them?"

He smiled at her confusion. "I assure you I'm not; don't make me protest too much."

"Are you going to tell me who you think killed Lewis?"

His face darkened. "That's a bit more difficult."

"Why?"

"Because I know you're not going to believe me."

"You think you know me that well?"

"It's not that. I just know it would be hard for you to swallow."

"I've swallowed a lot of stuff in my life, including my pride. Try me."

The flick of Chip's eyes was so brief, she didn't realize at first he had answered her question. When his face froze, waiting for her response, she turned and looked over her shoulder. Twenty feet away, still in the company of Audrey Dalton, Steven Wald acknowledged Chip's gaze with a lazy nod of his scowling face.

Nora knew there was no way she could avoid talking to Wald. His monumental head bobbed around, throwing off loud, self-conscious laughter as he worked the room. He had greeted Ben as a long-lost brother, putting his arm around his shoulders and walking him off into a corner, presumably to set up a more private rendezvous. Watching his machinations gave her a feeling of helplessness. Then she saw him leering at her, possibly his idea of a friendly approach.

"The country suits you." He spoke intimately as he approached her. "You must be enjoying yourself."

"I am."

"How's the play going?"

"It's a lot of work."

"I don't know what the religion is you actors seem to feel for the stage. Seems like a lot of work for something that goes up in smoke every night."

"As opposed to my old movies that are run night and day across the land."

"Now, now, now, don't be bitter. I'm sure someone somewhere is watching one even as we speak."

In full smile his teeth looked wooden.

"Anyway," he continued, "I'm glad to see you decided to start over."

"Do you mean after Lewis or my film career?"

"Both, I suppose. What choices, exactly, do you think you have?"

"I can live my life away from scum like you." She watched as his entire head turned red; even his eyes appeared bloodshot.

"I will give you one thing." His voice was low and controlled. "You've got bigger balls than your husband."

Neither of them saw Coleen approach. "My, my, my, what strange bedfellows." She looked at Nora. "Are you sure you want to be having this conversation?"

"I've been trying to avoid it since Mr. Wald arrived."

Coleen turned to Wald calmly. "If I understand my friend properly, she'd like you to fuck off."

He looked at her dispassionately. "I think you're drunk. I'm looking at a once great actress who's turned into the town lush. And a pitifully small provincial town it is."

"And what do you think you are? Right now, you're the town bully. And so far kids are afraid to fight back. But believe me, brother, that won't last. I've seen bigger than you float down the toilet in one flush."

She cupped Nora's elbow in her palm and steered her away from the studio chief, who had once again begun to look like a fire hydrant. They hadn't gotten far before they were intercepted by Nancy Shannon.

"We do seem to attract the high and the mighty, don't we?" She clasped her hands and pressed them against her middle as she stared at Russell until she caught his eye. Then she blew him a kiss. "I suppose we must seem quaint to them. In fact, I must seem quaint to the both of you."

Coleen and Nora assured her that wasn't the case.

"You both protest so beautifully, but I know it's true. And why not? I've lived here all my life and raised my family here, grew my business here, saw my husband reach the heights of local politics here. Partridgefield has been very good to me. It's the whole world, really. That's why Ben's book was so successful. He understood that. He knew to look behind our paneled doors. He understands that while we may look and act like old magazine covers, we have our own games, our own agendas, just like in the big cities. Only we exercise them with a little more discretion. Coleen knows that, she's almost a native, aren't you, dear? Partridgefield's been around over two hundred years and it just seems to give us all strength. Anyway, we adore having you actors here. I so look forward to it. Spring flowers, the returning birds, and our theatrical community, all descending on us in a rush of color and excitement."

"That's very poetic, Mrs. S." Coleen's voice had dipped into its famous pitch and cadence.

"Well, there, you see? We all have a little artistic blood in us. Even me." Suddenly she reached out and clutched Nora's hands. "I do hope your work here and our countryside are helping to heal your wounds."

Nora smiled and nodded.

"You know, Mrs. S," Coleen said, "all this countryside makes me kind of thirsty. You don't suppose we could slither to the bar and ask the nice gentleman to fill our glasses?"

"No need for that." She snapped her fingers much like Dorothy tapped her red shoes, flagging the witchlike presence of the serving woman. "We'd like some drinks, Betty. Do you think you could help us?" The woman forced a smile and left. "By the way, the Governor and I are going to have a quiet dinner, just for all you VIPs. I do hope you'll be able to come." She looked about as if spying on her other guests. "I know, why don't we go out on the terrace and sample the simple little buffet Isabel's prepared."

As they approached the open doors, they saw a line of linen-covered tables traversing the width of the terrace. The night was fresh and clear and the darkening sky promised a field of stars.

Thirty minutes later, an increasingly nervous Coleen strongly suggested to Ben and Nora that they leave.

Nancy Shannon's regret as the trio said their good-byes bordered on the indignant. She couldn't understand why they had to leave so early, especially as everyone else appeared to be having such a lovely time. Ben explained that he had notes to make before morning rehearsals, Nora pleaded that she had to work on her lines, and Coleen simply smiled at the hostess and said, "I'm old. And I drink too much. After a couple of hours of this, I don't consider myself fit company." Then she laced arms with the couple and navigated them through the door and into Ben's car.

Coleen's face went serious as she slipped silently into the backseat. Ten minutes later, when they were in her kitchen, she put a snifter of cognac in front of each of them.

Then she began to speak with astonishment of her conversation with Chip Walker.

The moment Steven Wald had set eyes on Audrey Dalton in the Shannon living room, it had brought back memories of the most spectacular blow jobs he'd ever received. Standing next to her at the party, mentally thumbing their bed experiences together, had actually elicited a hard-on.

Now, as he parked in the driveway of her rented cottage, his heartbeat revving, anticipatory dampness on his forehead, he felt like a teenager.

"To think, one of the most powerful men in all show business, pick of the litter at his fingertips, has actually chosen to come home with moi." She made the declaration to the tall shadowy trees as they walked around the side of the house. "Of course, the competition at that dreary party wasn't exactly devastating." She searched for her key, sweetly looking at him out of the corner of her eye, her tongue moving self-consciously over her glazed lips. "Quite provincial, I'm afraid." She pushed the door open and strutted into the kitchen, posing hands on hips before a row of glass-paneled kitchen cabinets. "Well, what do you think?" Her bosom heaved incongruously in the midst of the kitchen clutter.

"I'm sure you've gotten to know intimately every pot and pan in the house."

"Absolutely," she said, turning and leading him into the stair hall. "Seems cozier entering through the kitchen, don't you think?"

Wald was thinking of other things. He picked up the tail of her question; her pause indicated she was waiting for a response. "Hmmmnnn," he half-grunted, lowering his head and staring at her from under his pale eyebrows in a weak attempt at seductiveness.

"Yes, well I see you're a man of few words *ce soir.* Why don't you just follow me?" She stretched out a soft white arm languorously on the banister as she climbed the stairs. "The bed is just dreamy. It must be made of feathers. And I've been sleeping under this delicious comforter. The night temperature drops, you know."

She was teasing him with her innocuous remarks; that was all right. He was prepared to endure her little game for what was to come. The bedroom looked like a page torn out of an Americana magazine: four-poster, painted wood chest at the foot, stripes of garlands papering the walls, ball-fringed curtains covering the windows. She pulled the covers back, white and appetizing as a whipped-cream sundae.

"You know the routine, I'll just be a minute," Dalton said as she walked into the bathroom, reaching behind to undo her necklace.

Wald felt happy as a small boy about to be tucked in and read to. He quickly got out of his clothes and shoes, leaving on a thin cotton pair of baggy boxer shorts, and placed himself on the bed, casually drawing a corner of the sheet over him. There were three pillows beneath his head, one of which he slipped out and forced under his hips. A seductive breeze coming in the open window made him reach down and slip off his shorts. Then he put both arms behind his head and waited.

"If you want to pee or anything, there's another loo down the hall," she called out to him.

He closed his eyes, not responding, anticipating her familiar moves, her timing, the tensile bliss she provided. When she appeared, she was wearing only her bikini underpants, her newly reconstituted breasts poised and air-brushed perfect. She'd removed much of her lipstick and taken off her wig, which had made her look like a gypsy girl. Her own hair, flattened against her head and tied back in a small pony-tail, had an unappetizing wiry look. After daintily posing with her stomach sucked in so tightly her rib cage protruded, she moved coltishly to the side of the bed and shut off the light.

"Mmmmnnn," she said, climbing on top of him. She smoothed her tongue over his lips, tracing the edges until she was ready to insinuate the tip into his mouth. She worked their tongues together a moment before playing her long fingernails along the sides of his chest. Then, as if responding to a silent command, she lowered herself, her fingers picking up their deft tracery, working the inside of his thighs. Soon her tongue interceded, moving around his testicles. Her fingers kept up their stalking action as she reduced her touch to that of a feather, teasing more and more sensation out of him. Gauging the effect she was having and the need to retard him, her head moved up, pressing against his mouth, bringing the smell of him with her.

As they kissed, her hand resumed its activity around his crotch, maintaining its exquisitely delicate filigree. Then she whispered, excuse me, and descended slowly, pausing to to plant small kisses along the way. When she arrived at her destination, she immersed his erection in her mouth. As her head began to pump, her hands busied themselves like spiders, spinning, weaving along his body.

Then she went into what he remembered as her helicopter maneuvers, her mouth making trips between his nipples, his lips, his thighs, his scrotum and penis. As she continued her dreamlike navigation, he felt himself drifting, interplanetary, intergalactic, floating toward orgasm.

Suddenly she put her lips to his ear. "What's the matter?" she asked sweetly, ingenuously.

He made a moaning sound, rubbing his large hands over her back.

"I'd forgotten how nicely we fit," she said demurely, her own cooing sounds reflecting his. "Isn't this yummy?" she asked, working his organ into her. Once again, she began modulating his responses until she found the frequency she was after. She kept him on it, orchestrating his reactions, until she heard him begin to whimper.

When he came, feeling like a dirigible experiencing a sudden rupture, she quickly got out of bed and went to the bathroom, returning seconds later with a warm damp towel. "There," she said, gently passing the cloth around his groin with the delicacy of a geisha, "wasn't that fun?"

Chapter Nine

Ben Bradford had arranged to meet Steve Wald at a diner that stood behind eight large bays dispensing diesel fuel. Wald parked his borrowed Porsche; it looked to him slightly inconsequential among the sixteen-wheelers. Ben was already seated in a booth lined with quilted chrome.

"'Morning," the writer called, waving his hand in the air.

"'Morning, Ben. Perfect spot for a power breakfast."

Ben wondered at the studio czar's seemingly playful mood. "How about we get you some coffee?" He squinted at a heavy-set dark-haired woman behind the counter and nodded. The waitress came forward with a thick cup and saucer and placed it in front of Wald. Then she poised a pen above her green pad and waited.

"Pancakes and bacon," Wald said enthusiastically. When she left, he said to Ben, "Bet they don't stick bananas and kiwi in the batter."

"No chance."

"Was that a good thing to order?"

"Long as you don't like bananas in them."

"How's Nora doing?"

"She's doing great; she's a very fine actress."

"You mean she has talent?" He shrugged. "A quarter of the population has talent. From playing the spoons to cocksucking.

Which is quite different from making it. In Hollywood it doesn't matter how good your widgets are if the others sell more."

"It does to me."

Wald looked at him with mock surprise. "Oh, but you're a three-star commodity. That goes beyond talent. That goes beyond coasts. It makes you more than an artist; it means you can be merchandised."

"I've been schmoozed on both coasts, Mr. Wald. I'm as susceptible as the next guy. I like how it feels, but in the end, I'm ornery enough to resist it."

"You mean perverse. Looking down your nose at an earned compliment is more than ornery, it's dumb."

"That's me," Ben said with some satisfaction.

Wald reached calmly for the syrup. "Oh, I get your game. The modest iconoclast. Plays outside the system. Comes around just enough to suck off some of the honey, then runs home to his art. I believe it's called integrity."

"First you try compliments, now you're insulting me. What else have you got in your bag?"

"Money."

"That's a good one. What do I have to do for it?"

Wald gratefully received his pancakes and began cutting into them with the side of his fork. "Just what you've always done," he said casually, "just go on about your work. Aren't you eating?"

"I did about an hour ago." Wald appeared to be taking great pleasure from the pancakes. "Are you here to do a deal or just pick my brain for breakfast places?"

"Both. Business and pleasure. The serious business of finding the right places to eat and the pleasure of working with an important writer."

"Oh, *that* was a good one, Mr. Wald. I'm going to have to be a lot more wary of you than I thought," Ben said sarcastically.

Wald dropped his fork dramatically. "Just put your guard down and relax. And stop the Mr. Wald crap." He shook his head forlornly. "The coffee shop at the Beverly Hills Hotel in the seventies . . ."

"What about it?"

"The best pancakes in the world. The silver-dollar ones." He drew his thumb and forefinger together in a circle. "Actual size. And thin. Little piece of heaven."

"That's a diversion, Mr. Wald. This breakfast is on me, so you owe me straight answers."

He looked at Ben with dismay. "Come on. We're both in show business. What's with the straight answers? Oblique, indirect, elliptical; that's where the sweetness lies. You want to take away all the fun?"

Ben's face flushed with irritation.

"Yes, I can see that you do. Well, seeing as I'm a stranger in a strange land, I'll play by your rules. I want to start working with your book from scratch. Scrap anything you developed with Lewis. And any ties with Nora. And for all that I'll give you . . ." He swung his great head around in the air like a desktop model of a solar system. ". . . I'll give you a half million bucks."

Ben's ears reddened. "You make it sound like a tip."

"I didn't mean to. It's a substantial amount of money." His face tightened. "Old or new. Look, I don't understand your New England ways from a hill of ant turds. Just don't shine me on about the project. What I'm telling you is that I think I can turn your vision into a successful TV series. An update on the American dream. There's so much talk now about this one's roots and that one's roots and all this multicultural crap. I think most Americans are *dying* for a good dose of our *real* roots. What this country is all about: work ethic on up, and the struggle people are having to live it at the end of the twentieth century. Is that big enough for you? Can you pacify your integrity with that approach?"

"I can't tell whether it's high, low, or middle concept, Mr. Wald, but it sounds like a lot of extreme right-wing crap to me. Besides, you just want to show people what goes on behind the shades of so-called nice folk. You want it to be prurient and you want to put it down."

"Really, Mr. Bradford? That's not quite it. I actually want to pay you for your integrity. I'm depending on truth to make this thing bulletproof. Do you think I'd come all this way to kiss your ass if I *wasn't* interested in what you've got to sell?"

"How do you know I'm selling?"

Wald's sneer said he wasn't about to dignify the question with an answer. Then he spoke softly. "Give me credit for some insight. We all milk the human condition for a few bucks. By the way," he added politely, "at the risk of being vulgar, money's no object."

Ben noticed that Wald had managed to eat all of his pancakes throughout the conversation. "Do you consider what you did to Lewis Rosenthal part of milking the human condition?" He eyed Wald steadily. "At the risk of being vulgar."

Half of Wald's mouth rose in a smile. "Now you're beginning to sound like dialogue."

"We're talking something pretty melodramatic."

Wald began shaking his head. "Don't tell me I'm listening to the results of generations of inbreeding. I thought you were beyond all that."

"I'm asking if you had anything to do with Lewis Rosenthal's death."

"Holy shit. You're not making this up. You really mean it."

"It's a simple, direct question, Mr. Wald."

"Why on earth would I want to bother, care about whether . . ."

"Fear and greed are the two main reasons, usually."

Wald appeared to relax. "That settles it, then. I certainly had nothing to fear from Rosenthal. And God knows, there was nothing to be jealous about. It's very interesting, Ben. If you imply something like this over breakfast, I can't imagine what you'd accuse me of over dinner. Incest? A traitor to my country? Very vivid, your imagination."

"I didn't make it up." Ben watched a dimple form in his cheek.

"What a lousy poker player you are. You've just overextended your hand. What possible reason could you have, beyond your own hallucinations, to accuse me of something I had absolutely nothing to do with?" Wald wiped his mouth and put the napkin down with finality. "Well, we seem to have traveled far afield, and I don't quite know how to get our conversation back on track. Let's just say you aren't the only ball I'm juggling and forget the whole thing. Frankly, I thought I'd find you refreshingly down to earth compared to the Hollywood loonies I usually deal with. But, I must admit, by comparison . . ."

Ben's fist slammed the table. "Hold the putdowns. All right, I did misplay my hand."

"What does that mean?"

"That I shouldn't have expected a confession to fall trippingly from your lips."

Wald's look had the empathy of a wise parent. "Nora put you up to this. She convinced you I had something to do with her husband's death. And the sad finale to her career. And you've probably got some sort of a deep, repressed crush on her that makes you want to believe it. Well, I got to hand it to you; such decisions don't come cheap. As we both know, you could've easily talked me up to a million dollars. And that's just up front. Personally, I wouldn't call that integrity; it's more like stupidity. Give my regards to the grieving widow. Grieving for her career, no doubt." Wald gracefully slid his large frame from the booth. "By the way, you're out of your mind, Mr. Bradford. I had no idea. My sincerest condolences. And thank you for the hearty New England breakfast. Loved it."

Billy Carroll slid his thumbed copy of *The Limner* into the back pocket of his jeans and skipped down the makeshift steps from the stage. "When Father Stanislavsky remembers his words, call me." The young actor stuck his hands into his front pockets and strode to the back of the theater.

"Billy, stop it and come back." Ben's voice boomed through the auditorium. "You're not only acting unprofessional, you're being rude."

"I'm being unprofessional? How can I act with someone who hasn't the decency to know the words let alone try to find meaning in them?" He spoke slowly from the back of the theater.

"He's right, Ben." Tony Newland stood at the edge of the stage, a harsh overhead light making his thinning hair all but disappear. "It *is* unfair. The boy is correct. There's no reason he should be putting up with this so late in rehearsals."

"I'll be the judge of that. Billy, get back on the friggin' stage," Ben said harshly.

The young actor walked down the aisle quietly. "Hey, I like that. Very director. I must say, I was getting sick of all that would-you-mind crap." When he reached the footlights, he extended his hand to Newland. "Sorry, old bean, just seem to have lost my temper. You're doing a ripping good job other than remembering the goddamn words."

The older actor shook his hand and chuckled. "Thank you, my friend. And try to remember, it's easier remembering your lines when you're playing a deaf-mute." Carroll chuckled back and swung himself on the stage. "Right, now, where were we?"

"I was about to walk in and catch you with my wife in flagrante."

"Of course, that was it."

Nora rose from Ben's side and accepted Tony's hand as she climbed the steps. "Okay, Billy, let's flagrante."

They sat on two chairs that were later to become an Empire loveseat. Both held scripts, though neither looked at them. Billy sat straight arrow, his concentration focused on her lips.

"What do you see when you paint me?" she asked, exaggerating the movements of her lips.

He rubbed his knuckles, then pantomimed wiping his brow.

"Hard work," she said.

He stared at her in silence.

"Am I simply chattel?"

His eyes blazed, as though he'd been wounded, then he shook his head furiously.

"You see a woman, then?"

He nodded shyly.

"An attractive woman?"

He smiled and wagged his finger at her, as though she were a naughty child. Then he pointed to a mirror behind him.

"I'm being a bit coquette, aren't I?"

He nodded slowly.

"Can you put that in the picture, too?"

He arched an eyebrow and smiled.

"What do you think about when you're painting me?"

He stood, placed a fist on his heart and tapped it rapidly. Then he opened it extended, as if offering her a gift.

She shook her head at him. "Do you have any brothers or sisters?"

He held up four fingers.

"And are they all normal?" She clenched her eyelids. "I mean, do they hear and speak?"

He nodded, yes. Again he touched his heart, then held himself and shook side to side.

"You're very close. And do they approve of your being an artist?"

He shook his head smartly, sending his long brown hair into his eyes.

She extended her fingers to his brow and brushed it back. "I would be proud if you were my son."

He scowled.

"You are a very good artist. And yes, I'm old enough to be your mother." He turned away from her. "Does it bother you?" She touched his shoulders and leaned against his back. "You have courage and you put magic in your pictures. And I care about you. I only confess it now because you can't understand what I'm saying." Suddenly she looked stage right where Tony Newland was standing.

"But unfortunately, I do . . ." he said softly. "I think you'd better get the boy out of the house."

She turned Billy toward her, indicating Newland with her eyes. The young actor swirled around and jumped up, actually blushing as he did. Newland stepped forward and patted him on the arm wanly. "It's all right, son. Nothing happened. None of it is your fault. I'll give you your money and perhaps it's better you move on."

At that, the limner went into a paroxysm of denial, shaking his head wildly. He indicated the feeling of money with his fingers, then shook his hands as if erasing the image.

Newland stared at him for a long time, then flung his hands in the air and said, "Damn! I've done it again, gone up on my lines!"

"Shit," Billy said, leaving his character. "No, scratch that, it's okay. I can deal with it. They'll come, the lines, if I stop fucking yelling at you."

Newland smiled at him, "I thank you for that, Billy." He paused and the moment seemed to fill him with confidence. "There's something in this play that I've been thinking about and which we all might want to think about. It's when the crowd turns on the limner and . . ."—the thought appeared to bring tears to his eyes—". . . gouges his eyes out. I think I understand why they want to see him blind." Again he paused to find the courage to go on. "It's because people are always trying to diminish an artist. Convince themselves he's no better than they. In the middle of the night, when their unspoken, unspeakable fear comes sweeping over them; all the self-loathing; their sense of utter worthlessness becomes too much, they must rise and destroy the stranger among them, the artist, instead." He looked around embarrassed. "Sorry, but I just had to say that. We're all of us artists, and wouldn't it be nice if we could all love and protect each other. . . ." Then he smiled shyly at Billy and left the stage.

Chapter Ten

While *The Limner* was having its premiere, Congressman Neil Sheedy was making love to Tim D'Amato. He'd met the young man the previous summer at Reed's, the local hardware store where Tim worked weekends to supplement what he made working for his father, a local plumber. Then eighteen, guileless and sincere, he'd instructed the congressman on the replacement of his toilet tank float. The next day, they'd met again at the lake, Neil in the company of his wife and three children. This time the young man helped him repair his daughter's water wings. As thanks for the growing list of favors, the congressman invited Tim to join him and his wife for a beer. For their third meeting, Sheedy had invited the boy to his office to plunder his expertise on leaky sinks. As it was after hours, he had offered Tim a drink in appreciation for his labors. After the second, Neil had noticed the nascent plumber, who was six feet tall and of athletic build, was, surprisingly, showing the effects of the alcohol. Tim had readily confessed to hardly ever drinking and explained that he was subject to light-headedness and lack of coordination when he did. Clearly it had been the congressman's responsibility to drive him home, which he did, but not before a detour to a secluded area that seemed almost magically primeval.

Tim had been appreciative when Sheedy had steered the car

off the road and parked, thinking the congressman sensed his impending nausea. He'd jumped out of the car quickly, just in time to run into the woods and throw up behind a tree. When he had finished, he saw Neil a few feet away, relieving himself and staring at him with a smile. When the congressman had finished urinating, he shook his penis, then removed his hand, allowing it to dangle in a state of semitumescence. In that moment, sobriety had returned to Tim D'Amato and, angling his body modestly away from the congressman, he proceeded to relieve himself as well, also neglecting to return his member inside his trousers. Within seconds, the congressman had taken charge, walking up behind Tim and lightly rubbing his hands over the boy's chest, his stomach, then encircling him from behind and floating his hand over his groin.

Everything had happened so quickly, Tim felt as though he'd been caught up in a tornado, fingers and lips rushing about his body, paralyzing him with sensation. It was when he felt Neil's mouth on his own that reality set in and he allowed the congressman to initiate him into the taboo rituals that would then occur, largely undiscussed and regularly, over the course of the following year.

This night, the auspicious premiere of *The Limner,* Sheedy had told his wife he'd have to pass on the glittering event in favor of a position paper he was writing supporting a cogenerational plant. Instead, he'd met Tim behind the hardware store and taken his blue pickup, as the vehicle was ubiquitous enough to drive around unnoticed. They'd gone directly to the home of a friend of Sheedy's, a lawyer who'd befriended the congressman after they'd met at a gay bar in Albany.

Neil and Tim had dined at the lawyer's home, the congressman doing the cooking and most of the cleaning up, allowing the lawyer to excuse himself in order to go off and meet friends.

The ritual that followed between the two men had become so practiced and comfortable that both had fallen asleep afterward. When he woke, Sheedy realized the theater would be breaking soon and hurried to shower and dress. Tim, who had come to live for these evenings with his friend, did not rush to dress, preferring to watch the older man's activities fondly from under the covers.

"I'll leave you here for Alistair," Neil said to the grinning boy.

A look of hurt brushed Tim's face. Without responding, he pushed the sheets off and swung his legs over the side of the bed away from Sheedy. "I'll be dressed in a second; you didn't wait for me to shower."

"That would only lead to more stuff and I've got a deadline tonight."

"I wouldn't mind more stuff," Tim said, grinning over his shoulder.

"Next week; I'll find an excuse to get back from D.C. and spend more time with you."

"Because I want to or you want to?"

The congressman always grew annoyed at the boy's forays into commitment. "No mushy talk. Put your clothes on."

He watched as Tim stepped into his baggy shorts, old-man shorts, Neil thought, but extremely sexy against the young lean body. He, too, was ready for more stuff, in fact, he probably would have succumbed to the slightest physical provocation, but his ill-thought-out excuse for the evening demanded he be home before his wife. When the young man was dressed, he felt it safe to go to him and hold him tightly. He waited until he was completely still, then he closed his eyes and memorized the feelings until the time he could repeat then.

The moment appeared to pacify Tim's needs as well; he could feel the boy's soft face heat up against his cheek. He waited another minute, then gripped Tim's lean arms and pushed him away.

"It'll be easier when I'm married, have some kids," Tim said absently. "Then we can run around together much as we like. Nobody'll think anything of it."

"That's right," Neil said in his political voice. "But don't go rushing into anything just for the sake of appearances. Nobody's about to put two and two together. I don't see there's anything much to worry about."

"Except not spending enough time with you."

The boy's ingenuousness, which at first had seemed charming, had become, Neil thought, the price one paid for the feel of young flesh. "You spend any more time with me, you'd be bored out of your mind. Most of my waking hours are spent on the job."

"That's right. How's it going to look for you to get buddy-buddy with a plumber, even after I'm married."

"It'll look like I care about the people in my community. That I'm one of them. I don't see any problems with that, do you?"

The young man shrugged. As he walked toward the door, Neil looked down at his perfect, round ass and realized how unaware he was of his own incredibly appetizing presence. "You're going to drive me back to my car?"

The boy nodded and fished in his pocket for the keys. "Ten minutes to your car, ten minutes home; no problem."

"Ah yes, exactly as life should be."

Tony Newland had just finished consoling Nora over the blinding of the limner. He'd walked off stage, leaving her bereft and consoling the actress playing her daughter, who'd also become smitten, on and off stage, with Billy Carroll. Having spoken his last lines, he returned to the dressing room he shared with the young star and began taking off his makeup. He knew Billy Carroll would be watching the play's conclusion from the wings.

While it was customary for actors to remain in costume for curtain calls, Tony Newland had no intention of honoring the tradition. In fact, he had no intention of taking a curtain call. He felt in his heart that any applause he'd receive would be unearned, that he'd just managed to stumble through the performance without total embarrassment, covering up where memory failed and barely missing subverting his fellow actors. Several times he'd noticed Billy scowling at him or, even worse, mocking him with commedia del arte expressions. Even still, while he'd managed to acquit himself without total shame, he realized the sum total of his acting amounted to very little. Worse, he'd actually begun to understand why the industry had done such a thorough job of rejecting him. He had drifted far away from the satisfying world he'd inhabited and which had given him his identity. The un-made-up face in the mirror frightened him. The surgical procedures he'd submitted to had resulted in a bizarre effect: instead of looking younger, he simply looked like an aging man with a bad facelift.

He dressed himself in the crisp shirt and stylish Italian suit he'd planned to wear to the first-night party, except for the tie. This he placed over the back of Billy's chair, carefully arranged so the young actor would know he'd not simply tossed it there. Then he wrote on a small piece of paper: "I envy you your brilliant start." He felt tears burn the corners of his eyes as he left, once and for all, the world he'd spent his entire life trying to be a part of.

Unable to contain his boredom, Wald quietly rose from his seat just after Tony Newland made his final exit. As Nora sobbed on stage, he walked to the back of the theater followed by Chip Walker. Outside, on the gravel walk to the parking lot, both men looked up at a sky heavily riveted with stars.

"You don't see that in L.A.," Wald said.

"Incredible."

"As opposed to the play."

"A drag." Chip enjoyed the momentary feeling of complicity.

"These period things are big in local theater; people confuse long skirts with culture." They'd reached Wald's loaned Porsche, which in the moonlight shone like amethyst. "That asshole would rather write this crap than work on something that might actually keep people awake."

"You're not fascinated by deaf and dumb painters?" Chip asked cheerfully. "After they blinded him, he should have fallen in love with a crippled ballet dancer."

Wald smiled at his assistant.

"He could carry her around the dance floor and she could point him to his canvas." Chip glanced at the nearby road as two cars whizzed by in rapid succession. "I guess the locals get in their cars, tank up, and go on kamikaze missions to amuse themselves on a Saturday night."

"That would be the highlight of their week. After they graduate from fucking chickens." Wald unlocked his car, then squinted into the glare as more cars passed. "They turn on the high-beams permanently as soon as twilight hits."

"Want me to drop you off?" Chip asked.

"You don't know where I'm going." The meanness returned to his voice. "And I'd just as soon keep it that way." He got in

the car and started the engine. "Have a good night," Wald said
to him in mock surfer-ese and took off like a stunt driver.

The assistant walked to his rented Cavalier. His money was
on Wald heading for Audrey Dalton's, and for reasons that were
unclear, he decided to follow and see if he would win.

Neil Sheedy preferred to let Tim drive so he could run his
hand down the boy's thigh at leisure. It did not take long before
he could see the erection in his jeans.

Even if he got home after Catherine, Neil reasoned, he could
tell her he'd run out for a container of Heavenly Hash or the
paper. Now he regretted not doing more stuff with the boy; he
began rubbing Tim's crotch until he could feel the heat coming
through the denim.

"Shall I pull over?" the boy asked in a low, hoarse voice.

The congressman looked around to see where they were. Tim
had taken several turns, disorienting him. They were on a road
that could have been any of several in the area: secluded and
dark. His mind hung with indecision. "Where do you tell your
folks you are?"

"With friends. They don't question me."

"Maybe they should." Neil started working the boy's groin
again, causing Tim to swerve, then correct the car. "I don't
mean to distract you. Relax," he said as he moved his hand back
to his thigh.

"Sure you don't want me to stop?"

"Keep going; I'll just tune you up a little more," he counseled
as his hand slid back between the driver's legs.

Tony Newland had left the theater unsure of where he was
headed. He preferred being alone, even if it meant walking the
unfamiliar country roads. After a short while he began to find
his surroundings intoxicating. The temperature had dropped
considerably since daytime and the chill air had a fortifying
effect. The starry sky seemed surreal; disorienting but beautiful.
Only the silhouettes of the trees along the side of the road and
going up the hills seemed ominous.

He wondered how long it would take his fellow actors to
realize he wasn't among them at curtain call. Nevertheless that
was precisely what he was planning to do: take his final bow.

This stage was foreign to him, more rustic than he would have deemed appropriate and, of course, the audience had diminished to no one. Who would have thought it would come to this: Alone. Failed. Lost. Looking back, what his career had amounted to was merely a handful of films, now dated and relegated to barely rifled shelves in video shops; a period of social desirability he'd always felt was due more to what he could offer than who he was; and a brush with materialism that even in its most indulgent form had seemed foreign to him. Now all of it was fraying, or fading in the hazy limbo of memory, much like himself.

A car shot by and startled him. Then another, swerving as if it had seen a startled animal. As they passed he heard the sound of raucous young voices and something metallic bouncing on the road.

The exertion was starting to make him sweat, in spite of the chill air. In front of him he could see swatches of fog hanging over the road, the effect not dissimilar to that of studio dry ice. He began to wonder what animals beside himself might be out prowling the night, looking for succor. Then he remembered that solace was not the reason he'd come. He was there because his life had reached the point of diminishing returns. All the effort required to exist brought nothing but disappointment. Living had become a daily act of frustration, embarrassment, even humiliation. And most frightening, the chances of change seemed almost nonexistent.

He had come, as they say, to the end of his rope. Where better, he thought, than in this place that was so remote from his worlds of New York and Beverly Hills as to be another planet. Here, isolated from everything familiar or comfortable, was the perfect place to end his life. In a manner so mundane as to be ambiguous. His last gesture would be to turn himself into road kill.

Chip Walker found little satisfaction in proving himself correct. The house Audrey Dalton was staying in was brightly lit, as though the star were entertaining, even though he knew she hadn't yet left the theater.

The Porsche had been abandoned at the bottom of the drive. Chip smiled, noting how consistent Wald was in the imperious manner in which he treated his vehicles. Out of curiosity, Walker left his own car and walked over to the Porsche; faithful to his nature, Wald had left the keys in the ignition.

Again on impulse, Chip returned to his car, drove it down the road, and parked. There he waited for Dalton's return, after which he would indulge his childish whim to take his boss's car for a spin.

Tim was past imploring the congressman to allow him to stop. It had become clear that Sheedy was getting his kicks titillating him, working him into a state and not allowing him to inhabit it, even though there were signs that he also was sharing his frustration.

Tim had slowed to a cautious thirty-five, frequently checking the rearview mirror for cars. At that speed, he could deal with Neil's games, even allowing the driving to enhance them. He'd tuned into a local station playing willowy new age music. The sounds seemed to suggest a state of suspension, which was exactly what Tim felt.

He looked down and saw Neil was playing with himself, as well, parallel action making him more excited. Then he felt his belt being unbuckled, Neil's fingers unfastening the metal button on his jeans. He began rocking his groin back and forth, realizing Neil's plan was for them to do more stuff, now, in the car, as he drove.

It was just as Sheedy's hand slid under the elasticized band of his shorts that he saw it, something on the road, moving, the eyes at first caught in the headlights, then turning away, hiding from the glare. He couldn't make out the shape; it looked to be a tall animal, or something rearing, or a ghost.

Now as it hurled itself at the car, the body curled into itself like a fetus and Tim thought it was a man. He saw it as if in a mirage, so persuasive were the sensations between his legs. Until he hit it. Then he heard the thud of flesh and bone against blacktop. In that one acoustic instant, the entire world seemed fragile, totally destructible. Whatever he had hit decompressed and fell aside into a ditch.

Tim barely altered the car's speed. In the rearview mirror, the thing had disappeared from sight. Only Neil's voice attested to its reality.

"What in fucking hell? Did you hit something?" The congressman sounded harsh, scolding, as though he'd just arrived on the scene. "Well, for Christ's sake, what are you doing? Aren't you going to stop?"

In his mind, Tim had pushed Neil aside as well, into that realm of unreality that existed in the periphery of his mind. He'd reduced his purpose to the simple act of driving straight ahead, away from whatever had occurred. The congressman's instructions had become gibberish. The only thing he was aware of was Neil buttoning himself up, then roughly trying to do the same to him.

When he'd finished, both men sat up straight in their seats, staring ahead of them as though hypnotized by the patterns the fog was making. Now there was silence, except for the celestial humming coming over the radio.

"What happened?" Neil asked disingenuously.

"I don't know. Must have hit something."

Neither of the men spoke again as they drove to Sheedy's car.

Chip had kept a healthy distance between himself and the blue pickup truck in front of him. Because it had been moving so slowly, even erratically, he'd assumed a problem with the driver, alcohol he thought vaguely, and gave him room.

When what appeared to be a man jumped out of the woods, Chip had braked immediately. Then he heard the thud. He turned off his lights and let the Porsche drift to the side of the road. Chip stared at the scene as though it were a TV show. He waited for the truck to return, other cars to pass. But the silence held, except for the croaking of deep-throated frogs. After several minutes, he drove to the shape at the side of the road.

Suddenly Chip felt the same rush as when he spoke with his potential suicides: the feeling of danger, of risk, the toppling of the equilibrium of living. He stopped just short of the body and got out.

The silence and the extraordinary clutter of stars gave the scene a sense of peacefulness that even spread to the man lying beside the road. The body was surprisingly unsullied, the eyes open, staring at the glittering dome. Even the position of the limbs was graceful, as if the man had gently reclined. Only a trickle of blood at the side of his mouth hinted at what had occurred.

Then recognition set in. Chip was sure it was the actor in the play he'd just seen. His face had somehow managed to look blissful. There was a dignity about him in death, Chip realized, that had escaped him in life. The air of desperation apparent even across the footlights was gone.

Chip stood over the actor observing him as though he were a statue. Dried leaves were blowing into crevices about his body, wedging in the long strands of his thinning hair. His gaze toward the sky had a religiosity about it. Chip lowered himself slowly to his knees, fascinated by the hieroglyphics of death etched on the man's features. That was when he saw it: a slight tremor in the delicate flesh below his left eye. At first Chip was uncertain whether it wasn't a flickering shadow or an insect. But when he moved his face closer to the actor's, he not only verified the quivering flesh, he heard a low, shaky moaning sound as well. Then his eyelids flickered, not quite cutting off the man's stare. A second later he saw the actor's lips attempt to form a word. The face was addressing him with a conspiratorial look, as though letting Chip in on a great secret. He was asking for help: whether to let him live or die Chip wasn't sure.

Instinctively Chip raised the actor's head and rested it on his knee. He lowered his ear to the injured man's mouth and listened. All he could hear was the faintest breathing. Whatever the man had to tell him would be said with his eyes. Under the bright sky they took on a luminosity with the depth and agitation of twin vortexes. Chip realized they were either seeing the faint remnants of this life or the formidable unknown of the next.

Then Chip thought of a plan. Slowly he lifted his thigh, raising the man's head until the actor's neck rested on his knee. He surveyed the ground with his right hand, reaching down into the stony ditch. There he found what he was looking for: a rock half the size of the old man's head. He brought it up and placed it alongside them. Then he cradled the actor in his arms, resting the head on his shoulder, and felt the warmth from his body. As he stared at the taut, curious young-old face, he lifted the rock into the air. Just as he felt his arm begin to shake, he brought the stone down full force onto the actor's skull. The body jerked violently against Chip's and a soft grunting sound came from the throat. Chip held his breath, waiting until all sound and movement subsided. Then he placed the rock on the side of the road and lowered the actor's head to meet it.

Now Chip could hear the sound of his own breathing, forced and rapid. He stood, brushing himself, checking his shoulder where the trickle of blood from the man's mouth could have soiled him. Except for a certain dampness from his own perspiration, he was clean.

Once he caught his breath, his mind moved to step two of his plan. If it was to looking convincing that the Wald car had hit the actor, there would have to be a sign of impact. He stood, unlocked the trunk, and removed a picnic blanket in which he placed the rock he'd used on the actor and carried it several yards into the woods. Holding the heavy parcel at his waist, he raced for the car, throwing himself and the stone against it; the thud was almost identical to the one when the actor had been hit.

Chip maintained his position until he caught his breath, then slid himself and the bundle off to inspect the dent. It seemed convincing to him, enough to suggest a frail man had been struck at moderate speed. He opened the blanket and replaced the rock by the man's bleeding head.

Chip smiled, pleased with his reenactment, and backed off into the woods to survey the scene. He could actually replay it in his mind, inserting close-ups of the actor's face as the car hit, see in slow motion as the skull cracked on the rock.

Content, he returned to Wald's car and turned on the ignition. Now he backed up fifty feet, reversed, and accelerated toward the body, jamming the brakes just short of it. With the engine still running, he got out, inspected the tire marks, and smiled again. Then he lifted Tony Newland so that his midsection made contact with the dented fender and rubbed the body against it. Clearly, he thought, he had a knack for staging deaths.

Then he returned the car to Audrey Dalton's darkened cottage, where he picked up his own and drove it to his dreary motel.

*　*　*

By the time Tim D'Amato had dropped off the congressman and returned home, his entire body was wet with perspiration. As he walked the short distance from the garage to his house, he could feel his jeans crusty and damp, his cotton shirt sticking to the small of his back.

All the lights were on in the kitchen and living room, evidence of guests. He stopped outside the screen door to listen. The rumble of conversation turned into laughter and he could make out the voices of his brother and sister-in-law, then the squall of his infant nephew. He pushed the long brown hair from his forehead and entered.

His parents looked up at him pleasantly, then returned their attention to the squawking baby. Tim greeted them and went directly to the kitchen. The baby sounds subsided as he gulped a glass of water, leaning on the sink to steady himself. He felt light-headed, the sounds from the living room orbiting about him. He realized his legs were wobbly as he started for the hall stairs.

"There's your Uncle Timmy," his sister-in-law said in baby talk. "Don't you want to say hello to Uncle Timmy?"

He turned to see her shaking the baby's arm at him.

"I think I'm coming down with a cold or something," he heard himself say, "I'd better stay away."

"Did you take any aspirin?" his mother asked in her sharp parrot voice.

"I'll take some upstairs," he answered.

"Don't forget. Don't want you sick on me next week," his father said with a show of impatience. "Big job, very big job," he said, as though trying to impress someone.

"I'll be fine," Tim answered, pulling himself forward on the banister.

"The boy's probably drunk," the father said raucously. "Hope he got lucky first."

As the small group responded, Tim hoisted himself to the landing, listing forward as he entered the bathroom at the top of the stairs. He flicked on the light and confronted himself in the mirror. It was as though his features had taken leave of each other, the skin holding them together a mottled pinkish-white. His eyes were imploring him, filled with fear, as though he were a stranger. As he turned, he felt the vomit well up in his throat.

He swung and fell to his knees alongside the toilet bowl, heaving chunks of the dinner Neil had cooked for him. When he finished, the sides of his chest were tight with pain.

After stripping and washing up, he went into his room, carefully lowered himself onto the bed and pulled the covers up around his neck to fight a sudden chill. When he closed his eyes, it brought a black dizziness that made him sit upright. The taste of bile returned to his throat. He sat motionless, waiting for everything to subside. Then he began to whimper with laughter as he thought of the evening; finally, all his sins had caught up with him.

He ran the accident back and forth in his mind, trying to convince himself it hadn't happened, but the dent on the truck said otherwise. A deer, he would tell his father, and that he was lucky it had shied away after glancing off the fender. He knew there'd be little discussion, his father having been inundated with deer stories, some his own, over the years.

Over and over, Tim tried speculating on what he'd hit, finally confronting himself with the truth. He'd hit a man and driven away. He also knew that Neil had made only a halfhearted attempt to stop him. Even Neil wouldn't be able to explain what he was doing in a hit-and-run vehicle driven by a nineteen-year-old while his wife was at the theater. The thought brought Tim's second attempt at laughter, during which he lay back against the pillow. The dizziness was gone, even when he closed his eyes. Now he pressed the lids together tightly, clenching his teeth and wishing mightily that everything that had occurred that evening had never happened. He wished he could make a deal: stop seeing the congressman in return for obliterating the memory of the old man in the headlights. He would accept the wrong of his ways and return to the life that was expected of him. He would give up a reality that made him feel sharp and alive for the comfortable lull of existence as he'd always known it. If he could get through this one big crisis in his life, he would live the rest of it without risk. That was the bargain he formed in his mind and on which he fell asleep.

Chapter Eleven

Happy the first night of *The Limner* was over, Nora had fallen asleep easily, content to table her concerns to an indefinite future. So it was with peace-shattering fatefulness that she was drawn out of that sleep by the ominous buzzing of the phone next to her bed.

"Hello," she said clearly, not allowing herself to sound as though she'd been awakened.

"Congratulations. You pulled it off."

It was frightening how familiar the voice sounded, although she'd only spoken to it twice before. "You woke me to tell me that?"

"You don't sound like I woke you. Beside, I thought your comeback would keep you going till dawn."

"Who are you and why are you so intent on torturing me?"

"That's two questions. The first you'll have to guess at. As for the second, I hadn't realized I was. I thought I was helping you."

"How?"

"By cutting through the crap and feeding you little pieces of reality."

"What you're doing is stirring up fear."

"Truth is like that, fearful. But it's still best to confront it."

Nora had the urge to reach for a cigarette, something she

hadn't done in ten years. "You must have a giant revelation to wake me in the middle of the night."

"I thought you'd appreciate the drama of it all. Besides, for me it's just the end of my day. I've been busy, busy, busy."

"At what?"

"Ah-hah! Thought you'd catch me there. Sorry."

"How long do I have to wait until you're finished toying with me?"

"Shouldn't be much longer. I'm actually getting kind of sleepy."

She decided not to say anything, give him anything to play off; but she was curious to see where he was going. The frightening thing was she was getting used to him; his words were even beginning to take on some sort of elliptical meaning.

"Fall back to sleep?" he asked loudly. "That would be impolite. Especially since I'm about to hand you proof of our last discussion."

Now the fear began to take hold. "You have information about Lewis's death?"

"I said that, didn't I?"

She sat up against the padded headboard. "Listen. Let me be straight with you. You sound too intelligent to be getting into this sick conversation."

"I suppose that's a compliment. Now, could you, just for a moment, consider the possibility I'm telling the truth?"

She was perplexed by how sane he sounded.

"Only, as in most cases, the truth is going to hurt."

She tucked the pillow behind her head, concentrating on the voice, trying to place it.

"Well?" he asked.

"Am I ready? I'm not sure I have a choice."

He chuckled, sounding youthful, even friendly. Then she realized he'd never actually sounded threatening.

"The reason I'm hesitating," he continued, "is that it involves your friend Tony Newland."

Nora felt herself flush. "What's happened to him?" she asked quietly.

"He's dead. I don't know how else to say it."

She felt the warmth in her body intensify. "How did it happen?"

"How do you think? Why the fuck do you think I'm calling? Wald killed him, that's how it happened. He was staggering along the side of the road and Wald went after him with his car. For fun. Hunt the fucking has-been."

"And how do you know this? How are you so omniscient that you know what he was thinking? Were you there? Or are you making all this up, like when you suggested Ben Bradford had something to do with my husband's death?"

"You want proof? The body's lying alongside the road; I couldn't make that up."

Now she knew who she was speaking to. "You were a witness?"

"Not so as I'd testify. But I don't have to. Just have the police find his car; it's evidence."

"Where's the car?"

"Oh, do I have to do *everything* for you?" he asked mockingly. "I know it's the middle of the night, but you're still being awfully dense. I believe Ms. Dalton's having her own private cast party, for herself and guess who. Do I have to draw a map?"

"Sorry, I don't function great at this hour. So, explain something to me: what does Tony Newland's death have to do with my husband's?"

Suddenly his voice became raw and taunting. "Your husband's murder. Murder. Get it through your head. Your husband was killed, murdered. Only you don't want to fucking deal with it. Believe me, it happened. I know, I was there."

She felt his sudden silence well up as though it were tangible; clearly he'd said more than he'd intended. "When? Before, after, during?"

"Oh, come on, don't get cute with me. Don't waste your energy trying to tie me in. Don't you get it? A man who would kill another for sport, because he was there, maybe asking for it; if he could do it to one man he could do it to another. Newland was out there begging to die, just like your husband. Neither he or your husband had the balls to do it. That's where Wald comes in; his balls are big enough for the two of them."

"You really do have firsthand knowledge."

"Oh, come on; you're being cute again, toying with me. I'd strongly suggest you give it up. I'm better at this game than you are. I'd don't think you'd want me to prove it to you."

She tried to control her voice, to calm him down. "Your friend Mr. Wald seems to have a nose for would-be suicides."

"They're not difficult to come across in this business. Tell me you haven't thought of it yourself, in one of your in-between periods. Like where you are right now. You think they're missing you in Hollywood? Saying, how marvelous, she's doing *theater.*" He played with the word. "Just think about how many new ones came to town in the time you've been here. How many body parts are being stroked tonight under the Lotusland moon? How many promises are being made to turn those ripe, writhing, fleshy commodities into movie stars? Think how many deals went down, how many points promised, how much cash and fame and power changed hands while you were out here acting your ass off? Who knows about it? Who cares? Back there you're comatose and nobody's even looking for a heartbeat."

"Are you enjoying yourself?" she asked hoarsely.

"Not really. Believe it or not, this isn't how I get my jollies. I'm just telling you this to make my point. That it is Steven Wald who killed you. Pulled the plug on the entity that was Nora Howard. He can do that, you know. A few of them are plugged-in enough and strong enough and mean enough to do it. And for them it means no more than cracking their knuckles. They do it to prove how big they are. If they can get away with career assassination, if they can get away with pulling the plug on people's lives, they can get away with anything. It gets so heady that they don't even consider their own mortality. And that's what I'm handing you: Steven Wald's head on a silver platter. If you don't want the pleasure of cutting it up and throwing out the pieces, than I'm sorry for wasting your time. Spoiling your beauty sleep. I just thought you of all people would want, forgive the archaic nature of the word, revenge."

Nora had listened silently, intrigued by how little emotion he had put in his voice. She also realized he was smart enough to know that his own identity had escaped, that he could no longer be the anonymous avenging angel.

"What do you expect to get out of all this?" she asked him. "In fact, you'll probably wind up losing a job."

The silence was shorter than she'd expected. When he got back on the line, he sounded cheerful. "Bingo! Okay, you marked me. Now forget it. From now on, all roads lead away from me. Someone saw the accident, followed the black Porsche that didn't stop, saw it pull into where the movie star is staying. They reported it to the police without identifying themselves because they weren't supposed to be out themselves. Cheating on their whatever. Let your playwright knock off a little scenario. Let him make a citizen's arrest for all I care. I just want to see the frigging thing over. I'm tired of screwing around with you people, first your husband, now your costar. I'm bored with this gig. Fate's given me the opportunity to end it on a high note. I'm taking it. Got it?"

Nora could hear his nerves becoming spastic; the rhythm of his words, the edge in his voice saying he'd lost control. "I understand." She could hear him trying to catch his breath.

"Just use your head. I get a lot less friendly when I'm threatened."

And a lot less sure of yourself when you're found out, she thought. She heard the line being disconnected. It was then she let herself think of Tony Newland and allowed the tears to come.

Everything Nora had told Bradford on the phone had been confirmed by the sheriff: Tony Newland had indeed been killed by a vehicle that appeared to be the car being used by Steven Wald and found in the driveway of the home where Audrey Dalton was staying. When Ben Bradford had the news played back to him, he shook his head, uncomfortable that it had all played itself out so neatly.

The sheriff went on to tell him that he'd brought Mr. Wald in for questioning and that he'd denied any knowledge of the incident. Ms. Dalton had insisted on accompanying the studio head to the police station and had urged anyone who would listen, which turned out to be the entire force on duty, that the charges were all a lot of crap and that Wald, who she described as a highly important personage, should be released immediately. As for the suspect himself, he'd declined to say anything in the absence of his lawyers. The Porsche in question had been impounded and was to undergo a forensic examination.

Apparently the sheriff had some sympathy with Wald's declaration of innocence as well as empathy with Dalton's arguments and released the VIP on his own recognizance. The pair had struck a final deal with the law enforcement officer: that their names be kept out of the papers, local and otherwise, until the facts came in, although, the sheriff noted, the actress appeared less adamant about that particular condition. While the officer knew this to be difficult, given their high profile and the amount of attention they'd attracted at the station, he agreed to do his best. Ben felt he would just as soon attribute the accident to a plastered local and proselytize to the press about the dangers of drunk driving. In the end, he'd cryptically suggested to Ben that he speak with "the powers that be" before the whole thing got out of hand. The notion that Ben could somehow trace Wald's connections seemed at first improbable, but then a thought took root in his mind.

Within ten minutes, Ben had obtained the Connecticut phone number of Michael Russell and was surprised at how quickly the press mogul got on the line.

"Your play was absolutely stunning, or so I've been told. My wife absolutely adored it, said I was a fool to come down with indigestion and that she simply wouldn't speak with me until I saw it. But I can't imagine any of this has any connection with why you're calling this morning. Am I correct?"

"That's true, Mr. Russell. But I appreciate hearing your wife's words anyway."

"Is something wrong? Author's don't usually call hours after their triumph unless it's to complain about a bad review, which I don't think I've published, have I?"

"No, you haven't. I'm calling regarding an entirely different matter."

"Which is?"

"Mr. Wald."

Russell paused, than said, "Yes, I suppose in a way he belongs to me. What's happened to him?"

"He's allegedly involved in an accident. He denies it."

"What sort of accident?"

"Car accident. A man was killed."

"Hit and run?"

"Apparently."

"And Wald was driving?"

"His car is being gone over."

Russell paused to think the matter over. "I'm not sure why you're telling me this, Mr. Bradford. Is there anything you're *not* telling me?"

Ben wondered just how much more to tell the man.

"There is more, isn't there, Mr. Bradford?"

"Yes, Mr. Russell, there is." Ben recognized the man's gentle, encouraging tone as highly persuasive.

"Mr. Wald is a significant person in my company. As such, I've more than a casual interest in his character, for financial as well as moral reasons."

"This can't be totally substantiated, but this isn't the first time he's been involved in someone's death."

"Also an accident?"

"A suicide."

"That would strike me as a pattern. Wouldn't it you?"

"I suppose that's why I called. At any rate, giving him the benefit of the doubt, hit and run is still pretty serious."

Again, Russell seemed to be mulling over the situation. "It shows rather poor judgment, doesn't it? An inclination to panic. I never would have guessed it, would you? Seems steady as a rock, don't you think?"

"Unrelenting."

"Yes, that's it. We must talk more about this sometime. I suppose now I ought to bring in the lawyers if he hasn't already done so. I want to thank you very much, Mr. Bradford."

"Good luck, Mr. Russell."

"The same to you. I did say how much my wife adored your play?"

"You did. Thank her for me."

"I will indeed. Good-bye now."

Ben hung up, knowing the man was the only match for Wald and wondering why he felt he could trust him. Perhaps, he realized, because the alternative was so frightening.

Chapter Twelve

The morning after Tony Newland's death, Dick Shannon got the call he'd been dreading for years. Much as he knew he'd been overshadowed by his wife's entrepreneurial abilities in recent years and that his own fondness for alcohol had given him the appearance of a benign fool, his acute ability to read people, a characteristic to which he owed much of his early success, had survived largely undiminished.

For example, it hadn't taken the Governor long to realize that his daughter Catherine's decision to marry Neil Sheedy would prove to be a horrible mistake. In fact, he'd sensed disaster well before the wedding, but his fear of disillusioning someone he loved had inhibited him from asking that she reconsider.

When the first of their children came along, he'd tried convincing himself that he was wrong, that his son-in-law was everything he would have liked him to be. Unfortunately the doubt remained. After the second and third child, and the rise of Neil's political fortunes, Dick Shannon had become quite content to hide his own acuity from himself. Until the phone rang.

In order not to disturb Nancy, who was still asleep after her premiere activities, he rushed to pick it up while pouring himself his third cup of coffee of the morning.

"Dick?"

"Yes?"

157

"Neil."

"Sorry you missed the play; all the ladies seem to love it."

"I was busy."

"So Catherine said."

"Dick, something's come up that's made me realize I can't beat about the bush with you anymore."

The ex-governor gently put his coffee cup on the counter, and placed his hand over his eyes as they were beginning to tear. "Please don't. How can I help you?" He surprised himself with the strength of his voice.

"There was an accident last night."

"And you were involved?"

"Indirectly."

The Governor remained silent, knowing the story wouldn't be forthcoming if he did otherwise.

"I was in the car."

"Was anyone hurt?"

"Yes."

"How bad?"

"I'm not sure; the driver didn't stop. The man could be dead, for all I know."

"I can easily find that out."

"And anything else about the accident that you can."

"You want me to find out if they know who did it?"

"Exactly."

"And if they connect you with that person."

Now strain sneaked into his son-in-law's voice. "Yes."

"Do you want to tell me who it was?" As he feared, Sheedy remained silent. "I'm sorry I asked that; it wasn't to pry. I thought it might be helpful if I had a little knowledge of what happened."

When his son-in-law spoke again, his voice had gained its usual vitality; it even had the familiar arrogance. "A young man named Tim D'Amato."

"I see."

"He's local. He works for his dad, who's a plumber."

"I'm glad to see you're working at the grass roots level."

"Dick . . ." Neil said the name as a warning.

"Do you know who the victim was?"

"I haven't a clue."

As the Governor reached for his coffee cup, he realized his hand was shaking. "Does Catherine know?"

"What do you mean?"

"About last night."

"No. I was home before she was."

"Good. Will your friend lie for you?"

"I think he would; I'm not sure he can."

"I thought you said he was a plumber, not a priest."

"I'm giving you my opinion." His voice had taken an edge.

"Can he prove anything?"

"Not really, unless we were seen."

"And I should think you would have taken precautions not to be."

"I tried. But you never know."

"Does that make it more exciting?" Shannon could feel the years of loathing he had for the man well up in his throat.

When his son-in-law spoke, it was with utter calm. "Dick, I know what you think of me. I would never dream of asking you to do anything like this if it was just for myself. But, as we both know, it isn't."

"Obviously."

"I think it can be contained. First of all, I don't know if the man is dead. If he's alive, I doubt he could identify the vehicle. It's a blue pickup, by the way, like a thousand others around here. If he's dead, I don't see how they could connect the vehicle to the accident. But you can't be too sure, right?" he added with a chuckle. "Cover them bases. By the way, there's one thing about this little incident that was sort of strange."

"Just one thing?" Now that Neil had stated the terms of their collaboration he saw no reason to contain his feelings.

"I'd appreciate it, Dick, if we just stuck to the accident. . . . The man seemed to leap out at the truck, like he was trying to throw himself in front of it."

"Why didn't you stop, then, and call for help?"

"Two reasons. I wasn't driving. And it would mean I'd be caught in a lie to Catherine; I told her I was home working on a speech."

"So you did. She fretted to me that you work too hard. At least that's one thing she needn't worry about."

Now Sheedy seemed to ignore him. "The boy panicked. He

just kept driving. I'm not sure I could have stopped him if I'd wanted to."

"Anything else? I realize this can't be easy for you."

"Funnily enough, it's not nearly as difficult as I thought it would be. Much of this isn't news to you, is it?"

"I'm afraid not."

"How about Nancy? Have the two of you ever discussed it?"

"No."

"Do you think she knows?"

"I couldn't say. In some ways she's a very worldly woman; in others, she's naïve. It's hard to say. Perhaps she simply chooses not to think about it."

"Dick, I'll make you a promise. If we come out of this okay, I'm going to do everything I can to control my behavior."

The Governor shook his head wearily. "It's good of you to say that, Neil. But I'm not sure you can."

There was silence at the other end, then, "Thanks, Dick. I appreciate your help."

"You're family. I have no choice."

"I know that. That's why I called."

"What did you say the boy's name is?"

When his mother knocked on the door, Tim D'Amato was surprised to find himself wakened by the sound as he was certain he'd spent the night without sleep.

"Timmy, we're going to church. I assume you're sleeping in . . ."

"If you don't mind, Mom."

"If I did, it wouldn't get you in and out of the shower in time anyway. We'll see you for lunch."

He put his hands under his head and listened to the abstract sounds of his family's departure. Like a sitcom, he thought, dog barking; a voice asking if anyone knew where the car keys were; the door opening and closing several times; finally the sound of a car starting up. The sound made him jump up and run to the window. The blue pickup was sitting in the bright sunlight, its dented fender hard to discern from a distance. Apparently his father either hadn't seen it or hadn't been concerned enough to question him.

When he went downstairs, he saw they'd left the automatic

coffee maker on for him, but more importantly, the newspaper was lying untouched on a kitchen chair. He looked at it as though it had magical powers. He poured himself coffee, accepting the fact that the die had been cast.

With some relief, he saw there was nothing about an accident on the front page. Carefully he read through the local news, through the trivia of appendix operations and bowling contests. Finally, on page eleven, there was mention of an accident concerning an actor appearing at the Hartwood, his condition and the cause of the accident unknown at press time. It was the sort of story most people would miss. So much for his fate, he thought; he would still have to wait for the die to be tooled.

Wald had been on the phone all morning, raising lawyers from the Hamptons to Bel-Air. He did not take threats to his status quo lightly, especially from a two-bit, officious, incompetent bureaucrat. Having alerted everyone he could think of to be in a state of readiness, he decided it was time to prepare his own offensive. By eleven he was in a rented car arriving at the generously landscaped, sprawling Russell estate. As he exited his rented car, Russell himself came out the front door.

"Good morning. I see you had no trouble finding the place."

"Not at all. It sort of declares itself."

"Let me presume that to be a compliment." Russell was carrying a delicate china cup, from which he sipped. "From the tone of your phone call I'll assume you'd rather save a tour of the grounds for another time." Wald gave him his half smile, half sneer. "Right. Perhaps than you'd like to come in and have a cup of coffee." His extended arm encouraged Wald inside. "So Early American, don't you think?"

Wald couldn't be sure if he was teasing. "I'd no idea our founding fathers lived so well."

"True. All this lovely foliage and no taxation without representation to boot. They knew exactly what they were doing. Did you like the play last night?"

"It was tolerable."

Without Wald noticing, a woman in a black uniform had poured coffee and put the cup before him on the large round mahogany table.

"Aida loved it. But then she's into everything Americana."

He lifted the silver coffee pot the woman had left behind and refilled his delicate china cup. "Could your visit have anything to do with the accident?" He turned to Wald to watch the surprise on his face. "Yes, well you see, I'm not a press lord for nothing. Did you do it?"

"What exactly do you mean?" Wald asked, trying to adjust to the rapid turn in conversation.

"Did you hit and run?"

"I didn't hit anything. I didn't run from anything. I don't know how that screwy town works."

"I should think by the same laws of order as everywhere else."

"Really." A look of disgust came over Wald's face. "I'm not aware of many places that pull innocent people out of bed and accuse them of vehicular homicide."

Russell sipped delicately. "Is that the charge? I thought it was aggravated vehicular homicide."

Wald looked at him warily. "Do you know something I don't?"

"Possibly."

"Are you going to tell me or just play games showing me how smart you are?"

"Neither, unless you tell me the truth." He could sense bits and pieces of information spinning in Wald's head. Then the man leaned into him.

"Listen. You're probably more aware of the kind of justice meted out around here than I am. First this sheriff handles me with kid gloves, now you're talking aggravated whatever. I'm beginning to think it doesn't matter what I did so much as what people want to believe happened. If it's gone this far, I'm sure they'll have no trouble linking my car to the accident."

"Come now. You're implying some sort of surreal corruption. That's daft, not to mention paranoid. You either did it or you didn't; which is it?"

"I drove myself to where Dalton is staying, hitting no one along the way, fucked her, and fell asleep. Until the New England gestapo marched in this morning."

"That's it, then. That's the version you stand by."

"That's the truth."

"I see. Good. I gave you my studio to run because I found

you the best man around to do it. If you tell me you're innocent I will believe you and try to help you. Isn't that what you want to hear?"

"Bottom line, yes. But somehow I get the feeling you think you're aiding and abetting a cover-up. Why do I feel that?" Wald stared at him intently, a smug twist to his lips.

"Perhaps it's my British accent; makes a lot of Yanks suspicious. Not to worry." He smiled politely.

Wald continued to stare at him. "You know, your knowledge of my alleged accident is very odd. And I don't think I'm being particularly paranoid."

"Let's just say news travels fast in small towns. Faster when there are important people involved. Your credibility is very important to me. What you are is a deal maker. If people can't justify their faith in you, your raison d'être falls apart. Which represents a very considerable investment on my part." Wald tasted his coffee for the first time as Russell watched. "Isn't it ridiculous? They've flavored it with strawberries; American ingenuity."

Wald put down the cup. "I want to leave here as soon as possible. Do you think you can arrange that?"

"I'll try. You've called lawyers, I trust?"

Wald nodded.

"You'll be going back to the coast?"

Wald nodded again.

"I wouldn't disappear too quickly, if I were you. You don't want it to look like you're running away. Have you handled your business with the writer?"

"He's not interested. It's either my breath or my personality."

"I see. Then, in essence, this awkward situation has arisen for nothing."

Wald retrieved his usual smirk. "Oh, I don't think so. Dalton was quite a good lay. Anyway, as they say, no risk it, no biscuit."

Russell drained his cup. "Well, let me see what I can do. You'll wait to hear from me, I trust?"

Wald nodded suspiciously. "How long do you think this will take?"

Russell chuckled. "I love the American sense of anxiousness. 'Do it yesterday, delay is death.' I'm afraid I have to move at my own pace. But I'll try putting you out of your misery as soon as I can."

Wald stood and extended his hand. "My little crap-ass assistant didn't phone you about the accident, did he?"

Russell shook his hand slowly. "That young man you're traveling with? No."

Wald grinned at him. "Well, as I have a vested interest in you as well, I'll have to believe that."

They both smiled before Wald turned to leave.

Governor Dick shook his head with confusion after putting down the phone. The sheriff hadn't been at all surprised at his interest in the previous evening's accident, particularly as the victim had been an actor associated with Mrs. S's theater, as he called the Hartwood. So it was with no hesitation that the law officer revealed the chief and only suspect was the visiting Hollywood studio head, Steven Wald. Shannon had noticed how the sheriff gave the name an ominous edge. They were waiting for some forensic reports, he'd gone on, to confirm their lead.

The Governor had listened with interest, waiting for the other shoe to drop. It never did. No mention of Tim D'Amato. No Neil Sheedy. Only Wald, the name coming out like an invective. The sheriff cheerfully promised to keep in touch, then added that no information would be released until he'd briefed the Governor. Not even to the District Attorney's Office. It was at that point the ex-governor had shown his pleasure with the man's report by alluding to commendations that would climb the state's law enforcement hierarchy. Even more importantly, he chuckled, he'd put in a good word with his wife Nancy, who employed the sheriff's only son as a factory manager.

Both men hung up in cheerful spirits, although deep down each felt they weren't playing with all the cards and suspecting the other of having more knowledge than either possessed.

Slightly unnerved, Dick Shannon felt himself thoroughly justified in going to the bar and fixing himself a bloody mary. Probably half the people in the county, he thought, were doing the same, it being brunch time, Sunday morning. He was preparing his third when the housekeeper came to tell him that a Mr. Michael Russell was on the phone.

* * *

"You can call me Governor Dick if I can call you Sir Mike," Shannon said amiably.

"I'd be delighted. By the way, congratulations to your wife; I hear the production at the Hartwood is superb."

"That's what I hear. As for myself, I can never tell whether the damn thing's any good or not. Though I did find some of the cast interesting, if you get my drift."

"Ah yes, precisely why I got in the Hollywood business my- self." The thought was so foreign to him, Russell had no idea why he'd made the statement.

"I only gaze, mind you," the Governor continued. "That highly successful wife of mine would throw me out on my head if I did more. Even at my age, I know when I have a good thing going."

"Absolutely. She's utterly charming. I'd pick her over an old movie star any day."

"The same goes for Amy . . . er, Annie; there's my idea of a real lady."

"I'll tell Aida you said so. Thank you very much, Governor."

Dick Shannon leaned back with contentment. He'd fortu- itously filled his bloody mary glass before the call, and, given the sheriff's words, knew precisely why the Brit was calling. "Only blemish on last night was the unfortunate death of one of our actors. Hit and run. I was damned sorry to hear about it." Shan- non sat up, pleased with the way he'd given his caller an easy opening.

"Dreadful. But now that you've brought it up, it's one of the reasons I'm calling."

"Now, there's a coincidence," the Governor said innocently. "I was soon going to call you on the same matter. Courtesy call, you might say."

"That sounds very kind, but *why* were you going to call me, Governor Dick?"

"Come, come, Lord Mike. We both know that answer." He paused. "I'd hate being underestimated. Especially by someone as important as yourself. Makes me feel like a fool, and God knows, an old fool doesn't want to be reminded of that too often. Might even make him less accommodating."

"Right. Well, Governor Dick, that's certainly one thing I

never intended to do. In truth, the very reason I'm calling is that I'm looking for your advice."

"Well now, that's very nice to hear. A man of my age and former position notices that people don't come around very often to partake of his wisdom. To tell the truth, most think I'm over the hill, to be tolerated, like a jolly but foolish old man. I appreciate it that a man in your high position thinks enough of me to ask my advice. Especially on such an important and touchy matter."

"I think, Governor, perhaps you know more about this matter than I. Perhaps I should just shut my mouth and listen."

Shannon's voice became richer and more intimate. "You know, I've always found the mark of a brilliant man was how well he listened. Most people are just too full of their own words to even *hear* the other fellow, let alone listen. But, of course, a man doesn't get to your position because there happened to be a vacant chair." Shannon smacked his lips and took a deep swallow of his drink. "Your man got himself into a good deal of trouble last night. It appears as if he was too anxious to get wherever he was going and ran into an unexpected obstacle. Problem is, in leaving, he didn't stop to consider the consequences of his actions." He took a small sip. "Bad trait in someone running a big business, wouldn't you agree with me on that one, Lord Mike?"

"It's irrefutable," Russell said mildly.

"Yes it is. At any rate, you don't need me to tell you how to manage your business. I'm sure that's not the purpose of your call." He sipped. "What precisely *is* the purpose of your call, Mr. Mike?"

"I'd heard about the possible charges against Steven Wald and I was going to impose on your good graces to find out if they had any validity."

Dick Shannon could feel the flush in his face; it was all he could do to keep his voice from disclosing his rapid breathing. To what, he wondered, did he owe this incredible stroke of good luck? It was as though the powers that be had sent in a sacrificial lamb to take the place of his abomination of a son-in-law. He took a long, solemn pause. "Then I'm afraid I have bad news for you. Folks around here move pretty fast when they have to. Even our forensic prowess might be a bit more sophisticated than folks give us credit for. In other words, Mr. Mike, the reports are in, and the D.A. is going to bring charges."

There was a sighful pause on the other end. "I see. Wald *was* involved with the accident?"

"I'm afraid so." He drained his glass before he continued. "Let's only hope it was an accident."

"Which is meant to suggest?"

"Well, as the sheriff pointed out to me, the automobile can sometimes be used as a weapon."

"And why would he even raise that theory?"

"I can't answer that. There are some things one doesn't discuss on the telephone. But this I *can* promise you, now that I'm informed of your interest, I will keep you aware of events before the public at large. Does that satisfy you, Mr. Mike?"

"If I may be perfectly honest with you, Governor Dick, the only thing that would truly satisfy me is to keep my company out of a scandal. Let me ask you this; how common are these sorts of accidents on a Saturday night? When the good people of Partridgefield imbibe perhaps more than they realize and, despite the best efforts of the state, roads are dark and in less than the best condition? How many small animals are accidentally run over because they inadvertently jumped out of nowhere? How many *big* ones, like deer, for instance? Isn't it possible that someone could hit something on a dark road, or feel something bounce off a fender, and not really think too much about it?"

"I suppose it's possible, if one's mind is distracted by larger matters. And the price of a fender isn't particularly meaningful. Or one doesn't really care."

"I must say, I'm not at all surprised, Governor Dick, how much we see things the same way. And what was that actor doing out there, alone, on a dark road in the middle of the night when he should have been at the theater and the ensuing festivities? We'll never know that part, will we? Actors are a funny lot —it seems to me it's even within the realm of possibility that the victim *created* the accident."

"Now, that's one I hadn't thought about. But it is possible, certainly."

"In which case, he would no longer be a victim, would he? In fact, it's the other party who inadvertently would be the hunted, no?"

"What a quaint way you have of looking at things. But even if that's true, the publicity in going to court to prove your scenario could prove, how should I put it, disruptive. Especially, even taking into consideration all your arguments, since the fact remains that Wald left the scene. Surely he knew he didn't bump into a hummingbird, Mr. Mike."

Against his own wishes, Michael Russell reached into his shirt pocket and pulled out a cigar that he proceeded to unwrap. "It strikes me, Governor Dick, that the two of us have fallen into some sort of negotiation. Would I be correct in assuming that?"

The politician had cradled the receiver behind his ear and walked to the bar where he began fixing himself another bloody mary. "Really? I suppose I've been out of the world of politics for so long, I'm no longer aware of these things."

"Let me put it this way, Governor. As you may be aware, among my holdings there are some interesting little enterprises such as newspapers and TV stations, all of which can be terribly useful under certain circumstances. I wish you to know that I put them at your disposal, if you think they can be of any personal benefit to you."

"Well, I must say that's very kind of you. Especially as we really don't know each other all that well. Or is it that maybe we do. Anyway, while I find your offer incredibly generous, I can't think . . . oh, of course. Not that he really needs any help, but that bright-eyed and bushy-tailed son-in-law of mine, just the other day, he was talking about how his ideals and principles could one day propel him to make a run for the Senate. Seems that good-looking son of a gun not only wants to walk in his father-in-law's footsteps, but maybe surpass him. Now there's an instance where, as capable and popular as he is, I don't suppose it would hurt to have a nationally respected newspaper supporting him. Or these TV opinion shows putting in a good word every now and then. In fact, I suppose it's never too soon to start laying the groundwork for those sorts of political maneuvers, is it?"

The idea of Neil's behind being pushed into higher and higher public office appealed to him; these days the brighter the spotlight, the more careful he'd have to be about where and for who he dropped his drawers.

"Quite right," Russell said.

"You know, I've been thinking about your remarks about deer and all those innocent little animals out there. Truth is, they *do* cause a mess of trouble for us human types. I can see where a man might be minding his own business, trying to figure out how to improve those bottom-line figures, that sort of thing, when from nowhere, clear out of the blue, in the black of night, this thing leaps out at him, bounces against his automobile, and disappears. Why, I suppose if you had the radio up loud enough, you'd hardly notice. Especially if you were jet-lagged or something. You know, I just might share that insight with the sheriff's office. Can't promise that it'll do any good. He's a very independent man and rightly so. But he's also a fair man. And if I can put a bee in his bonnet . . . well, who knows? How does that sound to you, Mr. Mike?"

"It sounds like a good place to start. Have a wonderful day, Governor Dick."

"Same to you, my friend."

The Governor stirred his drink with the fervor of a whirling dervish. It seemed to him, even with four drinks under his belt, that if his poor excuse for a son-in-law found out that someone else was being held responsible for the hit and run, there'd be absolutely no reason for him to owe the Governor any gratitude whatsoever. But if the story had a way of disappearing, with no one held accountable, well, that would appear to be a different kettle of fish. It would sort of show that the Governor still held quite a few favors owed in his back pocket. And with someone like Neil Sheedy, who was responsible for one's own child's happiness, and one's child's children's future, that was no inconsequential thing.

Chapter Thirteen

Coleen Copeland took it upon herself to arrange for the funeral of Tony Newland. As no one who could be considered immediate family came forward, and no one, apparently, in his less immediate family wanted to, she began phoning theatrical organizations to which he belonged to find the most promising venue for his remains. In the end she turned to cremation, deciding to keep his ashes herself.

By coincidence, as the last traces of his mortal existence were disappearing in a wall of flames, the envelope containing the forensic report on his accident arrived at the sheriff's home. He immediately took it to the room his wife quaintly referred to as his study, which, in fact, also served as her exercise room as well as a repository for two tanks of tropical fish that his daughter had lost interest in.

Upon opening the envelope, the first word he focused on was *inconclusive.* Apparently there were fibers from the victim's clothing clinging to the edges of chrome surrounding the headlights, but whether they had resulted from impact was open to question. It went on to discuss the issue of distress to the cotton strands and whether the force of a car going thirty miles or more an hour shouldn't have caused a higher degree of implosion. The sheriff tried imaging an imploded fiber and one that was nonimploded as he slid the document he'd only quickly scanned back into its envelope.

Like most people, the sheriff did not consider himself a good liar, let alone a falsifier of facts. So it was with some comfort that he realized the report would most likely not be put into evidence, let alone stand up in a court of law. That, combined with the virulent insistence on the part of the alleged perpetrator of his innocence, not to mention his threats to sue and expose the incompetence of the sheriff's command, had predisposed the law enforcement officer to look favorably upon the Governor's carefully worded request to tread gently before bringing charges. Not to mention the report of how well his son was doing in Nancy Shannon's operations. He therefore saw no reason that the death of Tony Newland and the circumstances surrounding it shouldn't vaporize in the morning mists so endemic to Partridgefield.

"What the fuck is going on here?" Chip Walker asked himself as he thumbed carefully through the last of the regional papers. Wald had kept him in the dark as to what was happening; if the wheels of justice were turning, it was out of the sightlines of journalists.

On the third day after the accident, he'd thought about leaking the identity of the driver himself, but some deeper impulse suggested that would not be in his best interest. Soon he began to feel that he hadn't been invited to the party he himself had thrown. So it was with some surprise and gratitude that he answered the phone in his motel room to find Coleen Copeland at the other end.

"Busy?" she asked in her acerbic voice.

"Yeah, right. I'm reironing my underwear to make the seams lie flat."

"You're turning me on. Your boss there?"

"You're kidding. I haven't seen him for days." He wondered whether his honesty was smart.

"Don't worry about it as long as you're getting paid. What happened to your story about him causing Tony Newland's death?"

He slapped the mattress in frustration. "All I know is what I read in the papers. Or don't read."

"Want to come over and talk about it?"

"Who else will be there?"

"What makes you think there'd be others?"

"Because you've obviously been talking to Nora Howard. And I don't think I'm at the top of your chums-to-have-over list."

"Talking to Nora? Oh, you wouldn't be the one who makes those peculiar phone calls to her, would you? Yeah, she'll be here. And Ben."

"Sounds like the grand inquisition."

"Nah, no racks, no thumb screws. Just scotch, vodka, and white wine." She took a beat. "Oh, I'm sorry, are you otherwise engaged?"

Her sarcasm struck at his loneliness; he'd played all his wild cards and nobody'd picked them up.

"Does Steven know what you've been saying about him?" Her voice was honeyed insinuation.

"Is that a threat?"

"Your secret's safe with me. I wouldn't holler if a ten-ton safe was falling on Wald's head."

"Can I join the club?" His silence had convinced Chip Wald had connected him to the frame-up.

"Come on over." She gave him directions, her manner even and friendly.

While his instinct was to resist, the surreal state of his isolation had begun to scare him. "All right. When?"

"Now."

"Can I bring a date?" He surprised himself with his bantering tone.

"Sure, just park it in the stable."

He hung up, returned to the bathroom, and dropped the towel he was wearing. The shower was a dismal affair with a low cement edge he'd repeatedly stubbed his toe on, but the water was plentiful and hot. He submerged himself in it, wondering if by joining the people Wald had screwed, he wasn't stepping in front of the wheels he himself had set in motion.

The door buzzer rang four times before it brought Chip out of his shower-induced haze. He rinsed quickly, shouting, "All right, hold on," thinking how filled his dance card was becoming. When he got to the door, he hesitated, plastered his hair back with his hand, then opened it.

"Screwing some local talent?" Wald asked, walking around him.

"I should be so lucky. Playing with myself in the shower."

"Spare me." Wald sat on the edge of the bed.

"What can I do for you?" He felt stupid as he pulled his towel tighter around him.

"Just wondered how you were doing," Wald said nonchalantly.

"Want me to book us out?" He reached for the pad beside the phone.

"No rush. We're having a great time, aren't we?"

Wald watched him, the crooked smile an unpleasant reminder of the man's nature. "Everything straightened out?"

"Like what? Oh, that I was accused of vehicular homicide? That? No big deal."

Chip found his tone eerie. "Just a misunderstanding?"

"Right. Tell that to Tony Newland."

"I mean that you had anything to do with it. I thought you would have contacted me, to make calls for you."

"Oh, I'm a big boy. Very self-reliant when I have to be."

He inspected the room with connoisseurlike concentration. "You know, I wondered where they got that notion in the first place, connecting me with the dead has-been. Or should I say who gave it to them? For that matter, who could have involved my car in the accident? Any thoughts?"

"People in your position have enemies," Chip said cryptically.

"Bullshit!" Wald's voice exploded. "You did it! You, you little fucking cocksucker. I did some checking, just began to scratch the surface. And what oozed out wasn't very pretty, you fucking creep. I know what you are, the scummy things you've done. I also know they put you away for doing them. Now listen to this: I'm buying you off with a ticket back to L.A. But I'm warning you, you ever come near me or try playing your sick little games on me again, I'll see to it you get your psychotic little head twisted around. You get it, you demented little bastard?"

Chip listened to his heavy breathing. Then he saw it coming. The large hand appeared swollen as it lowered its trajectory toward his face. First he felt the sting in his cheek, then the full impact of the blow to his skull. As the motel room blanked out, he heard the door slam shut, the amplified sound reverberating in his head.

When he opened his eyes again, it was to see his face in the mirror above the bureau. Oddly, one cheek appeared thicker than the other, but there was no discoloration where Wald had punched him. As other sensations subsided, he was left with only a slight buzzing in the ear that had shared the blow.

They sat around the table waiting for Walker to arrive as if they were at a séance.

"What do you suppose happened to the punk? Think he changed his mind?" Coleen asked.

"I doubt it. We're his best audience," Ben said.

When the gravel in the driveway hissed a car's arrival, the three turned to the door like anxious parents.

Coleen smiled and walked to the window. "Oh brother, he's got us on tenterhooks." She peered through the lacy curtains. "Yup, it's deep throat." She ran fingers through her thick hair, disturbing its neatness. "Do I look okay?" she asked mischievously before pulling open the door. What surprised her was how nervous the boy appeared. "You okay?" she asked.

He nodded, making no effort to enter.

"Are you coming in?"

He tried for a smile that failed him and stood his ground, each eying the other. "Hello," he said shyly. They nodded slightly. "Sorry I'm late. Walked into a door. Knocked the wind out of me."

"Here," Coleen said, her hand in the small of his back guiding him. "Sit down." She closed the door behind them. "Drink?"

He looked at her gratefully. "A beer if you've got one."

"Honey, when it comes to alcohol I've got it."

He joined Ben and Nora at the table. "Pretty somber group." Again he tried to smile, but let it fade. "I'm sorry; the actor must have been a good friend of yours."

Coleen pounded the bottle in front of him. "Here you go."

He raised it in a toast. "To all of you. I enjoyed your play very much, Mr. Bradford."

"Thanks," Ben said, brushing aside the compliment. "Mind if we ask a couple of questions?"

The smile returned. "Like they say, no such thing as a free beer."

"Did Wald actually do it?" Ben asked. "Or did you make the whole thing up?"

Walker looked incredulous. "Why on earth would I do that?"

Ben grimaced. "How the hell should I know?"

"Look. You've got to believe I wouldn't say anything like that unless it was true."

"Why do I have to believe?" Ben asked with some menace.

Chip placed the bottle down carefully. "It was stupid of me to come." He started to rise. "Look, I can't help it if he can buy his way out of these things. I should have known better than to think a mere trifle like the truth could get you anywhere when you're playing against a guy like that." He looked down at them. "I don't see any of you getting out the militia to find out what happened to your dead buddy. I tried. You know what it got me? Out on my ass; he fired me." He took a beat. "I've got a plane ticket back and that's it. That's what happens when you try telling the truth."

Coleen reached up to take his arm. "It also happens when you lie. Sit down. No point wasting a nice cold beer."

Her tone was so ingratiating, he obeyed. "I don't care what you believe." He appeared weary as he took a slug from the bottle. When he looked up, Nora was staring at him. It was as though she were trying to memorize every pore in his face.

"Did you kill my husband, Mr. Walker?"

They sat in silence, as though testing the air as to whether the question had actually been spoken.

"Did you?" Her voice was mellifluous and controlled.

"Your husband?" He looked almost pained. "I'm sure you have a perfectly good reason, to your way of thinking, for asking me that." For the first time, he appeared perfectly composed. "I'm sure grief has a way of making what appears irrational to most people seem perfectly logical to you. So I'm not going to let myself get offended. I'll just answer as though you had a right to ask the question. . . ."

"Of course I have a right!" she shouted at him. "He was my husband!" She waited until control returned. "Do you know what it's like, Mr. Walker, to have a piece taken out of you?

And there's nothing, nothing, you can put in its place? Of *course* I have a right to ask."

He had lowered his eyes, patiently waiting for her to finish. "All right. There's no sense arguing with you. I did not kill your husband." He blinked with frustration. "It seems to me I've tried to tell you people how Lewis Rosenthal died. Apparently I've been misunderstood. I really don't think there's any more for me to say."

She stared at him as though struggling for a sign of comprehension. "You called me in L.A. to taunt me about Lewis's death. You called me here twice, first to suggest Ben had something to do with it, then about Tony Newland." Her features contorted with confusion. "Why are you . . ."

This time he stood quickly. "I can't deal with this. I'm trying, but I can't." He looked to Ben, then Coleen. "I think you'd better get your friend help." He turned for the door, then stopped. "All right, I did call you."

"No shit," Coleen said despondently.

"I *did* suggest Mr. Bradford might have had something to do with it. But that was to get you to *think*. To understand that there was someone else involved. Somebody who was at the motel with your husband."

"And, of course, that wouldn't be you." Again, Coleen's voice was laced with sarcasm.

His expression appeared sympathetic. "I'm very sorry," he said softly. "I know what it sounds like, accusing the guy who just fired me of murder. But what I told Ms. Copeland, that was the truth."

"How do you know so much, bigshot?" Coleen's question came out a challenge.

"Mr. Rosenthal called me for help. I worked for a suicide prevention hotline. I tried to stop him. I thought I had. . . . Mr. Rosenthal didn't kill himself. I know."

"That's it? You know. And we're supposed to believe you?" Coleen asked.

He nodded, lowering his head.

"But why should we believe you?" Nora's voice was harsh, on the verge of cracking.

As he was about to speak again, Ben silenced him with a

hand on his shoulder. "Why don't you go, Mr. Walker?" Ben asked politely.

"I'm sorry I've caused all this ugliness," he said to them, walking away from the table. "Thanks for the beer," he added with a hint of sarcasm. "I was going to say, See you around, but I doubt it."

After he left, the three sat in embarrassed silence.

"You think there's a particle of truth in what he said?" Drawing an owlish look on her face, Coleen swiveled her head back and forth between them.

Ben looked exasperated and turned to Nora. "Do you?" He covered her hand with his own.

She looked at him, then nodded firmly. "Yes. I think he meant what he said to Coleen. I think, unfortunately, he's telling the truth."

She spoke with such certainty, Ben and Coleen sat frozen, waiting for her to continue.

"I have the proof."

"Nora . . ." Ben began until Coleen silenced him by touching his hand.

"There's a tape Lewis made just before he died. There *was* someone else there. I just haven't been able to face it. . . ."

Ben looked at her earnestly. "May we hear the tape? May we?" Ben repeated.

"I didn't want to involve anyone. . . ." she said softly.

"Honey," Coleen said throatily, "involve us, please."

"I think so, Nora," he said to her softly, then banged his fist on the table. "Damn that son of a bitch. Walking away from the whole thing."

"Hold it," Coleen said, as though taking charge of a meeting. "Even if there was someone with Lewis, we have only that prick's word it was Wald. How can we . . . ?"

"Because I think Walker was there. And I don't think Lewis would have been afraid of him, would have let him harm him. But I think he saw someone who did," Nora said calmly.

Ben's face rumpled into frustration. "What did Tony say? That there's enough injustice out there and we should love and protect each other?"

His eyes stared into infinity, the way they did when he was working out a scene, Nora thought.

"I think the theater owes Tony a little redemption," he said, smiling at them with some secret insight.

Chapter Fourteen

The Main Street of Partridgefield in the full Saturday sun appeared as neat and generic as those once found on studio back lots. And Congressman Sheedy, walking down it with his slightly overweight five-year-old daughter, felt not unlike the invincible leading men who used to inhabit them.

"You look very pretty, sweetheart," he said.

"Thanks, Dad. You look pretty, too," she said and squeaked into her small hand.

"Now, now, Victoria. Daddys are handsome, not pretty. Your mother's pretty."

"No she's not."

He was about to stop in front of the pharmacy to question her but decided against it, toting her along.

"Pretty ladies wear makeup and Mommy doesn't," she continued anyway. "And she always looks worried."

"Really?"

She shook her brown curls assertively.

"What does she worry about?" he asked for his own edification.

"If we're going to like dinner. And if I'm wearing the right clothes."

"Well, that's what mommies worry about, sweetheart."

"Then I don't want to be a mommy." The hand returned to the giggle. "I want to be a daddy like you."

"That's very nice of you to say, Vicky, that you admire your dad. But your mother is pretty wonderful and I'd think you'd like to be like her, too."

The curls floated about her head as she swirled it.

"Well, you will, dear." He stopped them in front of Reed's Hardware. "Daddy needs a paintbrush. Let's stop in here for a minute. Okay, precious?"

"Okay," she said, pulling him into the store.

As the handsome congressman and his chubby daughter entered, Tim D'Amato looked down from the ladder he was perched on.

"Hi there," Sheedy called out, assuming the tone he used on constituents. "How about this weather?"

Tim looked beyond him, through the front window, as if he were unsure of the season. "I've been working in the basement most of the morning," he said, as if absolving himself of his ignorance of the weather.

"Good for you," Neil said, pulling his daughter around the ladder toward the back of the store.

"Anything I can help you with?" Tim called down.

"No thanks. I think I can find it myself." Neil pointed to a rack of brushes.

"Let me help," Tim said, climbing down the ladder with a carton of extension cords.

"No big deal," Sheedy said irritably. "Just need a two-inch brush for latex."

Tim walked in front of the father and daughter, reaching out to snatch a brush before they could reach the display.

"Thanks," Neil said, taking it from him. "This is my daughter, Victoria." The little girl, who had been studying Tim, put her face against her father's hip. "Say hi to Tim, Vicky. Knowing a fellow who works in a hardware store can come in real handy." The young man smiled shyly at the girl. "Real handy." Vicky twisted her head to look at him, keeping it pressed against her father's body. "Why don't you go over there and pick out a nice pair of garden gloves for Mommy while this young man shows me where the primer is."

"What's primer," she asked reluctantly.

"It's like paint." He gently prodded her away.

"I don't know what kind to get her," she said combatively.

"Then ask that nice man over there, Mr. Reed," he said, winking at the owner, who was watching them from behind the counter. As Victoria reversed her attitude and flew down the aisle, Neil turned the young man around by the shoulders. "Primer in there, correct?"

Tim nodded and led them into the paint room. "What happened?" he asked, revealing a sudden look of desperation.

Neil grinned and shrugged his shoulders. "Nothing much. Of course, that was the general idea."

"There was almost nothing in the paper."

"What would you have preferred? A front-page story, with photos?"

"I mean, how come?"

Neil's look seemed to pass through him. "In a word, power."

"You were able . . . ?"

Neil smiled up at the paint cans. "Which one of these fucking things is primer?"

Tim reached for one, barely taking his eyes off the congressman. "That's it? It's over? We have nothing to worry about?"

Neil's expression grew aloof and distant. "We? I don't think it would be wise to refer to us as we."

At that moment, Tim knew, as much from the steely edge in Sheedy's voice as his words, that whatever the peculiar nature of their relationship had been, it was to be no more. "Sorry." His voice sounded thin.

"Part of the deal was I don't see you," Sheedy said, his voice suddenly soft and sympathetic.

"Someone knows about us? Me?"

Neil nodded faintly.

"Will they . . . ?" The boy seemed unable to pose the question.

"Not if I don't see you." He looked directly into Tim's eyes. "Will you miss me?"

Before Tim could reply, Victoria returned, holding a pair of striped denim gloves. "For Mommy." She stood staring at the young sales clerk with annoyance until her father led her to the cash register.

Chapter Fifteen

The theater stood cool and empty, the open doors allowing a breeze to pass through the empty auditorium. Billy Carroll paced up and down the stage. He appeared to be arguing with himself, thrashing his hand about in small wavelike motions. His agitation increased, seemingly unaware of the arrival of Audrey Dalton, who sauntered down the aisle toward him.

"I don't especially like getting up at this hour, particularly after a play's opened. Isn't there supposedly a tradition in the theater of *freezing* a production?"

Billy stopped and turned to her, placing his hands on his hips. "I take it that you feel you've reached perfection."

"My darling, I *am* perfection. Just my *being* is perfection. Besides, nobody watches me act; they just look at my tits and try to see if I have any wrinkles."

"On your tits?"

"My face, asshole. Who else is coming?"

"Our star."

"Oh. And?"

"Not Tony." It was Ben's voice from the back of the theater. "I wanted to run down a couple of scenes with his replacement, if I may."

"Is that all? I thought you had wonderful news, like we're moving to Broadway. Better still, going straight to the little screen."

"So where is he?" Billy asked from the stage.

"Perhaps he stopped to pick up our darling star. Where *is* our swan-necked leading lady?"

Ben shrugged and settled in an eighth-row seat, riffling his script and making notes as Dalton pursed her lips, looking as though she were about to stomp her foot. "Audrey," he said, looking up shyly. "I really think you're awfully good in the part."

"Of course I'm good. You don't think I've been around all these years for nothing, do you? Even if playing a mother is a bit of a stretch." Her scowl turned to a smile and she blew him a kiss.

"Really." Ben shuffled in his seat. "While we're alone, except for Billy who's busy motivating"—he looked at the actor and grinned—"would you mind answering a question?"

"Would I sleep with you? Sure. Have I slept with him?" She indicated the young actor. "Yes. His fault, not mine. Have I covered it?"

"Almost, but not quite."

She raised her eyebrows and parted her gleaming red lips in a pout.

"I wanted to know about Wald."

"Are you planning on writing my biography or just kinky about my sex life?"

"About the night Tony died."

The bravura of her expression disappeared.

"Did he say anything about it?"

"What? That he ran over someone but was so anxious to jump in my bed that he left him dying alongside the road? Of course not. Do you think . . ." Her voice had turned cross.

"No, I don't. I meant later. In retrospect, thinking back . . ."

"I know what retrospect means." She clenched and un-clenched her teeth several times. "You certainly couldn't tell from his performance. He was particularly cold that night, not that that means anything. He's a very brooding person. I only slept with him on the infinitesimal chance that he might come up with something for me." She looked up at the young actor. "You may laugh, if you like; I'm old-fashioned, I still believe in the casting couch."

"Do you think he might have hit Tony?"

"I think it's *possible,* given his manner when I arrived. He seemed meaner than usual, drinking my scotch and taking the opportunity to rip apart everyone in the cast, except moi, of course. He didn't spare you either, darling," she said to Billy sweetly.

"What did he say?"

"That you come across like a faggot. That he still hadn't gotten used to these straight sensitive types." Again she smiled sweetly. "Neither have I, quite frankly."

"Did you happen to notice his car in your driveway?"

"Of course. I thought it was a bloody shame to have dented that lovely little car."

"Did you ask him about it?"

"I was going to, but he didn't seem in the mood for criticism. He didn't seem in the mood for anything but fucking."

Billy Carroll had begun following their conversation. He walked downstage and lowered himself to the floor. "Why the fuck wasn't there anything in the paper?"

Ben gently closed his script. "I can't talk about it."

"Why not?" The young actor reddened. "It's okay for you to interrogate my friend the TV temptress, but you won't answer a simple question?"

"I will, later. But I can't now." Ben squirmed uneasily. "Mind if I ask you one?"

The actor grinned at him. "You working on a detective thing or what?"

"Has Wald talked to you since he's been here?"

The actor blushed as though he'd been found out. "Yeah."

"When?"

"At the fancy party. It wasn't a very pleasant experience."

"How so?"

"People think I'm this cool guy, that I'm probably stoned and don't know what I'm saying. Well, that's not the way it is."

"What'd he say?"

"He started chatting with me, talking like we were both in on some kind of dirty joke. At first I thought he was putting moves on me."

"Why?"

"It was, like, wink-wink time. He kept bringing the conversation around to like, you know, gay stuff. Gay people. Clubs. Dish.

Dalton reached demurely for a cigarette. "Really."

"Really. Like from nowhere. Like we were members of a club. But then I realized he wasn't after me, that wasn't it at all."

She blew out a long stream of smoke. "That's a relief."

"He was after information."

"What sort?"

"About someone." The actor seemed embarrassed.

"How did you figure that out?"

"He asked if I knew that large British guy that was there."

"Michael Russell?"

"The one who owns the studio."

"And?"

"He wanted to know if I knew his son. That's what it was all about."

"What did he say about him?"

"Apparently the kid's . . ." He hesitated at the word. "He lives in London and apparently he's sort of got the reputation of being . . ."

"A transvestite," Dalton finished. "Big deal. I used to see him around all the time. He's great fun. Does it as a lark. Everyone knows; what's the big secret?"

"Wald must have thought he discovered it."

"Did he say why he was interested?"

Billy shook his head. "When I said I had no idea what he was talking about, he lost interest. Blew me off. Like it had crossed his mind then crossed out again and he couldn't care less. Then he went over to Shannon, small-talking away, with this little-boy grin coming out of that big mean face of his."

"Sounds like he was skeleton hunting to me," Dalton said. "Checking out the closets, so to speak."

Ben looked at her appreciatively. "What did he say when the police came?"

Billy looked at them as though he'd suddenly found the light switch. "What police? What are you talking about? He was a suspect?"

Ben and Audrey looked at each other, then to the actor.

"There was an investigation, a rudimentary one," she said as though speaking to a child. "Apparently there was nothing substantive enough to make a case."

"Or there was a cover-up; take your pick," Billy said.

"I'd rather not," Ben answered quietly.

Michael Russell hunched down in the light booth at the top of the theater. His large frame had by necessity been contorted amid the unwieldy equipment. He'd listened to the conversation silently, almost with a feeling of déjà vu. Whatever feelings he'd harbored about Wald's innocence had been sadly laid to rest.

The author had suggested he come to the theater where he could listen unseen as Bradford drew out those who Wald had contact with. He agreed, hoping that Shannon's report would prove erroneous and that his own decision to obfuscate Wald's guilt would be justified; clearly neither was meant to be.

He watched as the actors paced impatiently about the stage, returning to the play after Bradford had dropped his line of questioning. Now he wondered if Bradford suspected him in the cover-up, and what he would do about it. The thought fed his growing claustrophobia and he turned toward the small door, waiting for the author's return. Minutes later, it opened.

"Sorry. Are you okay?" The author appeared genuinely concerned at the sight of him.

"Yes, certainly. I'm just not built for small places. You were awfully good with them."

"Actors open up easily. Given the drama of Newland's death, it wasn't difficult." Bradford appeared to study the floor of the small booth. "I'm sorry. I had no idea Billy was going to come out with that stuff about your son."

The large man smiled a moon grin. "Don't be. I have no bother where Bobby's concerned. The boy is a bit odd but I love him, very much, defend him with my life."

Ben smiled, then nodded toward the stage. "I hope that sorted it out for you, though probably not the way you'd prefer."

Russell raised his eyebrows in two clownish arches. "Right again. But I'd rather it be this way. Now I know what I'm dealing with."

Ben stared at him hesitantly.

"What are you thinking?" Russell asked.

Ben shook his head.

"Is there more?"

Ben's gaze steadied but still he did not reply.

"Well, is there?"

"I really think you ought to speak to Nora."

"Fine," Russell said, with businesslike finality. "Why don't the two of you lunch with us in Crofton tomorrow." He began angling his large frame through the door. "Bye, then."

He looked, Ben thought, like a manatee swimming through a shipwreck.

"Is this what I'm reduced to? Waiting for a stand-by to show up so I can run lines for him?"

Ben walked down to the foot of the stage. "It's all right, he's gone."

She pursed her scarlet lips and cocked an eyebrow. "Did we bury Caesar?"

"Very adroitly."

"What did he think about the son part?" Billy asked.

"Nonplussed. Except if someone mocks him."

"You know," Audrey Dalton said confidentially, "I think it's perfectly marvelous the way we actors stick together. I'd have felt uncomfortable fibbing that bit about the fender if Steven wasn't such a major bastard. The fact that he's cruel and heartless as well makes it just that much more fun. By the way, Billy, how did you know about his son?"

"Last year he asked me to dance at a party in Mayfair."

"Hope he didn't step on anything," she said, as though in a boulevard comedy.

The drive down to Crofton had produced almost no comment from Nora. She'd acknowledged the handsomeness of houses and splendor of the vistas they passed, but her enthusiasm for their task with Russell appeared muted.

"If you don't care to go ahead with this," Ben said solicitously, "we can just talk about the play, thank them for a lovely lunch, turn around, and go home."

She smiled at him fondly. "I couldn't do that. This may be the only chance."

"All right, then. He's a very nice man. He appears to be very understanding, even honorable."

"You don't think he helped Wald slip out of charges regarding the accident?"

"I think the evidence did that. There wasn't enough."

"But the car? The dent?"

"There are other ways for cars to get dented; Wald obviously convinced them of one."

"What if he convinces Russell he's innocent?"

"Then we'll have done all we can."

They approached Crofton from what was apparently the wrong side of town: a bending road lined with pleasant houses, two canopied service stations, and a small strip mall. Midway down Main Street, they came to a stop sign that appeared to signal the end of the more humble aspects of the village. As Ben continued across the intersection, the road became lined with immense lawns and stone fences obscuring the view of enormous homes spreading out in a network of wings. Ben slowed down, nodding to Nora to inspect them. Then the road did an S curve; even without directions they would have recognized the freshly minted splendor of Russell's estate.

Bradford directed the car up the curved driveway. Like the other estates they passed, the grounds seemed devoid of life, except for the whinnying of horses somewhere in the compound. But before Ben shut off the ignition, Aida Maxwell had materialized at the front door.

"Ben, Nora, over here," she called as if greeting family. "Oh, I'm so glad you could come." Her warmth was so effusive, Ben had the urge to hug her. "Nora, what a pretty dress!" Her accent wasn't as strong as her husband's, but gave her words an air of humor. "If Michael insists on the tour, just tell him no. If you're too accommodating he'll have you mucking out the stables." She kept looking back at them as she led the way, as though fearful of losing them. "I hope you don't think me foolish if I gush over you. I absolutely adored the play. And you Nora, are just wonderful in it. Truly. I've been back to see it twice." She'd timed her speech to coincide with their arrival in the living room, a vast space filled with islands of furniture centered around a half dozen sofas.

"I love your home, Mrs. Russell," Nora said quietly.

"Please!" She'd turned the word into syllables. "My name is Aida."

"Aida, do I congratulate you or the decorator?" Ben asked.

"I tell Michael everything's *his* idea; let's just leave it at that."

From behind a thrashing of newspaper, Russell rose from one of the sofas. His size appeared to justify the generous proportions of the room. "Leave it at what? Has Aida already started telling you secrets?"

He approached Nora and bent to kiss her with surprising delicacy. "Lovely," he said graciously, then turned and shook Ben's hand. "It's such a lazy summer afternoon; shall we have a drink?" His sideways glance appeared to conjure up a white-coated houseman, who took their orders and disappeared.

"So. This has become my home," Russell said, his gestures incorporating the acres of meadow visible through the windows. "The horses, of course, are my wife's. Never go near them, much to their delight. They've been known to groan just hearing my footsteps near the paddock. Aida's our rider; perfectly at home on the beasts."

"Horses don't buy newspapers, that's why he has so little to do with them," his wife said cheerfully, as if going through a piece of well-rehearsed patter. "Do either of you ride?"

Both guests shook their heads.

"Tsk, tsk, tsk. You don't know what you're missing. Michael had the stables built for me as a thirtieth-anniversary present. He never considered I had every intention of filling them. Now when he visits his, as they say, far-flung empire, I visit my horses. We have the most delightful chats."

"You should see her when they're foaling; up all night with sympathy pains," Russell said admiringly, as their manservant returned with a silver tray of drinks. "There," he added, "I've done my job as host. The rest's up to Aida."

"Mr. Russell," Ben said after the glasses were passed out, "we appreciate your hospitality. But if it's all right, we'd like to talk about the matter I mentioned."

Russell's eyes went into understanding squints. "What can I do to expedite things?"

"Have you a tape machine?" Nora asked, rummaging in her handbag.

"I'm sure Aida and the decorators successfully buried one somewhere. Any notion where it might be?" he asked his wife.

"I think so." She looked to Nora who handed her a cassette, then moved to a japanned secretary bookcase and opened the doors. She placed the tape in the machine and looked over her shoulder.

"My husband taped this just before he died."

"Oh," Aida said softly, turning to her husband.

Nora looked at the woman. "If you'd rather not, I understand."

"She's a strong soldier. And there's absolutely nothing about my business my wife doesn't know. Or have a hand in. It's quite a good disguise, really, charming county lady. But I can assure you, my empire would consist of little more than a row of East End tenements and a newspaper printed in Hebrew if it weren't for her. She's not only the brains, but the balls in Russell Communications, if you don't mind my language."

Aida looked at him with displeasure.

"Well, it's true, you see. She makes her decisions based on facts. Then sticks to them come hell or high water. No emotion, just logic. And a perfect sense of right and wrong. Once she makes up her mind, hordes of the most invasive, cleverest tormentors couldn't budge her." He eyed them skeptically. "Now that you know my deepest, darkest secret, I trust it won't go any farther than this room." He smiled gently.

Nora smiled back and began to speak. "Shortly before my husband's death, we were involved in a picture deal with Al Kimmelmann. When Mr. Wald took over, it evaporated. Which is perfectly fair; that's the way the game is played. But it wasn't enough for Mr. Wald just to kill the project. He felt he had to maim my husband as well. He knew Lewis was very well liked and respected in the business. He knew there'd be a backlash among talent, writers and directors and actors who might not want to work for the studio if he stole, I can't think of a better word, our project.

"So he took advantage of the one thing he knew would work —Lewis's vulnerability. Our last film had been a disaster; that's widely known. It's also known that it takes more than one to declare you moribund. Except Lewis didn't accept that. He felt it was the end of the world. That he'd brought shame upon us both. He'd overreacted, and Wald sensed it. So he threw poison in Lewis's mental wounds. He knew exactly which buttons to press. I can't tell you the state of depression my husband fell into. He functioned; politely, soberly, an absolute gentleman. It was even difficult to see there was anything wrong. Except for the times he wouldn't speak to anyone, including me. Especially me, because of the guilt he felt.

"So Wald developed the perfect scenario for suicide. But there was one catch. In the end, Lewis wouldn't cooperate. Somewhere within him he'd found the strength to resist death. That as much as he'd been turned against himself, there was still a piece of him that he believed in.

"Can you imagine how tempting it must have been to accept defeat? To relieve himself of guilt? But there was this other part that was strong, that wanted to prove he could still have a success."

Suddenly she looked up at them and began to cry. "I'm sorry. I don't mean to cheapen the memory of my husband by putting him on display."

Aida Russell went to her. "Don't feel embarrassed talking to us. I honestly believe I understand what you're saying."

Russell drained his glass, seemingly hesitant to speak. He sat looking at her with distress. "But the point is, my dear, can you prove any of this?"

Nora looked up at him levelly. "I think so."

It was Ben who stood to turn on the tape machine. The four of them listened in silence as Lewis Rosenthal's voice filled the room with surprising force: *My darling Nora. . . . what I'm going to tell you is both a confession and denial . . . So you will understand the whole truth, I must begin with a meeting between Mr. Wald and myself . . .* As the tape continued, Ben watched the expressions on the Russells' faces; both appeared uncomfortable, embarrassed by their voyeurism. Michael leaned forward, as though planning to rise, but began seesawing in his chair instead. He tilted his head attentively, with the alertness of a dog who expects a biscuit in return for compliance. Aida Russell, who sat with great composure, looked resigned, as though a longstanding prophecy had been fulfilled. . . . *for reasons I can't go into at this time, I believe I'm in danger. That the decision has been taken out of my hands. . . .* Ben looked at the Russells as the tape was taken over with the sounds of shuffling and loud thumps. Their faces turned to surprise when Lewis's voice returned, calm and controlled. *I am now free of paranoia. You've come to make sure. My days of fear and self-hatred are over. And in return, all I must do is die.* He punctuated the thought with a low chuckle. . . . *So this is to be my little claim to fame . . .* The unintelligible sounds that followed abruptly ended in silence. Ben went to the machine to retrieve the tape.

"How did you get that?" Aida Russell asked with astonishment.

"The man at the motel who found Lewis saw it under the bed. Lewis must have slipped it there just before . . ."

"And how is it you have it rather than the police?"

Nora looked at Michael Russell. "I agreed to buy it."

"And you haven't turned it over . . . ?" He let the thought drop as he studied her, his eyes barely peeping through the folds of his lids. "And how do you know for sure he was speaking of Wald?" he asked kindly.

"He began by speaking of Wald . . . that's all that was on his mind. . . ."

Russell shrugged and his body slumped like a pumpkin left outdoors to spoil. "You're right, of course, my dear."

"Michael, I expect you'll deal with this directly." Aida said matter-of-factly.

Russell's expression had turned bemused as he looked at his guests. "Once again, my wife has gotten to the point. I imagine you'll be turning that tape over to the police?"

Ben nodded. "Nora could only bring herself to listen to it recently."

"Of course," he agreed solemnly. "Well, I don't expect anyone really has much appetite. . . ."

"This must have been very difficult for Ben and Nora, after all, they really have no way of knowing whether or not they can trust you." Aida Russell turned calmly to Nora. "You can, my dear. Believe it or not, he's totally trustworthy. Especially when I tell him he must be."

During the drive back to Partridgefield, Ben began mentally cataloguing recent events. The play, the eagerness to avenge, the desire to impress; they were part of the same thing—his feelings for Nora.

Nothing had changed from the time he'd had similar feelings for an English teacher in college. After he'd met her by chance on a bus after school, he'd taken to making little lists of things to talk about should they meet again. The encounters gave him a heart-pounding feeling of adventure as well as inadequacy. The feelings hadn't changed; instead of topics of discussion he'd made a skein of conspiracies to weave them together. He would draw her closer by putting Lewis to rest. Win her admiration by vanquishing Wald.

She sat silently next to him, her hair covered by a scarf, jet-black sunglasses over her eyes. She had the same imperious grace of women in Italian films he'd admired as a young man, moving to lush, soundless orchestrations.

"Thank you. I'm very grateful."

He'd almost missed her words. How grateful, he wondered.

Chapter Sixteen

Tim D'Amato felt the same missing heartbeat of surprise looking at the front-page newspaper photo as if he'd seen himself. The subject looked so much like him that he had to search for differences, parts of the picture breaking up into dots before he could find any. HIT AND RUN DRIVER ARRESTED. *Alling "Chip" Walker was taken into custody hours before his planned departure for California. Recently discovered evidence links suspect to accident. Studio head's testimony cited.*

Tim read the article with the enthrallment of a dream. He felt godlike, fascinated, his own role mysteriously taken over by someone else. How, he wondered, had Sheedy managed it? Found somebody to simply step up and take blame? Instantly a shot of jealousy flashed in his mind. He examined the young man's face again. On second inspection he looked older than himself. Was he a friend of Neil's who had threatened him in some way?

Now he realized he'd scanned the article too quickly to pick up all its meaning. He went back to the text, trying to concentrate, still his nerves so he could understand the facts. Apparently the young man had been driving his employer's car, a Porsche, which had been scientifically linked to the accident. Tim blinked rapidly, part of his mind trying to determine whether he was actually reading or imagining he was. How, he wondered, had Sheedy managed to incriminate a perfect stranger, to physically connect him to the dead man.

Then he thought about another possibility. Whether the man, the actor, hadn't been hit twice. Once by him, and once again, the second time fatally. Which would mean he hadn't actually killed him. His mood brightened. The more he thought about it, the more logical it seemed. It was as though God had given him a second chance, relieved him of responsibility by putting someone else in his place. Perhaps it was no coincidence that the young man in the paper looked so much like him; it was like divine intervention. Now, the question remained, what would he have to do in return?

"I thought he was awfully hammy, didn't you?" Nancy Shannon placed the newspaper on top of her husband's breakfast setting.

"Who, pet?" the Governor asked.

"The actor who was killed."

Shannon looked at the photo. The face was vaguely familiar, but he didn't recall the young man acting in anything he'd seen. "Doesn't look familiar. What did we see him in?"

"Not that one," she snapped, placing her stubby finger on the newspaper. "He's the one that hit him. Newland. Tony Newland, the one that's dead."

"Hammy? Yes, well, you certainly know more about that sort of thing than I." He raised the paper, slowly bringing it closer so he could read the print.

"I certainly do. In fact, show me a politician who isn't a ham and I'll show you one who doesn't get elected."

The Governor tried reading the story, having to start over several times as his wife went on comparing actors to assemblymen and governors and presidents. "They're all the same," he heard her say as the contents of the article swept through his mind. To mask his astonishment, he raised the hot coffee to his lips and began drinking it down rapidly.

"Dick! What are you doing? Your throat will burn out!"

"It's just delicious. Have we changed brands?"

She looked at him curiously, backing off, as though he were manifesting some sort of weakness of the mind. "No, I don't think so. I'll ask Isabel." She continued looking at him strangely.

He put the paper down as nonchalantly as he could. "Just wondered why it took them so long to catch him. I'll have to call the sheriff and personally congratulate him."

She sipped her coffee, finding it bitter, almost greasy. "Why do that? It's his job. And, as you say, he's taken his good sweet time about it."

He looked at her with annoyance. "These things are far more complicated than you can imagine."

She returned his look in kind. "Please. How would you know?"

He lifted the paper and swatted it down. "I'm simply a ham who knows nothing about anything. I see, that's your opinion."

She took his hand. "Be quiet! Isabel will hear."

"Do you really thinks she bothers listening after all these years?"

The question seemed to absorb his wife enough to allow him to reread the article.

"This certainly gets your boyfriend out of the frying pan. How'd you manage to get his tits out of the wringer?"

"S-s-s-h!" Neil Sheedy looked about, trying to account for his wife's whereabouts. "Do you want Catherine to hear this?"

"He's your boyfriend, not mine. If you don't want her to know, don't fool around."

"How can you be saying things like that over the telephone?"

"No worse than doing it."

Sheedy found himself starting to sweat. "What's your take on this article?" he asked his father-in-law.

"Seemed to get right to the point. The question is, who the hell is Alling 'Chip' Walker and why is he taking the rap for your boyfriend's act?"

"Will you stop that! I have no idea, to answer either question."

"I see. I thought somehow you'd gotten so big and powerful, you'd set the whole thing up. But now I realize you're just running true to form. Lucky. You just seem to step in it every time and come out smelling like roses, if you'll pardon my mixed metaphor."

"I thought it was you," Sheedy whispered.

"Me? A hammy old drunk has-been politician? I couldn't set up my own funeral. Just keep your fingers crossed. Nobody's been convicted yet. And pray the boy really doesn't know anything."

The Governor hung up, enjoying the drama of it, hoping he'd pulled the plug on his son-in-law's fleeting moment of relief in reading the article. It was obvious this Walker had taken Wald's car and that Russell had at first thought his own man was driving. The real question was, why his son-of-a-bitch son-in-law had insisted that his little plumber friend had done it? That was the mystery: Why had Sheedy chosen such a bizarre way to reveal himself?

Shannon decided he'd just as soon forget the whole matter. He'd long ago come to the conclusion that the less he knew the better off he was. The thought cheered him enough to toast it.

"I'm terribly confused, Steven."

Russell had chosen to meet his studio chief in the dining room of the Willowfalls Inn.

"I am too, frankly," Wald said, trying to force salt from a shaker into his clam chowder. "Why on earth did you pick this godawful restaurant?"

Russell squinted and smiled, rubbing his hand over hair oiled to his scalp. "I rather like it. It's so American."

"It's tired and phony and you know it."

"Really?" He seemed bemused.

Wald thrust out his chin and he sampled the soup. "Ugh. This is as New England as Pasadena. How do they get away with this crap?"

"The same way you get away with your movies and TV shows. People don't know any better. Perhaps that's wrong; they don't *want* to know any better." Russell looked about the half-filled room. Above wainscoting, the walls were lined with shelves on which sat ceramic teacups, saucers, and pots.

"I'm leaving in the morning," Wald said abruptly.

"I know, that's why I've invited you tonight. What am I to think, Steven? Tell me. Did you or didn't you run over that poor actor?"

Wald looked at him with annoyance. "That sick-assed kid did. Don't you read the paper?"

"Remember, I *own* papers. I read what they want me to read. I'm asking if what the paper said was the truth?"

Wald looked up at him and began wiping his mouth with the napkin as though preparing to leave. "What possible purpose are these questions serving? The kid took my car, ran over the old man, and tried to put the blame on me because he knew I was on to his weird act."

"Did you turn him in?"

Wald stared at him, his mouth forming its familiar mocking half twist. "Sure I did. It was *my* car, *my* dent; I'm notorious for leaving keys in a car. Who else could have done it?" The ridicule spread to his eyes.

"But you don't know that for a fact."

Wald shrugged. "Someone killed the old fart. They needed a perpetrator."

A short pudgy waitress came to their table and began struggling with a bottle of wine. Wald watched in silence for a moment, than took it from her and eased out the cork.

"Thank you," she said cheerfully and poured a small amount into his glass.

Wald's eyes returned to Russell as he motioned her to fill both glasses. When she'd finished, Russell asked, "And obviously they believed you rather than Mr. Walker."

Wald smiled as the waitress neatly wrapped the bottle in a napkin and left. "True. It's absolutely amazing that someone who runs so many newspapers doesn't put very much stock in what they say." He smirked at Russell.

Russell stared back. "That's quite true." He leaned forward in mock intimacy. "You know, I truly believe that between myself and a few colleagues, we actually run the world. Decide who becomes president or prime minister. The one thing we find difficulty doing is deciding who becomes king. But, of course, we can see to it that someone doesn't. How about Lewis Rosenthal? Did you stage manage that one, too?"

Wald shook his head patronizingly. "By dropping him? With a little sophistry, you can make the case I'm guilty of his death." Wald sipped genteelly. "Of course, why I would care whether someone like Rosenthal lived or died is beyond me. What's my motive?"

"Oh, I can think of several," Russell said with the enthusiasm of someone warming up to a game. "He'd threatened to sue. That wouldn't look good on my balance sheet or your reputation. You wanted to take the project from him, which you've already told me. You were interested in his wife, although I wouldn't put that high on the list. Oh, here's one; he had something on you, which he was going to spread as his revenge for your stealing his project. I'm sure there are a few skeletons even in *your* closet, aren't there, Steven?"

Wald shook his head with disdain. "What exactly is your point?"

"That I can't trust you. As I said earlier, you confuse me. If I don't understand how you behave and why, I can't be sure of you. And there are enough question marks about your behavior to have turned you into a conundrum."

Russell watched as Wald contained his rage and focused it into one low hissing sound, his large head and body writhing in serpentine fashion. "*I* confuse you? What about that epicene son of yours? *He* doesn't confuse you? Or am *I* confused? *Is* it a he? Or an it? You say *I* have skeletons? You talk like your life is so Simon simple and lily-white pure. What did *you* do that turned out that sideshow of a son? He's probably prancing around Chelsea right now whistling at sailors and offering to buy bum boys a drink. Or perhaps he's being fitted for a lovely new gown for your next gala celebrating your newest acquisition. I understand you've been on the queen's honors list. How does she feel about your son wearing more flowered chiffon and a bigger hat than her?" Wald stopped, short of breath, his eyes gleaming with hate.

Russell waited to see if he would resume speaking. Then, "My son doesn't give me one moment of pause. I have absolutely no shame or reservation about him exactly as he is. Which is to say, a rather unique person. It takes great strength and sense of self to live as he does. It takes enormous courage to live as he pleases in the face of people like you. You see, Mr. Wald, he knows exactly who he is and what he wants. I'm not sure the same can be said about you. If I had to choose, there's no question in my mind that my son is ten times the man you are, if being a man is a euphemism for character, strength, and convictions. Your behavior is what I would characterize as perverse. You've just convinced me how dangerous you are when you panic. You're out, my dear fellow."

Wald stood. He felt disoriented by the synthetic homespun quality of the room. He could feel the burning heat in his ears. From his full height, Russell appeared dwarfed as the room seemed to swim around them. He could see Russell calmly eating his salad, carefully shredding the leaves with his knife and fork. Then the older man looked up at him, as if wondering what he was still doing there.

Wald tried focusing on the exit, hoping the direction his legs were taking would lead him to it. He passed several of the long-gowned waitresses, each trying to jockey her overflowing tray out of his path. At the door, the hostess started into the room, questioning with her eyes his ability to navigate successfully.

"Do you want the men's room, sir?" she asked, extending her arm and pointing a long finger toward a passageway.

Wald took her direction, aware of the clumsiness of his movements, hoping he could reach the confines of the hall without incident. As his hand grabbed the doorjamb, he saw the door marked MEN in block letters and gratefully guided himself toward it. Before he could push against it, it opened and a small sunken man of seventy tried to pass him, looking up at his face without expression. Wald brushed past, hitting him on the shoulder to steady himself. Then he went into the farthest of three cubicles and dropped to his knees. The vomit emptied into the bowl immediately, small orange pieces splashing and sticking to his tie. His granite head hovered over the flushing water, waiting cautiously for the retching to subside. After the last barren heave, he reached for some toilet paper, brushing it over his lips and chin. Finally the only sensation left was a tight, intense pain in his forehead.

He lifted himself carefully, weighing each movement for its effect, until he stood up straight in the tiny stall. He let himself out, went to the sink, and began splashing his face with cold water. When he looked up, he looked as he always did, his features immutable, a permanent poker face. His shifting blue-gray eyes were fringed with red threads, intensifying his imperious stare. His breathing had returned to normal, his dizziness subsided.

He turned from the mirror, passed through the door, strode down the narrow passage, and walked through the exit nodding politely at the hostess. As he headed for his car, he wondered just how many Hollywood lives he had left.

Chapter Seventeen

Billy Carroll had just come, his damp head and chest fallen on top of her. She wiggled her shoulders, feeling his stickiness against her breasts. Even spent, youth, she thought, had quite a pleasant scent.

"That was won-der-f-u-u-l-l. . . ." Dalton said reassuringly, stroking the wet ringlets on his head. "Won-der-ful," she repeated.

He remained still except for soft quick panting sounds. Then he grunted and rolled off her.

"Oh, good, you liked it, too," she said.

He smiled, leaning over her and rubbing his tongue against her nipple. "Yummy," he said as he flopped onto his back.

Good, she thought, at least her venturing onto the boards hadn't been a total waste of time. Her foolish expectations regarding Wald had amounted to nothing but questionable publicity. *Accident vehicle found outside actress's home.* How ever did it get there? she imagined millions of Americans asking across the continent. Her culpability in the accident had been tangential at best; she'd fucked the car's owner. She wondered whether Ward's unannounced departure had been due to circumstances or his lost interest in her.

After all, what more could an aging actress expect? Especially one whose career had been built on allure. Allure dimmed, in

spite of the ministrations of the finest cosmetic surgeons,
makeup artists, and wig makers. It was meant to; that's why
beauty was so potent. Still, she had enough left, or reconstituted, to attract, even if briefly, Wald to her bed. Even sustain
the interest of a young and wildly attractive man like Billy Carroll. But the real magic, that which had fired the imaginations of
millions of fans, talk show hosts, and tabloids, that particular
potency had all but vanished.

As was usual for someone of her generation, she'd amassed
the requisite jewelry, collections of fine art, bits of real estate
here and there; enough to keep her comfortable and her dignity
intact even if her career had failed totally.

As it happened, the fame, the main byproduct of her allure,
was something she missed much less than she'd expected. There
were still the restaurant reservations when needed, the house
seats to hit shows, still the invitations; it all simply lacked the
brilliance, the inevitability, the excitement. They were now
more perks for dues paid. And that was quite enough; it had to
be.

There were still choices to be made: to gracefully disappear
into private shadows, or haul it out and parade it in front of the
lights, keeping the illusion alive for no one but herself.

This decision she would make another time. Now she could
see her latest award stirring below the young man's incredibly
flat stomach. It was an honor for someone her age to be appreciated, one that she greedily accepted.

Before lawyers could talk, before threats and accusations
could be made, coast-to-coast gossip had it that Steven Wald
was out. Even before a formal announcement was drawn up to
gracefully disguise the uglier facts, a surprising number of
mostly gleeful people were spending lunches and cocktails speculating on exactly what had induced the mighty communications
lord to bring his wrath down on Wald. And exactly how many
pounds of flesh Russell was going to extract for the transgressions.

Even Nora and Ben, whose names were never connected with
the fall, were surprised at the rapid turn of events. Now she
curved her body against Ben's. She was sleeping, snoring lightly,
her hair entangled over her face, exposing the gray roots she'd

come to ignore. He moved his fingers through the thick blond waves and stared at the paleness of her un-made-up face. Her eyes were reduced to slits, the barest fringe of lash outlining them. Her nose was slim and sharply defined, her waxy nostrils spreading and contracting with each breath. Only her lips fulfilled the promise of the made-up Nora. They were full, soft, tinged with pale pink.

Ben raised himself on his crooked arm, pressed his cheek against his palm and watched her sleep; a vantage he had employed other times with other women. From this angle he had examined their faces, made decisions, sometimes, though seldom, feeling the nervous tenderness of affection override the rational element in his musings. Now his own thin, weather-chapped lips smiled.

The smile broadened as he felt the familiar pattern emerge: the plotting to gain acceptance, to earn love. She'd been an important star and that impressed him. There would always be the persona of her achievements, and it would always, to some degree, intimidate him. He watched her sleep, thinking how his curiosity marked the newness of their relationship. Only when the wonder dissipated, when the thrill of having her in his bed subsided, could he begin to think serious, grown-up, permanent thoughts. And that was what he had to work on.

Steven Wald had underestimated the extent and virulence of Russell's wrath. Within days of his dismissal, his office and those of his highest officers were overrun by a phalanx of auditors. The formal, jocular Russell had given way to hardball Mike. It wasn't long before the scabrous bean counters had accumulated a litany of the usual transgressions: an island rental written off on the studio, weekend trips abroad, a circular routing of payments that wound up back in Wald's pocket. The cheesy flotsam and jetsam of greed as practiced by people who transgressed more for sport and custom than need. In their ordinariness and relatively modest dimensions, the forms of graft looked petty. In the eyes of the law, they constituted embezzlement.

As Wald lazed on the deck of his Malibu beach house, his mind wracked with the whirling incremental effects of his entanglement, he thought about the fragile fairyland he and his neighbors inhabited. The actor in the surprisingly close house to his right had released two films during the year, promising to gross him ten and twelve million dollars respectively. For him and those people up and down this stretch of sand, those numbers were reality. They carried the weightlessness of a parlor game, charades; with each successive word guessed, the *yeses* growing increasingly loud and resonant in the winner's ears, the normality of excess and justification grew. That the game would end, either through diminishing enthusiasm or pleasure or results, was inevitable. Everyone knew it was only a question of time, of how long one could keep on winning.

Wald sipped his wine, wondering how far Russell was willing to push. His reputation, cash flow, privileges had all been significantly diminished; the question remained, how much more was Russell going to extract? Humiliation? Prison? It was not a question Wald cared to ponder long.

He watched a spotted orange butterfly work its way around plants growing in wooden containers neatly arranged on the deck. It was a town of butterflies, some more brilliant than others, more fanciful, all coming from secret, hidden wombs of ordinariness, even ugliness. None, including himself, knew how long butterflies lasted. Or what ever happened to them.

The usual assortment of gold to brown bodies padded in the hazy surf, preening and posing, as if parading through the circles of hell. The longer Wald stared, the more they appeared to writhe, their ecstasy shimmering in the heat waves and the backlit ocean mists. No longer was he catnip to those perfect bodies, no longer would they smile and fawn and flirt. No longer could he seduce them with the balm of power, rubbing his hands over yards and yards of perfect, unblemished flesh.

He felt sadness at the thought of loss, anger for the pleasure his topple would give others. There were still variables, directly connected to how hard Russell would squeeze him. There were always jobs; the people who did what he did passed in and out of their positions almost seasonally. It would be more difficult, but nothing was impossible. The question was, was it worth it? And to what end? For the admiration never quite believed? The questionable camaraderie? The never quite knowing what was genuine and what was a form of bargaining?

The phone next to him buzzed and he anxiously, almost

gratefully, reached out to answer. But his hand froze midair and he could hear the answering machine clicking into action. His act of hesitation was such a small, pitiful assertion of independence, it saddened him.

Everything about his life was shrinking; he'd tried to find something positive about it, but the gain eluded him. Yet he had never really believed most of it, never questioned its transience; it had never fitted; perhaps the loss had really been discounted a long time ago.

Chapter Eighteen

New England

"Michael Russell here."

His telephone voice had a cheery inevitability about it, a benevolence that heralded joyous occasions, largesse.

"Mr. Russell. How are you, sir?" Ben could hear the deference automatically creep into his voice.

"Very well, thank you. How have *you* been?"

The voice sounded totally interested in the response. "It's been a nice few months. Nora and I are happy. How is Mrs. Russell?"

"Good. In fact, she's the reason behind my call. She wants to produce your book. The same idea Wald had, but her way. I think you'll find it a bit more acceptable."

Somehow the abrupt proposition didn't surprise him. Nor did Aida Russell's interest; correspondence over the past several months had signaled her intentions. "Mr. Russell, I'll be honest with you. Anything I commit to right now has to include Nora."

"Understood. Aida and I want her to be part of it."

The I'm-here-and-all-is-right voice massaged the words and Ben let them soak in. "You're serious."

"Of course. She's a very big star, Ben. You've seen her at her most vulnerable. To all the world, she's a legend. Impervious. My friend, the people who read my tabloids have no idea that those with fame and money have a worry in the world, let alone weaknesses. They don't believe me when I tell them. Each week my headlines scream how this one's a drunk, that one's gotten fat, he lost his job on account of drugs, she doesn't speak with her children. They don't really believe it. Except, they want to. It reassures them, even the possibility that someone famous might have a taste of the same lousy stinking life they lead. It comforts them; that's why I'm rich. But the next week they go right back up on their pedestals. We all need our heroes. And Nora is one of them. In fact, the tragedy of Lewis Rosenthal just made her more adorable to them. In other words, it's to your and my advantage to have her as part of the project."

Ben wondered whether he himself hadn't reversed things, convinced himself that she was the invalid and he was the strong one. Whether it wasn't to his advantage to accept her defeat; that it minimized the chances of losing her. "It sounds great."

"There's more. While you're developing and writing and trying to squeeze more money out of me, we'll be launching a perfume around Nora. Another of Aida's ideas. She recalled I picked up a small parfumerie in France a few years back, nothing but the scents of long-dead designers. No, I'm afraid that doesn't sound quite right. But you know what I mean. The plant and the technology and the distribution is all there. All we need is an appealing image. Aida says Nora is it. Ben . . ." Now his voice went plaintive. "Let's leave the lawyers out of it. Let's do a deal without months of posturing and trying to outsmart each other. Let's just get together and make it happen."

"It's quite a menu you're offering me."

"I know it. Excess is my biggest fault. But I'm a large man, my appetites are huge and my capacity is enormous. I overdo everything, I'm afraid. But it's not your problem. I've one other fault. When I want something, I want it yesterday. I think that's why I fit in the States so nicely. Americans are wonderfully impatient. They want instant everything, just like me."

"Except for us New Englanders; we're a bit more cautious."

"Damn. I was afraid of that!" Russell said lightly. "Then can you decide by morning?

Ben smiled. "May I have a few seconds to discuss it with Nora?"

"By all means. If it's any comfort, Aida has already thought it through and concluded it's in both of your interests. But, by all means, have your talk. And let me know within the week. Much as the delay goes against my nature, I don't want you to feel rushed."

Russell hung up without saying good-bye. A sane man, Bradford thought, would be ecstatic. Yet there was something tempering his feelings. Everything in his life had taken on an inevitability; never had the streams of his world flowed in such accord. Why, then, did he feel so uncomfortable?

It had taken months for Tim D'Amato to put the accident out of his mind. But Neil Sheedy would not be exorcised. He had come to understand the congressman's faults, to judge his character. On every level imaginable, he was someone to be avoided. Yet Tim D'Amato thought of him almost every last moment before he fell asleep. He thought of his body, manlike, rather than youthful like his own. He remembered his large hands, covered in fine reddish-blond hairs, running over his body at a demonically slow pace. Sometimes in bed, Tim lifted his hips in anticipation of what the congressman would do to him, only to relax them into the empty bed.

Tim began to think it was only Neil's absence that was tormenting him. That if he'd continued to see him, the man's remarkable lack of sensitivity, to his wife, his career, to him, would turn him against the older man. That even the pleasures he gave him would wear thin, that he himself would become knowledgeable enough in the ways of titillating flesh that he might want to go off and experiment on his own.

As it was, he was trapped in a void, a surrogate living out his punishment for the accident; Neil, the only human being he'd ever known with whom he could communicate fully, absent.

The months of living in this void had begun to take their toll. He had become sullen, resistant to the ways his family treated him, which seemed unchanged since he was a child. His taste of unbridled freedom had been like the apple to Adam. His surroundings seemed third-rate, hand-me-down. Everything, the reclining chair, the remote-control TV, the microwave, all concessions to function rather than enlightenment.

In Neil's warmer moments, he'd played CDs for him in his car, classical music that the D'Amato radio ground past. Once they'd driven to the museums in Springfield, which had had the affect of humanizing Sheedy. He'd responded with joy to the fifteenth-century paintings, uncovered for Tim the tenderness in a Madonna's smile, the deference in her adoring finger as it hovered in the air near the Christ Child. Neil's smiling silence during the drive back was one of the more palpable memories he held of him, the thought of which still could bring tears of frustration to Tim's eyes.

Tim had come to find his existence, shrouded by the past, so wanting, that after the initial shock, the new front-page story about Alling "Chip" Walker seemed sadly inevitable. At first the name appeared vaguely familiar, like a remnant of a once prominent local family. Even the face seemed foreign, unlike the months-ago photograph that had reminded Tim of himself. This time Alling "Chip" Walker looked worn, his eyes dulled by the dark crescents beneath them, his cheeks sunken into the residue of a numbed terror. His hair was long, plastered straight back on his head, either from lack of washing or caring. Even the upper half of his body was angular, with stress beneath the slouching drape of his denim shirt. Tim D'Amato had no way of knowing Chip Walker had come to look his real age.

Tim stared at the photograph for a long time, only allowing the horror of what it meant to him to seep in slowly. Then he began to read the text around it. Walker had been released from prison following his successful appeal. Mr. Walker had admitted being at the scene of the accident in a car loaned to his former employer. But, according to Mr. Walker, he had not struck the actor. There had been a vehicle in front of him, a blue pickup truck, that had hit Mr. Newland, throwing him off the road. The truck had not stopped. According to his most recent testimony, Mr. Walker had driven the Porsche to where he'd seen the body disappear into the woods, and was about to get out and see if he could help, when Newland suddenly lurched out of the shadows and flung himself against the car, then slipped off it, striking his head on a rock. When Mr. Walker got out to investigate, he determined the man to be dead. Feeling nothing could be done, he returned the Porsche and drove off in his own vehicle, afraid he would be incriminated in the accident. Later, when Steven Wald, the former studio head, was taken in for questioning, Mr. Walker still hadn't come forward, certain in the knowledge that Mr. Wald, being innocent, would be exonerated, also realizing that he would become the chief suspect. Forensic reports appeared to back up Mr. Walker's assertions. It was also determined that because of the remorse he'd expressed since being apprehended and the time already spent in prison, the remainder of his sentence would be commuted.

Tim's initial reaction was relief; he would no longer live with the specter of an innocent man penalized for his act. But a new fear crept up to replace it. Perhaps Walker *had* seen the license plate. Perhaps he had even seen him and Neil in the truck. As his mind spun out the possibilities, Tim withdrew from the extravagances of his imagination and began to relax. If Walker knew anything, he would have said so by now. He was safe. A lightness, almost a joy, asserted itself and he breathed more freely than he had in months. His body began to take on sensation again and feelings began to surge within. Suddenly Neil was no longer a stake in his heart, blunt and steely. He was simply an untrustworthy man, someone not to put one's faith in, let alone love. He had returned to his family, his career, his life in Washington. His sacrifice had been nonexistent. And he had left Tim alone to sort out the aborted strands of his life, to be strangled by them.

Without thinking, but as if he had rehearsed it many times before, Tim reached for the phone and began to dial a number he knew as well as his own even though he'd never called it. When a voice at the other end answered, he said, "Hello? Is this Catherine Sheedy?"

"Yes. Who am I speaking to?"

She sounded harried to the point of annoyance.

"A friend of your husband's. Perhaps I should say your husband's ex-friend."

"Who is this?"

"I won't give you my name. But I want you to know your husband's not everything he appears to be."

"Listen to me. This isn't the first crank call I've gotten. In fact, I've picked them up all my life, since my father was governor. Now if you don't identify yourself and explain what it is you have to say, I'm hanging up."

Her words almost overwhelmed his resolve. "Please. I'm not calling out of revenge or nuttiness or anything like that. I really believe I'm doing you a favor."

"What kind of favor?"

"A favor about your life. Your husband is making it a lie. You're living with half truths. He's not always where he says he is or doing what he says he's doing."

"Do you want to be more clear?"

She sounded like an officious operator at an emergency number demanding only relevant facts. "I was his lover."

Now she was silent. When she got back on the line, her voice was faint. "Who are you?"

"Does it matter?"

"You say you're revealing my husband; why don't you reveal yourself?"

He considered the logic of her request, then he said, "I can't."

"You can't because you're a coward." Her voice had grown in strength again. "You can call and defame another man, but you can't tell me who you are. Do I know you? Have I seen you around town?" Her questions were being hardened by emotion, their urgent stridency rising with her cadence. "I bet I have. I bet I'd recognize you if I saw you. Why are you saying this thing about my husband? What are you trying to do to me?"

Tim hadn't expected to unleash such a torrent in her. His own reaction was a mixture of fear that she could identify him and shame that he'd upset her so much. "Maybe . . ." He spoke as if to himself. "Maybe it's better not knowing . . ."

When she responded, her voice surprised him, as though he hadn't expected her to hear. "What makes you think I don't know?" The sound was low and guttural. "Do you think I could live with a man all these years and *not* know. Do you suppose I'm a fool? Do you suppose, living in the Governor's Mansion, I grew up naïve? I know what Neil Sheedy is. And I chose to live with it."

The silence became so complete, Tim wasn't sure whether the line had gone dead.

Then she continued. "Apparently you couldn't. Once you found out what he was really like, you had to do something. Hurt me. Get revenge. Anything but accept it. Well, it's too bad. Unlike you, I have no intention of letting him break my heart."

Tim looked at the receiver as if it had singed his ear. The woman's nasal breath was still audible in it. Then he returned the phone to its cradle as gently as he could, with full comprehension of how much he would regret this call the rest of his life.

Chapter Nineteen

The Shannon house, bedecked in snow, looked like a dentist's Christmas card. As they drove up, Nancy opened the door and stood backlit by the golden glow from within, broadly wiping away mock tears. "I'll try to behave myself, but I'm distraught already. Two of my favorite people leaving me for months and months," she called to them.

She watched them get out of the car, squeezing herself and shivering as broadly as she had wept, an orphan in the storm. Then she hurried them into the house.

"Don't you look gorgeous!" she said to Nora, her eyes slowly evaluating the outfit. "That certainly didn't come from around here!" she exclaimed, leaving it uncertain as to whether her statement was a compliment.

"Oh, just something I sent for from a catalogue," Nora said lightly.

"Like hell you did; my *business* is catalogues," Nancy whispered as she hugged her. "And Ben, who knew you were so handsome under that awful beard you affected. I used to say to Dick, I know it's trendy, but it looks *horrible* on Ben. Makes him look like an old man!"

"Quite the opposite." The Governor suddenly appeared at her side. "She used to tell me how sexy you were. That I should grow one myself." He kissed Nora on the cheek, then shook

Ben's hand. "Guess I should have expected it. How were we to keep a movie star down on the farm? In fact, why should we?" He laughed like a comedian cueing his audience to do the same. "What's Beverly Hills got that Partridgefield hasn't? And don't tell me 'cause I don't want to know."

A dark-haired woman helped Nora off with her coat, then tossed Ben's over her arm and left.

"We get 'em from those religious societies around here. The more they find God, the better they serve us, is what I've found." The Governor had lowered his voice.

Mrs. S's effusiveness ignited. "Well, come say hello to the other guests. They always think you made it up when you say a movie star's coming to dinner." She led them from the hallway into what appeared to be the set of a library. The couple within stood to greet them. "This is our daughter, Catherine. And her husband Neil Sheedy, who's a congressman."

Ben and Neil exchanged words about having met before while Nora allowed herself to be inspected by the daughter.

"See?" Nancy asked. "Isn't she as ravishing up close as she is on the silver screen?"

Before they could answer, Coleen's voice sailed over them. "Can't a person pee around here without some other broad showing up and stealing her thunder?" She went to Nora and embraced her. "I forgot just how good you can get yourself together. And now I'd like you to meet my date for tonight."

A wan-looking gentleman arched his brows. His fine gray hair was brushed in a dandyish arc over each ear, the thinning top composed of long-waved strands arranged bridgelike over his crown. At the base of his long bony nose, a thin, impeccably groomed mustache twitched as he spoke. "Nora." The word came out a caress. "Coleen has told me so much about you. I'm such a fan of yours. Have been for ages. This is such an *honor* to meet you. Justin Saint James." He extended his arm with the angular grace of a heron.

Nora moved her lashes vampishly, and smiled. "Mr. Saint James."

"Oh no! Justin! Please!" With some effort, he took his eyes from Nora and turned to Ben. "I'm a great admirer of your work, as well. I just loved *The Limner.*"

"And he liked the play, too," Coleen said. "Justin, for the

record, is Partridgefield's, nay, the county's, leading antiquar-
ian." She looked at him with pride and approval.

Nancy Shannon watched, her face a finely lined, powdered
grid, her parrotlike eyes trying to read the company she was in.
Suddenly she raised her glass. "To Ben and Nora, our golden
couple, going off to bask in the pleasures of California. May
they find their fortunes and dreams there."

The others raised their glasses and voiced approval of her
words.

"To think," she continued, "that in my infinitesimally small
way I played a part in this Hollywood saga."

Neil Sheedy looked at her with surprise. "Really, Mother?"

The Governor cleared his throat, inviting his son-in-law to
read his scowl.

"I did indeed. It was in this very house that Ben met Mr.
Russell, who would go on to make this wonderful dream happen. Imagine, Ben's book, written here in Partridgefield, and
about all of us in one way or another, being turned into a TV
series. Just be kind to blue-haired ladies, that's all I ask." She
toasted him again.

"If you can't find the right handsome devil to play me, I'm
available, Ben." The Governor raised his empty glass, flicking
his finger to get the serving woman's attention.

"And let's not forget the star of this exciting venture." Mrs. S.
raised her glass to Nora and smiled broadly.

"Well, let's hope we don't scandalize you," Ben said, toasting
the room back.

"Hey, come on," Neil said, "if it's not scandalizing, who's
going to watch?"

Justin Saint James grinned appreciatively. "If you need any
local dirty little secrets, please don't hesitate to call," he said
innocently.

"Like the night Justin appeared at my door starkers, holding
a candelabrum at each ear," Coleen said.

"It was a teensy-weensy little joke, really," he explained. "I
was delivering them and they were just so beautiful, I didn't
want anything to distract."

Coleen pinched his cheek appreciatively.

"Well, anyway," Nancy said, "it all started last summer at our
annual preseason party. Lots of bigwigs, including that awful

man who ran Mr. Russell's studio. I must say, even I, who's not particularly worldly, being content to spend most of my life within fifty miles of this house, could tell he wasn't the right sort. When people make you nervous, you just sort of know."

"Then you'd better stay here; in Hollywood you'd be shaking day and night," Coleen offered with wide-eyed helpfulness.

"And you, Ben . . ." Mrs. S eyed him shrewdly, determined to hold the spotlight, "I'd start thinking about tying Nora down somehow, before all those handsome hunks start sniffing after her."

Neil raised his eyebrows. "Mother Shannon! Hunks? Where did you learn that?"

"Hush." She dismissed him with annoyance. "You see the word every week in those newspapers at the checkout counter. You'd know about them if you engaged in a little family time, like shopping."

He smiled at her, as if returning a compliment. "Anyway, I think it would be in Nora's interest, too, to ward off all those starlets out there."

"Starlets?" Coleen seemed genuinely puzzled. "Do they still have starlets? I thought everyone was a star or a superstar or a mega-super-star; a starlet?" She shook her thick mass of hair.

"I suppose I'm sort of out of the show-business loop. A politician's always the last to know what's happening around him," he said disingenuously.

"That does seem to be the case these days," his father-in-law added.

"Anyway," Nancy continued, "I'm sure Ben will do us proud. And Nora. Have you been studying us, dear? You know, we talk and move and dress in a very particular way. None of that fancy stuff you always see on the TV. We like to play things down."

"I have noticed that," Nora said primly. "I'll try to wear only three ball gowns a show."

Justin laughed appreciatively. "Do, my dear. That's what sells. Leave this sociological reality crap to the young film makers out of school. We old dogs want *glamour!*" He emphasized the word with gestures recalling the opening of a flower.

"See what happens when you listen to people, Ben?" the Governor asked. "One says play it down, the other says play it up. That's why politicians have to talk out of both sides of their mouth. You two go off and knock 'em dead. We'll stay here and worry about reality."

"That's right," Nancy added, taking back the conversation and ignoring her husband. "Justin's absolutely right. I hope that perfume Mr. Russell is bringing out with your name will just *exude* glamour." She smiled at Nora. "I'd bathe in it if I thought it would do me any good."

Catherine Sheedy stood, as though to make a toast. "I see that boy was let out of jail," she said in a loud, firm voice.

The Governor looked at her strangely. "What makes you say that, sweetheart?"

"Well, you said 'reality,' and this talk about show business. I just thought of that poor actor and how he was run down like a dog. And how 'reality' is that whoever killed him is getting away with it, whether it was that boy or not."

"That *was* odd," her husband said, "reversing the decision. He must have done a hell of a job talking himself out of it."

"Or he didn't do it," his wife added.

"But this is a celebration! Let's not think morbid things," Nancy Shannon said brightly, as if her daughter were speaking of a dead cat.

"I had a premonition about that actor," Catherine Sheedy continued. "During the play, you saw he was at the end of his rope. I could feel that. Across the footlights. It was something that went beyond acting. I could sense that things had gone wrong for him. Desperation is something you can't hide."

"Catherine!" Her mother's admonition was like cannon fire.

"I remember wondering how many other people at the theater felt it too." She continued as though she hadn't heard the warning. "One is very receptive to people's feelings in a theater. That's part of how it works. We let down our guard and let the actors do our feeling for us. And if it strikes true, it's called a catharsis. Only in this case, the man wasn't acting. He was on the stage allowing us to see his own emotions running. Running dry." She paused to look into her lap. "There does come a point in people's lives when nothing is right and there's no place to turn. Because if you try, you stand the risk of hurting other people. So you're trapped. And events keep twisting on you, beating at you, until you're so weak . . ." She had let herself go on in spite of the threatening silence around her. "I recognized that in the actor. Perhaps he had wanted his life to end that night. That's what I thought when I read about it in the paper. That he'd jumped out in front of the car, that whoever was driving might have *thought* it was his fault, but it really wasn't. He'd just been the innocent victim of the actor's own emotions."

Neil Sheedy took his wife's hand. "You know, there just might be some truth in that. Catherine's a very sensitive person —she sees things most of us don't. Why, it could just have been some kid out for a joy ride, a little spooning, an innocent cruise along a back road, and this poor demented creature jumps out at them . . ."

"There was nothing demented about Tony!" Coleen's voice quivered. "He'd just given a performance. A very fine performance. You can't do that if you're demented."

"Confused . . ." Catherine said softly.

Neil ignored both women as though they were hecklers interrupting one of his speeches. "And this man jumps out and throws himself in their path. Can you imagine? The guy was probably all hot and bothered anyway, probably frustrated he couldn't get in his date's pants . . ."

The Governor glowered at him.

Coleen leaned over to watch the Governor's face; it had turned scarlet. She realized she'd never seen him so sober.

"Perhaps there's a more cynical explanation. Like they didn't want folks to know they'd been out together." His eyes burned into his son-in-law.

"Oh, this is hopeless," Nancy Shannon said with dismay. "If we must have these serious discussions, can't we talk about something different, like gardening or the Kiwanis? What difference does it make what happened? Catherine, you really shouldn't have brought it up. As for your suicide theory, don't you know Nora's husband . . ." She stopped to look at the actress, who shook her head as if to suggest she could go on. "I was just trying to . . ." The older woman shrugged. "Well, let's see, what is it we're having for dinner?"

"Lighter conversation, I hope," Justin Saint James said with worldly ennui.

"My point, exactly," Nancy agreed. "I just will not have these people going to Hollywood telling folks out there what doomers and gloomers we are. Angela!" she barked at the serving woman. "I see empty glasses. Will you please tend to the guests?"

Shortly before dinner was to be served, Congressman Sheedy allowed that he had need of the "little boys" room. His wife, who'd spoken very little after her mother successfully steered the conversation to talk of the local produce markets and antiques, subjects on which she and Saint James did not agree, wordlessly followed Sheedy from the room. Before he could enter the guest powder room tucked under the grand sweeping hall stair, she grabbed his arm.

"You can keep your hands off it another five minutes, I would think." She said the words imperiously.

He smiled at her. "You want to hold it for me?"

She wrinkled her face in disgust. "He called me."

The congressman's stare went from bemusement to blank.

"Your ex-boyfriend."

Now his skin reddened as his voice filled with annoyance. "Oh, come on. We're in your parents' home. They've got guests for dinner. I'm about to take a piss and now you tell me some crank called saying he was my boyfriend?"

"It wasn't a crank call. He knew you. I believed him." Her face was composed, serious.

"Whether you believed him or not, this isn't the time to discuss it. What did he say his name was?"

"He didn't want to tell me. He said he was calling for my own good."

"How considerate." His normal color returned.

She studied his face. "I think he meant it."

"What kind of scumbag would call a man's wife and tell her he was having an affair with her husband?" His eyes narrowed. "You sound like you commiserated with him."

She continued staring at him. "I could understand his motives more than I do yours. Hearing his voice, the pain in it, I began to think what a farce we are. How humiliating, degrading, to be playacting a hoax." She indicated the living room with a swirl of her head. "They get paid for it. What do we get?"

"My career, for one thing. Which has not been without its shining moments."

She sneered a laugh, then her features became serious again. "What you said before, about the people in the car not wanting anyone to know; you were driving. It was you who hit the actor." Her expression dared him to refute her.

"I wasn't driving . . ."

"But you were in the car."

A mocking smile came to his lips. "It wasn't a car. It was a pickup truck. And it was the young man who phoned you who was driving. Happy?"

Once she saw the ridicule in his eyes, warm tears set in hers. "How can you take pleasure in this?"

"How can you bring it up now?"

Her face lost color. "You got out of it; how?"

Sheedy intensified his sneer with a slight twist of his mouth as he looked beyond her into the living room. "Looks after me like his own son," he said with mock humility.

Her head began shaking in little shudders. The word *no* started forming on her lips, gradually becoming audible, growing in volume as the shudders increased. "No! It's disgusting! You dragged my own father into it? He knows?" Her eyes begged her words to be untrue, that he contradict them. But her voice held the tonality of resignation.

"Daddy knows," Neil said quietly. "Now may I pee?"

"There weren't any really *good* pieces of furniture in the house, you know." Justin Saint James delivered the assessment to Coleen as they were pulling out of the Shannon driveway. "Lots and lots of fabric all over, but not even a teacup of note in the entire barn. I'd like to meet the decorator that made off with that bundle."

"I heard Mrs. S did it all herself," Coleen said with mock innocence.

"I wouldn't brag if I were she."

"I dunno. I never question the landed gentry."

His brows flared. "But you're joking! They don't deserve to kiss the boards you've trod on. It's like that furniture; it's all phony. Or just old, with no particular merit. Pieced together like they don't really care. What they don't care about is spending money for the real thing. If it came down to them, that's one thing. Although these days, they'd probably sell for a good profit. Don't ever let them think they're better than you; you'd just be feeding their delusions."

She shot up in her seat and looked at him with her famous owl eyes. "Am I going through menopause again or was there something strange going on around that table?"

The car skidded on a patch of ice, causing Justin to make an adjustment. "Oh, you're quite right. Very chilly evening. The young Sheedys were well out of sorts. At least she was. Her poof husband didn't seem to care."

She saw the sly smile on his face.

"Are you just saying that or is he really . . ."—she searched for the right word, then shrugged—". . . a poof?"

"A one-hundred-percent-genuine poof. And we're not too proud of it. The sort that does everything behind bushes or in motel rooms. Really quite sordid."

Coleen nodded. "Think Mr. and Mrs. Gov know?"

"Well, there are all sorts of degrees of knowing, aren't there? The conscious kind and the unconscious kind. Then there's the actionable sort and the ones you sort of bury. I'd say it was the buried kind."

"Mrs. S is a pretty shrewd cookie; why would she let her daughter . . . ?"

"We don't always have the luxury of *allowing* people to do something, do we?"

Coleen tossed her mane as the ramifications of his statements fanned out before her. "Wow. Being in politics, that's a hell of a secret."

"Oh come, we all know the senator . . ."

"Yeah, but still . . ." She cut him off, holding the thought. "Still and all, he's married with a couple of kids."

"Three."

"So he must go both ways." She spoke tentatively, as though doing a crossword puzzle.

"I don't know. There are ways. . . ."

She looked at him skeptically. "You're not suggesting they've found ways I don't know about?"

A car was speeding toward them; Justin tensed and tightened his grip on the wheel. "Dumb bastard," he said as it shot by spraying slush on their windshield. "They drive like absolute animals in foul weather, like they all have a death wish."

Coleen slumped down in her seat. "Do you buy that part about Tony wanting to kill himself?" Her mood had turned morose. "It's not so easy for some people. Not everybody can just keep turning the pages; some people are afraid what they're going to find in the next chapter."

"Well, I think you just keep going and there's always a happy ending. Like your friend, Nora. She really is lovely, by the way. I wasn't just nattering on about it. Here she's suffered this horrible tragedy not even a year ago and now she's got her own TV show, a perfume, and this plaid-and-corduroy man's man to comfort her at the end of the day. I should be so lucky."

Coleen allowed him to go off in his reverie as she began to think of Lewis Rosenthal and what demons drove him. What if someone really had stalked him, knew of his intentions, and helped push him over the edge? That scenario set off a tingling in her arms and neck, an intuitive nod in its favor. It seemed to her she could even figure out who it was if she set her mind to it. And with that thought she brought her attention back to the road and nodded approvingly at what a superb foul-weather driver the smiling antiques dealer was.

Neil Sheedy looked at the newspapers spread about him and smiled expansively. There was no question about it, he'd been born to be a politician.

For weeks he'd feared his wife turning into a loose cannon. She was perfectly capable of using his involvement in the death of the old actor against him. No matter the cost. Fortunately his father-in-law had intervened, using his considerable influence on his daughter to calm her down. In the end, Catherine had realized they had little choice but to close ranks and protect him.

But the stroke of genius had been his, turning his knowledge of the incident into an act of honor. He'd stepped forward, telling the world how the *real* driver involved had come to him asking for his help. Sheedy had explained how he'd spearheaded a quiet investigation with the help of the sheriff's office, corroborating the driver's account that it was an accident, the actor irresponsibly walking out in front of the vehicle. Sheedy himself declared he would assume personal responsibility for the driver's innocence, implying extenuating circumstances had justified leaving the accident scene. The sheriff's office had nothing but praise for his involvement, stating that if more citizens got involved in seeking justice, policing their own communities, following the congressman's civic-minded example, everyone would be better served.

Of course, there were those in the county who'd shrewdly suspected that Sheedy himself was somehow involved; perhaps the driver was fair and nubile and of more than passing interest to him. This theory, however, only brought sympathetic winks from those constituents, along with empathy and understanding.

Now, in bed, he sat basking in the glow of the media's coverage.

"Daddy, Daddy!" He heard a cacophony of grating young voices outside his bedroom door.

"Not now, kids, Daddy's working."

There was a low rumble of voices, then a rapid thud of feet as they made their way down the hall. As he was admiring a particularly attractive photo of himself in the paper, Catherine entered.

"No knock? My, you live dangerously."

She watched his grin in silence.

"Doesn't it make you proud, when you read all this stuff about your husband? What an honorable caring man he is? Citizen Sheedy. Sounds like the French Revolution." He inspected her face, trying to read some meaning in it. She'd somehow managed to avoid inheriting her mother's cloying prettiness or her father's granite handsomeness. Hers was a plainness so resolute, it was as though she'd never stopped to question or address it. "Well, are you just going to stare at me all morning?"

She shook her head sadly, making no effort to divert the tear crawling toward her mouth.

"Now, now, no need to be so joyful. I know how delighted you are that this little episode is over and you've got me all to yourself once again. All together, just one big happy family."

He could see the rage flicker in her eyes, the frustration tighten her lips.

"I'd cry too, if I weren't so macho."

She brought her knuckles to her lips, trying to control her expression.

"Now, now, my love, don't get so emotional. You knew what
you were getting into when we pledged ourselves to one another. Who says you can just up and change your mind? Besides, I *need* you." A half smile twisted his face. "And our little
progeny. Makes real nice campaign pictures."

She appeared stuck to the floor, isolated, like a trapped animal.

"Now, what we have to start doing, pet, is drawing up our
Christmas list. I think this year I should make a point of thanking folks for all their trust and faith, don't you? He watched her
shoulders hunch up; the loneliness of her pose almost made
him feel sorry for her. "Things aren't all that bad. What would
you do without me? Be a single mother with three young children? Forever indebted to your parents for looking after you?
You call that a life? No. I think you're better off as things are.
Respectable. Even envied, married to a good-looking young
stud like me. Here, just look at this photo. Can you imagine
how many young women would like to be in your pajamas?" He
waited until her wet eyes looked into his. Then he gave her a
dazzling smile that matched the photograph he'd just shown
her.

"Eighteen inches. And I'm not talking size, I'm talking
snow." Coleen sipped her bourbon slowly, smiling at the steady
stream of flakes outside her window. She pictured Nora at the
other end, poolside. "It's a veritable winter wonderland; get me
the fuck out of here." She turned her head to watch the log
she'd just added crackle and spark, then she moved her hips
snugly in the chair. "Nothing but howling winds day and night.
Every time they clear my driveway, it starts falling again. So I'm
not going anywhere. Fortunately I rented a shitload of tapes
before I became entombed in this white hell." She took another
sip, letting the warmth prowl through her. "So, what do you
think? Are you going to save a bawdy old lady from her icy
prison or what?"

"Absolutely. And I promise no snow," Nora said.

"That's all I ask." She looked out the window and smiled at a
row of sixty-foot spruces spiraled with white. "Is the pool guy
cute?"

"It's a woman."

Coleen growled. "And the gardener's a what?"

"We're not sure. Maybe you can help. When do you want to come?"

"Yesterday too soon?" She felt the pang of denial as she said the words and leaned forward to stir the logs. "Actually, I'm thinking a week. Does that fuck up any grand monumental plans you and Ben have?"

"Not at all. It's just work for us. You sit at the pool."

"Right. I want lots of vapid conversation and tanning tips. I don't want to be one of those old ladies that slips on her front walk and breaks a hip."

"Bring your bikinis and I'll make an appointment for you to be waxed on arrival."

"Dandy. That's just what my wrinkled old flesh needs."

"You'll be surprised how many of your old friends are here selling out and loving it."

"Just warn them I'm pretentious and unforgiving. And probably broke by their standards."

"Just let me know when you're coming."

"Thanks, doll." Coleen hung up and shook her head sadly, both at the thought of leaving the perfect tranquility of her home and what possibly waited for her where she was going.

Chapter Twenty

The images of Nora's face and a perfume bottle hovered around the room in giant blowups, blurred sparkles emanating from the crystal, the star's eyes, and the abundance of jewelry she wore in the photos. The real-life Nora appeared dwarfed and far less contemplative.

"Ms. Howard, what would you say your scent offers that Ms. Taylor's doesn't?"

"A savings of about forty dollars an ounce."

"What do you feel it will do for a woman?"

"Whatever she's too shy to do for herself."

The reporters and Nora seemed to be engaged in friendly sport, like Ping-Pong.

"How would you characterize your fragrance?"

"Romantic top notes, gutsy low ones."

"Do you feel it's a fair reflection of yourself?"

"I don't know. I've never approached myself romantically."

"Is it something you'd take with you to bed?"

"It and my hot water bottle."

Several of the women reporters appeared bored, if not slightly displeased, and began eying the buffet.

"Have you field-tested it on men?"

"It was unavoidable; it just seems to attract them."

"Beside yourself, what sort of women do you see wearing it?"

"The enlightened kind."

Ben Bradford listened nervously to the repartee from the back of the room. The confidence Nora displayed before the public and press still surprised him. As the questions turned increasingly inane, he returned to the bar.

"Does she look fabulous or what?" Danny approached him from behind. "And that frock; only Nora could look like a lady in it."

Ben appeared embarrassed by the thought.

"Listen," Danny counseled, "if some broad's going to shell out over a hundred bucks a bottle, one must pique the imagination."

Ben looked at the hairdresser uncomfortably. "Well, I think you've succeeded. How did you make all those wispy pieces stand out like that?"

"We baked her head in an oven last night." Danny sipped his club soda. "No. Spritz, spritz, and more spritz. As I've told you, Ben, I'd be only to happy to do you if you'd let me." His hand moved toward the author's hair. "I could make you a real turn-on," he coaxed.

"I'm not sure I'm ready to be turned on." Ben smiled and began to walk away. "Tell Nora I'll see her at home." He tried catching her eye to wave good-bye, but her vision was obscured by strobes going off around her.

"Oh, thank God!" Danny exclaimed. Ben looked at him puzzled. "The TV cameras just arrived. I thought we were going to have a major floperino on our hands."

Ben cuffed his shoulder and left. With the arrival of the TV press, the excitement in the room picked up, as did the illumination as portable lights were hastily set up around Nora. Danny's face turned serious as he craned his head, focusing his attention on the aura of hair he'd arranged about her face. His judgment was harsh: too much heat, too many responses to photographers prodding her to change angles, too much time away from his fingers. He twisted with frustration. Where was someone to call a break so he could disappear with the star and return her to a serene state of perfection before the TV cameras took over? All her handlers seemed to be engaged in seducing reporters into realizing the enormity of the event. The momentum of the party seemed to be changing, focused on capturing the insular magical world of star and product trapped within the sweaty chaos of the surroundings.

He resigned himself to the hopelessness of the situation, feeling annoyance with the lack of professionalism that kept him from his charge. And then he saw the young man.

His face looked wan, even sunken, but it made him appear more beautiful than ill. His blond hair was short and followed the contours of his perfectly shaped skull. He wore the sort of Italian suit that only worked on someone of his height and wiry build. He appeared removed from everything around him, neither a participant nor observer, more like he was there only to be seen himself. But everyone around appeared too preoccupied to notice. Everyone except Nora. He'd caught her eye and they stared at each other, separated from the activity around them. Danny was fascinated by the miragelike nature of their contact, which lasted only seconds before Nora returned her concentration to pinning down the elusive qualities of her fragrance.

Only Danny seemed to realize that, as much as she bantered, attempted to charm the stolid young interviewer and through him much of America, her awareness of the pale figure never diminished. Only Danny saw the panicky eye movements now as she sought him out, the almost imperceptible tremor in her bare shoulders. The only thing Danny didn't realize was who she was looking at. It was a surprise Chip Walker had kept secret from all but the woman who was the center of attention. And his strategy appeared to be as successful as the event it was disrupting.

When Ben had first moved into Nora's home, he'd recognized her houseman's face from dozens of black-and-white movies of the forties; the man usually played a mercenary or a gangster or a Nazi. He had fallen into domestic work decades earlier and Nora had explained that it was considered a coup to have landed his services. Among his many unique attributes, Ben had noticed, was the affectation of a British accent when they had guests. Now he greeted Ben with the news that Miss Coleen Copeland was waiting in the living room.

"Does she have a drink?" Ben asked.

Allen smiled shyly. "She does, sir."

Ben smiled back and approached the living room. Where the façade of the house was almost fortresslike, the rooms behind it swam with light as the opposite wall was almost entirely glass. The long expanse of linen-colored carpet was dotted with a good deal of white-and-gilt carved furniture. The walls were hung with paintings of indeterminate impressionistic origin and, even in the daytime, were kept lit, as was the fire within the large pink marble mantel. As he entered, Coleen looked up from a magazine, her face obscured in a cloud of cigarette smoke.

"I didn't expect a marching band, but I was starting to wonder if you forgot."

Her voice and face were so plaintive, Ben felt the need to bend down and hug her. "I'm so sorry. Nora's hawking her perfume at a press conference; otherwise we'd have carried you off the plane."

She inspected his face like a fortuneteller eying tea leaves. "It's okay. The driver you sent was kind of cute. He even recognized me at the gate. And your majordomo has been plying me with booze and scandal sheets." Her eyes were registering disappointment. "So, how have you been?"

"Busy. Adjusting. So far, Partridgefield's winning."

"Don't tell me. The minute we began driving up these hills, I felt I was in Shangri-la. Sort of creepy." She smiled sadly. "Well, as an alternative life-style, I guess it's not too bad."

"Which is worse, skidding on ice or getting shot on a freeway?" Ben smiled and shrugged.

"You know what the really spooky thing is?" Her head turned slowly as she observed the room. "I sense Lewis here. I can feel him. Unexpected stuff. Delicate." She fingered a white porcelain Oriental figure next to her.

Ben gazed at it, then turned to her. "So how are things in Partridgefield?"

She tilted her head back to smile. "Like a paperweight. Snow, snow, snow. And that twit Congressman Sheedy. Declaring everyone innocent of Tony's death like it was an act of God. How do these people get away with rewriting history? Can you imagine what happens in Washington if a shit like Sheedy could pull this off?" Then she focused her familiar saucer eyes on Ben. "I *do* prefer to believe the part that Tony jumped out. Somehow it makes me feel better that the choice was his."

Ben squeezed her hand. "Other than that, all's quiet?"

"Ain't much happening, that's the beauty of it." She looked toward the pool and stroked her arm. "Why does Beverly Hills give me the willies? Everything's so perfect, every leaf, every blade of grass. The water in the pool is spotless. It seems sort of perverted, living idyllic nutmeg-brown lives."

"I'll be honest, it grows on you."

"Like skin cancer." She shook her head sharply. "I'm sorry, some guest. If I open my mouth again, pack me up and send me directly into a snowdrift." He could see a small shudder attack her body. "Lewis managed to fit in," she said softly. "I could never figure that out. Definitely not your West Coast type. Every time I saw him out here he was dressed in some pin-striped blue business suit like he just got off the plane. Those thick, wing-tip cordovans. But I think he truly ate it up. He liked playing East Coast type temporarily lolling. But the lolling went on for years, didn't it? I think he simply liked playing." Her voice became even softer. "What's all that?" She jumped up and went to a wall of shelves containing small figurines behind wire mesh. "Nora's porcelain collection?"

"Lewis's."

Coleen examined the little ceramic men and women, aristocrats in wide skirts and satin britches, little peasants, almost all with salacious expressions. She seemed at first mystified by the collection, then her mouth curved into a knowing smile. "Curious," she whispered.

"Why?"

"I don't know. Collecting something so perishable. Maybe because deep down Lewis saw everything as fragile, needing to be protected."

Ben stood behind her, encouraging her with his silence.

"On the outside he was a businessman, playing hardball with the rest. But inside he was so sensitive it was frightening. If he saw a scared puppy, he'd get down on his hands and knees, talk to it until it stopped crying, then clean up its crap." She shook her head, making clucking sounds. "I miss him, Ben, really."

When she didn't continue, Ben said, "I didn't realize you knew him that well."

"Nobody did. He could be captivating. But distant, which didn't hurt in keeping your interest. I think he was just shy. There was a Middle European darkness about him, as though the Cossacks were just outside the door." She appeared to be blinking away knowledge she didn't want to think about. "Nothing was ever easy for him; he never expected it to be and I don't think he really wanted it to be. If something was easy, it wasn't worth it. Do you understand that kind of reasoning?"

Ben nodded.

"Maybe you do. But not to the extent Lewis carried it. Once he told me he'd never wanted any children, that he wouldn't make a good father. He was afraid he'd ask too much of them, destroy them with his ambitions for them. Isn't that odd? A man knowing himself that well? Admitting that about himself?" She sighed softly. "Maybe he had to kill himself. Maybe life was getting too complicated. I don't know." She shook the mop of curls. "But God damn it, Ben, why doesn't Nora try to find out what happened? How can she live with the uncertainty?" Her look was almost pleading.

"That's why you're here, isn't it? To find out what happened?"

She nodded her head and placed Ben's arm around her shoulders.

"I understand," he said.

"Right. That I'm a busybody old broad." Her glistening eyes crinkled at her attempted smile. "So what's wrong with that?"

Chapter Twenty-one

Steven Wald had found himself being inexplicably polite when Ben Bradford called. The author had been direct in asking to get together and Wald had flashed on their diner meeting when he had thought he held all the cards.

Now he watched the action on the beach, anonymous silhouettes, some waving, marching in the haze, the sun chewed away by thickening gray clouds. He recognized the Olympian advantage of his deck; at the moment, it, too, was being mired in fog.

When Bradford arrived, he realized he was actually glad to see him. "Hi, Ben," he said, adding a hearty handshake.

"Steven." The author made an obligatory gesture of looking out at the beach. "Great view."

Wald nodded. "If you like sea gulls and tight tushies."

Ben smiled back. "What else is there?"

Wald cocked his head. "Well, gin and tonic, vodka, bourbon, scotch . . ."

"Scotch."

Wald went to a small tray table set up in a corner. His large hands appeared to have difficulty dealing with the ice cubes. When he returned, Ben noticed the glass was offered with a tremor.

"How have you been?" Ben asked.

"Fabulous. Humility suits me. Who needs power this and

power that? Now, a breakfast is a breakfast, a lunch a lunch. I do my biggest deals at swap meets. People love me for what I am, which is why I'm alone. Who cares if I have to wait for a table?"

"At least you've developed a sense of humor."

Wald looked surprised. "Well, a bitter one anyway." He watched the writer lean on the rail, drawn to the scene below. "It's like television, boring but hypnotizing. There's two or three hours of my day. Another couple talking to lawyers. Russell's suing the ass off me and my counselors are jerking off my front. All in all, not a bad life."

"Well, as you've discovered, it can turn on a dime."

"Why did you want to see me? You don't have another book for me, I hope."

Ben smiled and shook his head. "Nope. I wanted to know more about Lewis Rosenthal. What you really thought about him."

Wald looked at him skeptically. "Since when am I an expert on Lewis Rosenthal?"

"I have to assume you had good judgment. That you were good at reading people."

A slow smile broke on Wald's lips. *"Had . . . were . . .* Those really are sad words."

"I'm sorry . . . I . . ."

"No, no. I *did* have a business sense. Yes, I *did* read people well. What can I tell you?"

"Who killed him?"

Wald looked at Ben in the solicitous manner of a doctor breaking bad news. "Who killed him? Why do you make that assumption? The papers lied? Another conspiracy?" He grinned. "I may not have known them, but Lewis was no J.F.K. or Malcolm X."

Ben appeared embarrassed.

"Nora believes it was murder," Wald said. The statement had a conciliatory tone.

Ben nodded. "She's been getting calls."

"Calls? *Anonymous* calls?"

Again, Ben nodded. "They were. We know who it is now." His discomfort appeared to increase.

"I couldn't take a wild guess, could I?"

Ben's face reddened.

"And you believed him, my Mr. Walker?" Wald smiled his old smirk. "My *ex*-Mr. Walker. That's very interesting." He cocked his head at Ben. "Can I have another whack at it? He said *I* was the murderer." Wald waited patiently for the answer.

Now Ben's face showed anger. "Give us some credit, Steven. It wasn't just the guy's ravings. There was a tape Lewis left at the motel. He made it to say good-bye to Nora. He talked about you at length."

Wald raised his brows calmly. "Well, that's some sort of fame, being part of a dying man's last testament."

"He wasn't dying," Ben interrupted, "he was explaining to Nora that he'd intended to take his own life, but that he'd changed his mind."

"Isn't that where Mr. Walker comes in? The suicide maven? Chip talked him out of it, no doubt."

"I don't think so. I think he talked himself out of it. But something happened, someone got into the motel room . . ."

"How do you know this?"

"It's on the tape."

Wald's eyes grinned at him. "How very handy. And what did the police make of all this?"

"They haven't heard it."

Wald threw him a skeptical look. "No police? Interesting. And what did he actually say on the tape?"

"There are sounds of a scuffle. Then he accuses someone of coming to kill him."

Wald grinned. "Sounds like those old radio shows I used to listen to as a kid. I bet Lewis did, too."

"You don't believe it?"

"Do you believe me? All right. It doesn't really matter if you do or not. Let me give you another piece for your puzzle. I got a call from Rosenthal that night. He didn't say where he was or what he was up to, but he wanted to get together. Not being a total asshole, I asked him, why? He said it was about a project, a new project. This is like ten o'clock at night. I told him to smoke better stuff and shove his new project. Then I hung up." Ben stared at him. "Got it? If I had been insane enough to bite, he would have had me meet him at the motel. I think he was looking for a make-believe murderer, to set me up and make me be it." He waited until his statement settled in. "You've got the tape. Do you really believe someone was there, murdered him and left the tape behind? Why? The killer left it as a sweet farewell present to Nora?" He shook his head with disbelief. "Lewis was maybe a shrewder deal maker than I gave him credit for. He wasn't going to miss an opportunity. I think he had every intention of killing himself that night. But he was going to leverage it, take me along with him. Have me identified at the flea bag motel and get even. When that failed, he tried plan B: your tape." He sipped gently at his drink. "As for Walker, he's tried pointing the finger at me for every suicide since Marilyn Monroe."

"Why?"

"Sociopath, is that good enough? Maybe he didn't like me seeing through him. Maybe he couldn't help himself."

"Did you do anything to him?"

"I was nice to him. Gave him a peek at the view from the top. No, I didn't do anything. The little fucker likes to turn everyone into a victim." He looked at Bradford soberly. "If I were you, I'd turn the tape over to the police and stop guessing."

Ben swallowed, realizing the effect the liquor was having on him. He stared at Wald, puzzled. "Why the hell didn't you say anything about Lewis's call?"

"Why? Life is complicated enough. Why crap it up with details. He killed himself; what difference did it make?"

The darkened sky and fog had discouraged most of the beach strollers. "Bet it gets terrifically romantic here on a stormy night," Ben said, without looking at him.

"Yeah. As long as the waves and mud slides don't knock the pylons out from under you."

When the call came, there was no surprise left in Nora. Before Allen could get it, she picked up the extension in her bedroom and heard the voice she'd been expecting.

"I thought you were fabulous."

Nora stared at the phone.

"Really. You handled yourself beautifully. Great poise. I ran out and bought three bottles."

She listened in silence, unable to take the receiver from her ear.

"Well, aren't you going to say thank you? No? Anyway, it was good seeing you again. You look great. Do you think I've changed?"

"What do you want, Mr. Walker?" She could hear soft breathing at the other end.

"My, my, I've really come a long way. A magical lady of the silver screen actually knows my name. See what notoriety will do?"

"What do you want?"

"Hey. Aren't you going to ask me what it was like? The slammer?"

She waited for him to continue.

"I've got to tell you. All that stuff about sadistic guards and slipping it to you in the shower are a bit exaggerated. Actually, I found it kind of boring. Like spending a semester with a dull professor. I'm sure there was a message, but I didn't get it." Now his voice lost its mocking edge. "You wouldn't know it from the papers, but that Sheedy guy came forward and saved my ass. Like a blooming miracle."

"I'm very happy for you, Mr. Walker. Why are you calling me?"

"Hey! No need for you to get that tone in your voice. Especially to me. Not after what I've done for you."

"What are you talking about?" Nora allowed the exasperation to show in her voice.

He snuffled into the phone. "There are no lights, no cameras. This isn't make-believe. It's just the two of us."

"Not for long. Say what you have to say or I'll hang up."

"Don't get cunty with me."

Indignation made blood rush to her head. "That's not necessary, Mr. Walker."

"I'm trying to be a gentleman. What I really need is an invitation, so I can tell you what I have to say in person, privately."

"You must be out of your mind."

"You know, for a while I actually thought that was true. But it turns out I was only a bit confused."

Nora relaxed; his voice had lost its terror for her. "This is harassment, Mr. Walker. I'm going to call the police. They're used to cranks like you."

"I knew you'd say that." He sounded relaxed, confident. "In fact, I was waiting for it. But I don't think so."

"Why not?"

"Because you'd be foolish to write me off as a crank. I have information for you. About the night your husband died."

She felt another stab of pain in her head. "Haven't we been through this enough? I'm not interested in your theories anymore."

"Who says it's a theory?"

She made an effort to control her voice. "That means you were there."

"That's quite correct. I was there."

"Then, you . . ."

"No, I didn't. Let's not be coy, Nora. I said I was there. I know he had a visitor."

Now his silence seemed gracious, expectant, waiting for her to fill it.

Coleen Copeland got out of the cab on a quiet street off Sweetzer and walked to the apartment complex: two-story buildings built atrium style around a pool just small and turquoise enough to appear tacky. Several sunglassed loungers eased their bodies off their towels to witness her arrival. She climbed the stairs and walked down the cement gallery until she reached a door marked 28. She caught her breath, crossed herself, and knocked.

When Chip Walker opened the door, she was surprised to see the sheepish look on his face, until she realized it reflected his embarrassment over the furnishings beyond.

"Hey, what a great surprise." He stepped back with a courtly gesture. "By all means, slum away."

"Nora told me you called. From now on you talk to me." She took no pains to disguise her curiosity about the surroundings.

"This is it," he said casually, as though hoping his comment would dismiss the inspection. "Sit anywhere."

The choices were limited to a slab of foam on wooden slats and two bright, frayed slipcovered chairs. "I'll stand, thanks," she said.

He nodded acquiescence. Now he appeared nonplussed by her visit. "Oh, what the hell. You've come all this way to see the hopeless, the wannabes, the rejects and outcasts, the mentally mauled and emotionally maimed, as we cling to our last dollop of hope. Here we are, in all our tawdry splendor. Not a real pretty sight, is it?" He scratched his hand over what seemed several days worth of stubble and observed his surroundings as though a stranger to them. "It seems only fitting that I wind up here, in the land of make-believe. But, hey, if it wasn't for make-believe, I'd have absolutely nothing at all to believe in." He sneered. "Cut the crap, Chip. Sure you won't sit down?"

In the dusty afternoon sunlight, he looked both older and more vulnerable than she remembered. "Did Lewis really turn to you for help?"

He looked up, indignant. "What's that supposed to mean?"

"No offense. I just never knew Lewis to ask for help."

"Well, I must say, he did it in a funny way. Sort of like a cock tease. He did and he didn't."

"Did you try to help him?"

He seemed stopped short by the implication of kindness in her question. "Yeah, I guess. At first. He seemed scared and tired."

Coleen kept her silence.

"What do you want me to say?"

"What you've been threatening to tell Nora for almost a year. What you really know about Lewis's death."

He shrugged. "But that would take all the mystery out of our relationship."

"Quit fucking around."

He seemed resigned to the outcome. "Your friend Nora—this is going to sound so fucked up—she was always my mother's favorite actress."

Coleen rolled her eyes. "Oh, please. You're not that young." She advanced, putting her face close to his. "Are you?"

He wiped his hand over his eyes and turned away. "She was. People used to tell her she looked like Nora Howard. Only my mother got older and Nora didn't."

"It's a trick we great stars learn in kindergarten."

"Right. Except I'd like to see Nora if she drank like my mother did." He gave her a knowing smile. "Of course, she had good reason."

"I'll bet."

He wiped his hand through the air, dismissing some thought. "Yeah. You're looking at it." His face went blank.

Suddenly her eyes lit with the sort of insight she'd get studying for a role. "Nora reminding you of your mother, that isn't especially a compliment, is it?"

He responded with a small smile.

"What did she do to you . . . ?"

His smile grew into a leer. "Come on, you're warm. . . ."

"Oh, shit." She moved back and lowered herself onto the foam slab.

"Come on. . . ." He forced himself to look at her.

Coleen shook her head. "You poor fuck."

"Well, look, we all have our little crosses to bear. Mine just happened to have body odor and lousy breath." He slipped into the chair opposite her.

She looked at him with concern, then doubt. "You shining me on again?"

The small smile intervened. "Don't overestimate me. Even the most genuinely fucked up among us have our limits. I'm treating this as time out from game playing."

The sunlight created a barrier of dust in the air between them. "I don't remember ever moving. Like I just let her do it. That's what I thought good little boys were supposed to do."

"Is she dead now?"

"To me she is." Suddenly his body came alive, his swagger and the glint in his eyes returned. "Aren't you glad you came to visit? Nothing like a little gossip to help kill a dreary afternoon."

"Look, fella. None of these people, particularly Lewis and Nora, had anything to do with that stuff. I hope you realize that."

"Why, of course I do, Miss Copeland. It's just a little childhood memory I carry around close to my heart. But then, you really came here to talk about Lewis. And, darn, somehow I managed to steer the conversation around to me. How boorish."

"Come on, don't make it any harder on either of us."

"Oh, is this difficult for you? I thought nothing in the human condition was alien to an artist."

She leaned into him. "What did Lewis say to you that night?"

Now he deflated. "He said he hurt as much as I did. That sometimes we had to take the blows for things that weren't of our doing. He said he understood all the guilt and regret I had and that he hoped I could live with it better than he could."

Coleen nodded gently. "You went to see him at the motel?"

"At the motel," he repeated thoughtfully. "He told me a story about a puppy he had when he was a little boy. He thought of it because its name was Chips. He swore it, Mr. Chips. The dog was four or five weeks old when his parents brought it home. They put it in a cardboard box by his bed during the first night. But the puppy wouldn't sleep. It kept crying, keeping everyone awake." As Chip recited the story, his eyes moistened. "In the morning, he dressed Mr. Chips in its collar and leash and took it for a walk. He told the dog everything would be all right, that he shouldn't be afraid and that he loved him. The dog seemed to have understood, kept licking his face. But that night, it started crying again. No matter what he said to the puppy, it kept whimpering.

"After three nights, his parents took the dog back to the shop. He told me he never forgot Mr. Chips. That he'd always wondered what had happened to him and that he would pray that he'd found a home where people loved him. He said he'd saved Mr. Chips's collar and lead, that he still had them. Can you imagine, living in Beverly Hills, saving a puppy's . . ." He looked at her embarrassed. "We just talked like that, telling childhood war stories. Then he told me something so dumb, I just stared at him. He said he'd let down everything he'd every loved. Can you believe a guy like that saying such a stupid thing? Here he'd given Nora Howard the world, but to him he'd let her down."

She nodded. "I know, I know. For some people, no matter what they do or how well they do it, they feel they fucked up. And God forbid, one time they really do, they show themselves no mercy." She screwed her brows together and looked at him. "You didn't kill him, you swear to God?"

He shook his head. "Swear. For what that's worth, coming from me." He caught her stare. "I didn't."

She leaned back and sighed. "I don't know, I guess I believe you." She gave him a sly smile. "You should have been an actor, bozo. I'm convinced half of us would be psychotic killers if we didn't let it out on stage." Now she looked at him fiercely. "Who else was there?"

He seemed fascinated by her stare, looking into her eyes obediently. "No one. There never was anyone. I just said all those things to Nora . . ."

"Why? Why did you say them?"

Now he broke from her gaze. "I don't know, I'm not sure."

"Yes, you are. You wanted to play with her, torture her, torment her, get even for what your . . ."

He looked back at her calmly. "Is that why I did it? A few sessions with you, I'll be as wholesome as an Annapolis graduate."

"Why did you work at the hotline? To find people worse off than you? But they weren't, were they? They were just poor suckers who happened to turn their rage at other people or circumstances back onto themselves. But your rage, your feelings about your mother; you're too much of a coward. You had to find someone like Nora to fuck with, get back at. Did it do you any good? Make you feel like a big man, making sick, anonymous calls to someone, playing off their grief?"

For a moment, he looked as though he was about to cry, but his eyes had simply taken on a peculiar glint.

"He tried to help you, Lewis. He tried to help you even if he couldn't help himself. And you go after his widow like a pit bull."

"I couldn't help it." His voice was soft and weak.

"I know; you found your mother in a pretty package and there was no stopping you." She went to the door without looking back at him. "So what you're telling me is that after Lewis spent his last hour trying to make you feel better, he killed himself." She opened the door without waiting for an answer. "Good-bye, Mr. Chips. I really hope you find some people to love you."

Chapter Twenty-two

Allen Thompson sat in the spacious kitchen of Nora Howard's home tending to his scrapbooks. He'd long ago stored his own away, but he'd been diligent about commemorating the activities of his employers. Since his absence from the screen, he'd worked for some of the most distinguished people in the industry, staying away from the shooting stars, the flashes-in-the-pan, no matter how dazzling their trajectory, or seductive their offers.

The tragedy of Lewis Rosenthal had affected him deeply. But, happily, things appeared, now, to be working out, and the new turn of events, the TV show, the perfume, were providing fresh fodder for his albums. It was these articles that were claiming Allen's attention when he heard the ringing of the front doorbell. He looked up, trying to remember if there was an expected caller or delivery. It was then he noticed how bad the weather had turned. From his decades in L.A., he sensed it was the sort of downpour that could continue for days, like a seamless gray shroud.

He stood, feeling the weight of his years, and went to the intercom. "Who is it, please?"

"A package from Ms. Howard's studio."

His scrapbooks and thoughts that they spurred still occupied his mind. "Ms. Howard is at the studio."

"Yes, I'm sure," the voice said solicitously, "but I was asked to deliver this here."

"One moment, please." It was not for nothing he'd been an actor. When there were people around, he was able to make a show of being light on his feet, brimming with energy. It was only when he was by himself that he allowed the reality of his old man's body to emerge. And so it was with a sigh and slow shuffling steps that he made his way through the house.

When he'd reached the barred, glass panel of the large wooden door, he peered out and saw the back of a closely cropped blond head. He tapped on the glass and watched the young man turn around. "May I see your I.D.?"

The man smiled and placed a plastic-coated card with a matching grinning image opposite his fingers.

Allen unlatched the door and saw that the young man, who was soaked despite his umbrella, seemed intent on protecting a blue plastic-wrapped package against his body.

"The Devil Squad, 1952," the messenger said.

Allen smiled and lowered his eyes. "That's correct."

"You, and what was her name? The Italian actress, Alida Valli."

"That's remarkable. I can't imagine anyone of your generation remembering us."

"See? Some things are eternal. You look pretty much the same."

"Hardly," Allen said. "Uh, the package, please."

"Oh, God. Sorry. Here." He carefully removed it from beneath the cradle of his arm. "Feels like scripts to me."

"I wouldn't be surprised," Allen said, reaching for the envelope. As his hand went out, the young man raised the package like a shield and rushed toward him, pushing it against Allen's chest, sending him backward onto the floor, as though he were weightless. Then the man stepped over him, kicking Allen's legs aside so he could close the door.

"Oh, sorry about that. I guess I was a little overzealous." The man grinned down at him.

"What are you doing?" Allen asked as the man wedged his foot on his stomach, looking around.

"I'm getting even for all those people you bullied in your old movies. Right now you look to me like an S.S. officer and I'm

part of the American liberating army. Die, Nazi scum, die!" He
raised his foot and kicked Allen's rib cage. "Doesn't this bring
back memories of your glory days?"

Allen drew his legs up to his chest, listening to his own short,
heavy nasal breathes. It *did* remind him of scenes from his old
movies.

"Here, let me help." The young man leaned over, extending
his hand. "Come on. You don't think you can get away with one
take, do you?"

When he didn't respond, Allen felt him pulling at the
bunched fabric of his shirt and coat.

"Get up. The director's not happy with that one."

Allen found himself obeying, pressing his palms against the
marble floor and raising himself. "What are you going to do?"

"Don't be so nosey. We're only into the first reel." He steadied the houseman by grabbing his shoulder padding. "Where do
you usually hang out? In your room? The kitchen? Show me."

Allen gently massaged a pain in his side with his elbow. "I
was in the kitchen."

"Good. Lead the way."

The young man took Allen's right arm and yanked it behind
him, using it to urge him on. Allen felt himself stumbling, weak
and clumsy, very differently from the way he would have done it
for the camera. He led the messenger down a side hall that had
been designed for staff use. His mind drifted in and out of the
situation, remembering moments when he himself had played
the captor. Now the stranger twisted his arm, pulling him back
to reality. The pain made him feel faint and he realized how
unequipped he was to deal with such circumstances anymore.
But for some reason, he was unafraid, trusting the scenario
would play out as it always did; that good would triumph. When
they reached the door to the kitchen, the man yanked him to a
stop.

"Is anyone here?" he whispered in his ear.

The question gave Allen a shot of energy. "What's the matter? Are you afraid the cook will hit you with an avocado?" He
felt his arm being twisted with another jolt of pain. "No one."
He heard the remorse in his voice, then felt himself weakening
again. There was no longer any doubt in his mind that he was
not in a motion picture. The more he began to realize he was in

real danger, the more he felt his mind drifting, curious, expectant, encouraging reality to slip away. Then he felt a sharp blow on the back of his head, as though the director had called, cut.

Chip Walker looked down at the old man, thinking how gross he looked. He remembered him from watching old movies on TV, possibly from Saturday matinees at a local movie house when he was a child. Now the actuality of the icon lay before him, the pinpoints of white stubble on his thick, double chin, his large gut making the bottom of his shirt spill from his pants, his naked head covered with liver spots and small scabs. The man looked like an extra, reduced to playing shabby servants, the last stop on a career that had gone on too long.

Chip stepped over him, into the kitchen, and walked to a work table with clippings spread around a scrapbook. Pictures of Lewis and Nora, separately and together, pictures of Nora and Ben, stared up at him. "Sooner or later you guys were bound to have me over, you know that?" he said aloud. Then he went to the counter, opening drawers, quickly discovering everything he needed to tie the old actor up so he could accomplish what he'd come for.

When Chip re-entered the foyer and began climbing the grandly curved staircase, he sensed how much his exertions harnessing the old man had taken out of him. The realization made him smile in acknowledgment that his days as a juvenile were ending. The doors off the second floor landing were all ajar, making it easy to see which led to the master bedroom. He went to it quickly and entered as though he'd been summoned. With the same sense of conviction, he walked to the side of the bed, picked up the phone, and tapped in a familiar number.

"This is WAYS. My name is Penny. May I help you?" Chip looked at the phone Lewis Rosenthal had once used to cut his deals, nurturing his feeling of irony.

"Hello? Did you want WAYS? Hello?"

"Yes, I do," Chip said in a whisper.

"Can you tell me your name?" The woman's voice was pleasant, almost *too* sociable.

"My name is Allie."

"Hi, Allie. Penny, if you didn't catch it. What made you call us?"

"Is this a test, Penny? To see if I understand acronyms? Why do people usually call?"

"Because they have thoughts about ending their lives."

"Aaaaah. Then I do have the right number."

"Tell me about it, Allie."

"*Tell me about it, Allie.* You sound like a bartender twenty minutes before closing."

"That's good. I'd rather you vent your anger at me than yourself."

"You would? Gosh, I wish everyone felt that way. Be great to be able to vent your anger anytime you want."

"What is it that's making you call?"

"I thought we'd established that; I'm considering taking my life."

"Well, I'm glad you said you're still *considering.* Why?"

"Why? What, considering it, or taking it? I just don't see any reason to live it; how's that for an original thought?" He rubbed his hand along the edge of the bed, wondering if it was the side Nora slept on.

"Has something happened that's made you feel this way?"

"Maybe. Or maybe it's genetic. Maybe I'm programmed to self-destruct at . . ." He groped for an age he wanted to give her.

"How old, Allie?"

Still he hadn't come up with an appropriate answer. "I'm . . ."

"You'd rather not talk about it?"

"I'm twenty-five."

"Good. Now I'm starting to get a picture of you."

"Really? How do you like me so far?"

"It doesn't really matter. I'd prefer you tell me how you feel about yourself."

He looked about at the whiteness of the room. There was a molding circling the walls made to match the frames of the chairs and a chaise longue. "Well, let's say I'm not one of my favorite people."

"Why? Did you do something?"

"Like what?"

"That made you dislike yourself."

"I hope you can take shorthand, Penny." He worked his loafer off and rubbed his foot against the thick white carpet. "I do what I think people expect of me. People think I'm kind of slimy, so that's what I give them."

"What makes you think that's what they expect?"

"That's a good question, Penny. Don't you know how people feel about you? You can read it in their faces, their body language, their inflections." He lowered himself gently onto the pillow. "Of course, when they start throwing eggs and spitting in your face, you're sure."

"Come on, Al, you can't be that bad." Her voice was gracious to the point of being aloof.

"Now, what's that supposed to mean? Some sort of psychological ploy to make me defend myself?"

"Look, I know you're going through a mood now, lots of dark feelings, alienation, loneliness. It can be very powerful. I'd like to help if I can."

He sensed the sincerity in her voice now and wondered if he'd conveyed such a feeling. "I know. The question is, can you?"

"Maybe I can. I'd certainly like to try."

"Wow. I'm telling you I want to kill myself and you sound positively perky."

"Tell me something else, Allie. How do you plan to do it?"

"Pills."

"What kind of pills?"

"Norflex."

"Where did you get them."

"A sick friend. What difference does it make?"

"Do you have them on you now?"

He put his hand against his heart, feeling his empty shirt pocket. "You bet. By the gross. Enough to take half the neighborhood with me."

"What do you mean by that? Is there anyone else involved?"

He looked around the room; so very old Hollywood, he thought. "If there was, I wouldn't be calling you. You're for suicide. That would be murder."

"Has someone driven you to this?"

He surprised himself with abrupt laughter. "Driven me to it? Like making me a fool for love? No such luck."

"Is there someone, whether you love or hate them, behind your feelings?"

He pulled open the drawer of the bedside table, his hand idly playing with the contents. "I suppose so." He found what must have been a wallet belonging to Rosenthal.

"Who is it?"

He unfolded it and stared at a snapshot of Nora leaning over Lewis's shoulder. "Someone who's not very nice."

"Then you know what it is that's bothering you."

"I'd have to say you're right."

"That's good. You can confront your feelings. That's a big first step in working them out."

He closed the wallet and shut it back in the drawer. "You're very good at this, you know? What do you figure your batting average is? How many lives do you save a night? How many do you lose?"

"I'm not prepared to answer that. We don't actually know. Why don't you tell me more about yourself?"

"Like what?"

"Whatever you want to tell me. Preferably the things that led up to your making this call."

He spread his arms and legs out across the bed, as if he were floating. "Water."

"Did you say water?"

"That's it. That's what I said."

"What kind of water?"

"Bathtub water."

"I see."

"You do?" He closed his eyes, pretending he was immersing himself.

"Did you try to drown yourself?"

His laughter shook him out of the reverie. "No, Penny. Frankly, I think that's an awful way to go." He imagined himself underwater, eyes open, something weighing down his feet, his body too weak to struggle. The thought made him shiver. "I'm remembering a rubber ducky."

"Something to do with a child?"

"Yup."

"Whose? Yours?"

"Mine." He said the word softly. "Sort of."

"Are you the child?"

Her directness felt like a slap. "Bingo."

"And you're in a bathtub?"

"Don't forget my rubber ducky." He sat up. "You know, some guys charge a hundred bucks an hour for what you're doing."

She laughed. "I sound like one, don't I, a shrink? Shall we keep going?"

"Why?"

"So maybe you can see your feelings a little clearer. Frankly, I'm happy if we just keep talking."

"I wasn't the only one in the tub."

"You weren't?"

"No. Don't you want to know who was in the tub with me? Besides my rubber duck?"

"I'm sure you'll tell me if you want me to know."

"We played and sang in the tub. Washed each other's backs and sang 'Farmer in the Dell.' " He waited for a response. "Am I boring you already?"

"Not at all. I'm interested. Keep going. How do you relate that memory to how you feel now?"

"Oh, that's easy. Imagine someone's hands all over you. Someone whose hands you don't want on you. Someone you can't stand, touching you and rubbing you and feeling you all over. Then making you do the same to them. Someone you can't say no to, because they're bigger than you are. And they're your. . . ." His eyes had teared and the room appeared blurred. He stood, cradling the receiver between his shoulder and his ear. "This is bullshit. Why am I telling you this?"

"To get it out. Get it out. Get angry at it. Put the blame where it belongs. On whoever did whatever they did to you. Not on yourself." Her voice had become angry. It also seemed clear and honest.

"It's too late."

"No! No, it's not. Don't believe that. Don't. It's not fair; it's not your fault."

"Oh, yes it is. Lots and lots of things are my fault. Which is better? Punishing somebody who has nothing to do with anything or blaming myself?"

"Please. Listen to me. Get rid of the pills. Now. Flush them down a toilet. Don't give yourself any opportunity . . ."

He dropped the receiver on the bed and walked to the sliding door leading to a small balcony. Below it, Nora's pool glittered in the rain. Beyond it, on the sides of the curving hills, dozens of other pools and terraces clung to the landscape in neatly carved-out niches. The winds had come up, whipping palm trees into elegant curves. Everything looked fake, toy-size.

The glass door slid silently, easily, as he pushed it. He moved out to the small landing; it was like standing on the prow of a ship, before him the turbulent sea of Beverly Hills. Lights had gone on in and around the fantasy houses. It looked like a graveyard of power monuments. And now, here he stood among them, the celebrated, the wealthy; he could almost smell the scent of their lust in the wet air. Only he didn't belong, he was faking it, as he had faked his entire life in an effort to please. Only sometimes he had hurt people instead, as if it were the other side of the same coin.

From the small canopy above him, water dripped down on his head. He turned and walked back into the room, leaving the door open, enjoying the cool, damp, menacing breeze it let in.

"Allie? Are you there? Are you near the phone? Can you hear me?" Her voice was calm, even, as if reciting a mantra. "Please pick up the phone if you can hear me, Allie. Allie, if you're listening, please pick up the phone and tell me. I'd like to speak with you some more."

He looked down at the phone, feeling sorry for her. How had he sounded? Had he been as interested, as convincing? Keep them talking, get them over the hump, that was the main thing. You can lose them in a blink, in an unguarded moment. Don't let them make a run for it; the pills, the exhaust fumes, the oven, the gun, the razor blade. Keep them talking, keep them on their feet. Keep them breathing so they can have second thoughts.

Had he done that for Lewis Rosenthal? Had he wanted to? Or had he resented Rosenthal, because he had everything Chip wanted and was ready to throw it away? And why? Because a dildo like Steven Wald had thrown away his marbles. That had

made Chip angry. Didn't he see it was only time out? Where
was Wald now? Even Chip, a nothing, had managed to contrib-
ute to his downfall. Why couldn't Rosenthal have seen that?
What Wald had done to him was no reason to kill himself. It
was stupid and selfish; that's what had angered him. Why he
had finally lost patience. So-o-o-o self-indulgent. It was as
though he'd just been waiting for an excuse.

Had Chip pushed him over the edge by condoning it, encouraging him? That in itself was a kind of power. He looked about
Lewis Rosenthal's bedroom, master suite, with twin dressing
rooms and two bathrooms. Now rain was soaking the carpet
near the open balcony door. The picture perfect world of Hollywood royalty sullied; even more so by his presence.

"Hello, Penny." He spoke softly, breaking her ceaseless flow.

"There you are." She seemed out of breath, grateful. "I was
getting worried. That's good, you're still there. That's good.
You've gotten over the first hurdle, bought yourself time to reconsider. Now, if you like, we can go back and talk about what
you remembered, what came to your mind. . . ."

Abruptly he put the phone down, braking the endless stream
of her exhortation. "So, this is it, Lewis. Two ships that passed
in the long Hollywood night. We've managed to switch places.
I'm here in your bedroom where you belong and you're somewhere whipping about purgatory." He looked out at the cascade
of lights, the rain and smog washing away a sense of time. "I can
feel you, Lewis. It's like we're in the same place in our lives.
Broken beyond repair, no matter what Penny says. Some things
can't be fixed, don't you agree? Obviously you did, because look
where you are, out there, watching.

"I'm glad I got to see where you lived, what your life was like.
Just goes to show you can have it all and it's not enough. You
know what we never learned, Lewis, you and I? That you can't
please everyone all the time. You always wind up hurting someone, usually yourself."

Suddenly he heard the sound of a car below, an engine being
turned off, fragments of voices carrying up to him. For some
reason, he couldn't see any longer, although he seemed to be
incredibly aware of sound, of the rain on the tiled balcony floor,
the wind hissing in the room. He heard the front door opening,
being slammed shut. Then, as if a bolt of lightning was his cue,

he ran toward the open door, through it, going much too fast to stop even if he wanted to, feeling the jab of the railing cut into his stomach, then himself flipping over it, hearing an explosion of thunder, sailing, sailing, feeling the freeing, pleasant, pummeling rain, until there was nothing more to feel.

The rain had been relentless and torrential. The rapidly fluttering windshield wipers on Ben's rented Mercedes allowed only vague gray visibility. He drove slowly, pumping the brakes carefully, cursing and praying for the moment he would be seated in Nora's living room having a scotch. Coleen Copeland sat next to him, her head, covered in a scarf, leaning against the padded headrest.

"Christ, I'll take the fucking snow over this. Doesn't it ever stop?"

"After a couple of houses wash away and a few cars slide down to Santa Monica Boulevard."

The car in front of them stopped short and Ben feathered the brakes, barely touching his bumper. "Why the hell did he do that?" He shook his head and made little pounding motions on the steering wheel.

"Well, at least this weather's a change," she said. "Most of the time this town looks like a painted backdrop."

"Nora's working too hard."

"Can you blame her? They only let you be flavor for a month at a time. Did she say when she'd be home?"

"For dinner."

"For dinner? Hell, that's not bad; I lost husbands for weeks at a time."

"Thanks for being reassuring."

She cracked the window and lit a cigarette. "Tell me, Ben. What Wald told you and Mr. Chips told me; you think there's a grain of truth between them?"

"You believed Walker, didn't you?"

She slapped his thigh. "See? You've been out here too long, answering a question with a question." She rubbed the heel of her hand against the foggy windshield. "Yes, I believed him. There's honor among fakers. He's a pro and I'm as good as they get. He wouldn't dare lie to me."

"Then you're convinced Lewis killed himself?"

She turned to look at him. "What is that supposed to be, some sort of trick question?"

He smiled. "No. How about Wald's theory of Lewis wanting to implicate him?"

"Bullshit. Lewis wouldn't do that." Her eyes lit with a thought. "But he may have had a point."

"Like?"

"Like maybe Lewis wanted Nora to *think* there was someone else there."

"Why?"

"Why? You're the writer, you figure it out."

"You know, there was a moment the other day, I almost began to like Wald."

"Don't. He's a killer. A wounded killer, right now. But wait until he's back in the saddle. He'll be his same old treacherous self. Don't fall for his line of crap." She spoke the words demurely. "Once you thought he killed Lewis. Now he's your buddy." She pushed the scarf off her head and ran her fingers through her hair. "This is a very strange town; it's not like the East," she continued. "Here everyone who's a big player is a goon and the stakes are very high. They take each other out with regularity. Those that fold, get up, brush themselves off, and start over again. It's a game; if you take it seriously, you lose."

Ben turned off the main road and began a series of twisting climbs toward Nora's house. "You don't think Walker did it?"

"I really don't, Ben. He's one twisted puppy, but I don't think he did. The truth is, I felt sorry for him that day."

"Don't. They're all killers. Wounded, right now. But wait until they're back in the saddle."

She laughed as the sky darkened and a clap of thunder detonated above them. Once more, the force of the rain made the wipers almost useless. Ben hunched over the steering wheel, squinting at the pieces of houses revealed behind gates and hedges as the road became steeper. "Why does everything out here seem make-believe?"

"Because it is," she said, touching his cheek gently with the back of her hand.

*   *   *

"Where the fuck are servants when you need them?" Coleen asked, brushing the water from her hair. They stood in the entry hall of Nora's house, as if waiting for someone to respond. "What good is it being a movie star if no one runs out to meet you with an umbrella?" The house was silent except for the rolling thunder outside.

"I think I ought to put the car in the garage."

"Screw it. If we got wet, it can get wet."

Ben peered at it though the open door and decided to agree with her.

"Last one to the bar is a sissy," she said, making some quick adjustments to her hair in the hall mirror, then walking tentatively into the living room. The light was soft and pink, contrasting sharply with the lit pool beyond. Ben walked to the bar, unaware of the water beading down his forehead, and poured for both of them. He joined her at the glass doors, handing her a drink.

"Thanks. Look at that fucking pool," she said suddenly. "It looks black. And the way the rain stabs at it; kind of spooky, don't you think?"

Ben tried to follow her gaze, but could only see his own reflection in the glass. And Coleen's image sliding away from him. "That's real creepy. Listen?" She paused as a low, distant roll of thunder echoed outside. "And look at the palm trees . . ."

He watched the reflection of her face turning up, staring at the fronds being blown together like a clump of feathers.

"Back east, it's nice and scary. This is, like, weird."

He joined her. Now he was able to see the tableau she was talking about. The fading light had taken the dimension from the scene, leaving flat, posterlike outlines. It looked, he thought, like the cover of an old paperback novel.

"Oh, shit," Coleen said in a stage whisper.

"What's the matter?" His mouth touched against her thick waves as he tried to see what she was reacting to.

"Oh my God," she said thoughtfully, "there's someone out there."

"Where?" The more he squinted, the more he lost track of details in the shiny reflections.

"There," she said, pointing to the end of the pool.

He slid the door open, spoiling the serenity of the room with a swish of rain, then stuck his head out. "Where? Show me."

Coleen extended her arm, finding her voice with difficulty to accompany the gesture. "Over there." The sound was thin and flat, as though she were being dubbed.

Ben turned to look at her eyes. They'd taken on a fluorescent quality, their moist surface reflecting the smudges of light around the water. Then he turned back, following the path of her stare, and he saw him. He looked as though he'd taken a badly misjudged dive. The body was splayed almost gracefully three feet from the edge of the pool. But given the strange angle of the head, there was no question that Chip Walker was dead.

Chapter Twenty-three

"Go on, you and Anna May Wong? You gotta be kidding."

"Well, Miss Copeland, I didn't exactly claim . . ."

"Come on, just between us . . ." Coleen squinted into the morning sunlight and poured coffee for herself and the house-man as they sat beside Nora's pool.

"You'll just have to read my memoirs to find out," he said, his old man's face stretched into a naughty grin.

Coleen grinned back. "You know, my friend, you have marvelous recuperative powers."

He put his hand to a small bandage at the base of his skull.

"Well, you see, in the old days, they taught you how to fall, how to let yourself go limp. It was all part of learning sword-play, jumping on and falling off horses, that sort of thing. Believe me, I've done far more difficult scenes."

She gave him a doubting look. "He hurt you, didn't he, the scumbag?"

"I really don't remember. My consciousness had the good grace to slip away. When I woke, a young police officer was hovering and two interns worrying over me. Apparently I required nothing more than two aspirins."

Coleen faked a hook to his chin. "I guess playing thugs all your life toughens you up."

"Yes, and looking after the rich and famous makes you even tougher."

They both laughed, then she shook her head. "Not me. There we were, Ben and me, just about to usher in the cocktail hour, real cozylike in all that lightning, and I see Walker sprawled out like a kite." She turned her head to look at the spot where she'd seen him. "Right away I got nauseous. Then we run around the house looking for you and there you are trussed up like a giant turkey, if you'll excuse the expression. I thought I was going to have a heart attack. I couldn't remember if you're supposed to call nine-one-one or one-nine-nine." She rolled her eyes. "What is it with us thespian types? While Ben was calling, I fell right into playing a scene, like we were on the front lines and you were some sort of fallen soldier and I was a demented Florence Nightingale." She looked at him conspiratorially. "You know, for two old actors who haven't worked in some time, I think we did pretty good."

He put his hand to his wound again. "A bit too method for me, I'm afraid." He cocked his head to listen to something. "I believe Miss Howard and Mr. Bradford are coming." He stood, removing his cup and saucer from the table.

Before he could slip away, Nora went to him. "Are you sure you should be up and about?"

"Oh yes, Miss Howard. Energy breeds energy. Besides, Miss Copeland is very restorative. Talking to her is like spending a month in the country."

"Yeah, endless and boring," Coleen boomed.

"You sure you're okay?" Nora touched his arm.

"Listen, it could have been worse," Coleen interrupted. "I could have been in the pool skinny dipping and Mr. Chips could have swan dived on top of me." She hesitated. "Could you see that picture in the tabloids?"

"It probably wouldn't be a bad idea to take the day off," Ben said to the ex-actor confidentially.

"Lucky bastard, gets to watch the soaps all afternoon," Coleen said as Allen smiled and walked into the house.

Ben poured coffee for himself and Nora and sat next to the two women. The sun was energizing the azure pool water, etching its ripples in stark chiaroscuro, bleaching out the memory of what had happened. Suddenly Coleen's voice cut though the coddling serenity of the moment.

"Well, my dears, it's time to put Lewis to rest. Against my

better judgment, I've flown three thousand miles to stick my nose in places it didn't belong and I'm going to tell you what I think before I stick it back on a plane and resume my hibernation in Partridgefield."

Nora looked away, as though distracted by a distant sound, but Ben's smiling nod urged her to continue.

"You think Mr. Chips took Lewis's secrets with him? Like hell. I don't need a Chip to know what happened." She pounded her chest. "I know. Nora, what the hell do we do for a living? What do you think Ben does? We are lightning rods for truth. We catch it in the air and shoot it back at people. We show them what's real, their deep-down parts. And when we're really good, at our best, they say, holy shit! You mean I'm not alone? Other people feel that, too? That's why they come. To make contact. To find out they're not isolated.

"I came here to know what happened to Lewis. And I do." She raised her head triumphantly, looking as though she were sculpted of granite. "Ben and I put it together."

Nora made a small struggling sound, which Coleen responded to by speaking softly. "Please, hon, hear us out." She looked at her sweetly, resigned, and Coleen continued. "He was like a viola. Big and a little unwieldy, but such a sweet sound. He had a special radar for people, always conscious of what might hurt them, distract them, put them on track. I saw it when we were casting what's-its-face, *Dario's Revenge.* Even when you knew from the second some kids opened their mouth that they were wrong, or maybe not even much good, he gave them their moment. And then he thanked them. So they walked out with their pride intact. Left them something they could leverage the next time they had to get it up." Coleen felt the heat building in the air and scowled at the sun, remembering why she hated warm climates. "If he felt so much for these strangers, can you imagine what he felt for you? What it did to him when he fucked up? We all have a cut-off of vulnerability. We can take so much and no more. Most of us never reach it, thank God, but we come close. When the next rejection, the next hour of loneliness, the next catastrophe can spit us over the edge."

She wrinkled her nose. "Lewis decided to check out. But he had one big problem. You." She looked at Nora defiantly. "He didn't want you to feel in any way, shape, or form responsible."

She leaned over and rubbed Nora's shoulder. Her grin was tinged with sadness. "That tape, I'll bet you anything he made it *before* he went to the motel room. He had to have staged it himself. To make it sound like someone, some mysterious, ominous person was there, an enemy who'd come to get him. Anything, just as long as you didn't feel responsible. He called Wald, I think, as a final desperate effort to patch together a deal, which would have given him an out. But it didn't happen." She sighed slightly. "Then he made sure someone, the night manager or the police or whoever, found the tape." Coleen looked up. Mercifully the sun went behind some baby-cheeked clouds. She looked at Ben expectantly, encouraging him with her eyes.

He continued in a monotone. "Lewis couldn't go to you, Nora. You were the one he was protecting. The one he felt he harmed. All he could do was try to save face. Even if that meant giving up what he cared about most."

Nora looked at them calmly. "But why that motel?"

Coleen grinned. "Where better to meet your assassin? Lewis was raised on the same diet of films as Allen and myself. The Paradiso is exactly the sort of place you'd be lured to by some evil party. It appealed to his producer-imagination." She seemed pleased with the thought. "Show business up to the end."

Nora nodded, understanding. "He used to worry about his enemies; that he'd been too hard on them. Hurt them. People like Lewis, who worry so much about how others feel, do it because they're so fragile themselves."

Coleen scowled. "What was he afraid of? Being caught with his fame down? Worried about not bringing home a gold star?" She looked from Ben to Nora stymied. "Is it worth it?" she asked simply. "Is it? What does it all amount to? People staring at you when you walk into a restaurant? Guys kissing your ass over an expensive lunch when you'd rather be having a hamburger by yourself? Bold type in a column some dog pees on the next day?"

"I think it meant a little more to Lewis," Nora said kindly. "It entitled him to come to the party. To smile at people and be their friend. It enabled him to help people. He used his celebrity very gracefully. And when he was afraid he'd lost it, he felt like the invisible man when they unwrapped the bandages."

Coleen looked up at the sky and squinted into the sun. "What a shitty business life is. People either kill themselves trying to make it or die when it doesn't turn out as they expected. They should put up a sign when you enter Hollywood: 'Careful. You might find it here.'"

Coleen watched the tops of Nora's palms being pushed into disheveled plumes. "Here come the famous Santa Ana winds. What do you say I make us a pitcher of bloody marys and we toast all the survivors?"

That night Nora dreamed about Lewis and Tony Newland. They were walking together in a grove of tall pines, the sun cutting through a sieve of branches, creating a slanting pattern around them. Lewis was doing most of the talking and Tony was nodding appreciatively.

Mist moved about their feet and Lewis had affected a walking stick that seemed to pole through the fog like a gondolier's oar. When they came to a small clearing, Tony stopped and pointed. Lewis responded with a searching look, then stared solemnly in the direction the actor had indicated. Nora knew it was the place Tony had died.

In the dream, she could see their faces clearly. There was a sweetness about them. Their skin was luminous, contrasting with their eyes, which were blank. Both lacked expression as they turned to look at her.

Their mouths opened in recognition, Lewis immediately extending his hands to her face, meaning desperately trying to come through the empty eyes. Tony's head moved up and down in a craning motion. His hands moved to his heart, then out to her.

Seconds later, she felt herself disappearing, although she could still see them. They returned to their conversation, walking rapidly into the woods to be swallowed by the fog.

She tried to call after them, thinking that she had something to tell them. But they were gone in the sullen gray mist that had replaced the blades of sun. Then suddenly she heard the roar of an engine and Wald's black Porsche drove wildly through the forest, Chip Walker at the wheel. He stared at her and grinned with the demented look of a ventriloquist's dummy. She watched as the car careened through the woodland, wildly skirting the tree trunks then retreating into the fog, worried that he was going after Lewis and Tony. Seconds later she heard an explosion, followed by a pink smudge of light in the distance.

Then she heard Lewis speak to her, his voice against her ear. "Don't be afraid, my Nora, there is plenty of time. I will be here for you." A warmth took her and she felt herself struggling not to wake.

Ben listened as a series of small, startled sounds interrupted Nora's sleep. The pale yellow light had begun to sculpt the sharply delineated planes of her face, her unadorned eyes twitching slightly at whatever she was dreaming. Her skin was drawn taut and soft pink over the familiar features.

"You're up?" she asked, surprising him. He snuggled his nose in her neck, tasting the salty residue of her sleep.

"Hmmnn," he muttered against her flesh.

"Should *I* be?" The sleep in her voice indicated the decision hadn't been made.

"You don't have to."

She pushed her face into the pillow. "That's nice."

"But while I've got you . . ."

She smiled and rolled toward him, lifting her arm and placing it behind his neck. "Yes?"

"May I be my boring honest self a moment?"

"Yes," she said with apprehension.

"You know what I've decided?"

She shook her head, making herself more awake in the process.

"Don't take this wrong, but what's nice about us, is that we didn't start off with a bang."

"A thud?"

He continued without looking at her. "This way it doesn't burn itself out."

"What doesn't burn itself out?" She brushed the tip of his nose with her finger.

The question made him blush. "The mushy stuff."

"Does the mushy stuff have a name?"

"Oh, come on, you're not going to make me say it. . . ."

"Say what?" She moved her fingers over his face as though she were sightless.

"The *l* word."

"Which one, I don't get it?"

"Lo . . . lo . . ." He pretended to force the sound out, his tongue stuck to the roof of his mouth.

"Oh, you don't mean *love,* do you?"

He nodded as he extended his arm and leg over her and began kissing her ear.

"Let's play charades," she said quietly. "Do you want to go first or should I?"

"Why don't you go first?"

"All right. This is a four-letter word." She pushed herself up over him, her tumbling hair forming a frame around her face.

It had not ceased to amaze him that at moments like this she looked exactly like a close-up from one of her movies. "Four letters; that's a lot of choices. Let's see what a good actress you are."

"All right, smartass. Let's see you turn me into this vision."

Coleen sat in Danny's salon, squaring off with her image in the mirror, his head and raised scissors peering over her shoulder. He appeared lost in elaborate deliberations as he stroked her wet hair out to its maximum length.

"It may not feel like much, but at least there's a hell of a lot of it," she commented. "No mean feat, but you're going to make me gorgeous so I can get on the goddamn plane looking like a fucking movie star. I will drink for five solid hours and still arrive in Partridgefield looking like a dream. Then I will parade around town with the 'do' you're going to give me and watch their jaws drop.

"After that, I will turn back into the frump I was when I came out here and not worry about it one iota. So think of what you're about to do as art for art's sake."

He threaded her hair through his fingers, snipping at it with tiny scissors. "This whole little number with Lewis and Wald and Chip Walker is, like, incredible. I mean, like, fabulous. It's, like, the man kills himself and everyone's knocking into everyone to point a finger." He put his lips next to her ear. "Well, the truth is, *I* did it. Self-defense. I spurned him and he was out to get me."

She bumped her damp head against his. "Sure. And if frogs could fly, they wouldn't land on their ass." She sat back and he resumed his small snips.

"Come on, you must have inside dish about Lewis."

She caught his eye in the mirror. "Well, I hear he was a great fuck."

"Please, Miss Copeland, you're making me blush," he said. "Was he really? I mean, what makes a great fuck? I'd love to learn."

She arched an eyebrow. "Well, I've only known three or four in my lifetime. But from the looks of you, I wouldn't be too optimistic."

Small shards of hair fell on the towel he'd placed around her shoulders. "Too good looking, right? Great fucks are usually toads like Lewis. Compensating. The beauties sort of just lie there and let you look at them."

"It's something you're born with, so why don't you forget it?" They both turned at a shriek from across the floor. "I give Ben and Nora six months and they'll be clamoring to go back east."

"Oh, really? You're very sure of that? Not if the series is a hit. You know what success is like out here? You're Cinderella and the clock never strikes twelve. The greats and near greats are constantly asking you to dance and all the rest are your footmen. And with each passing day your coach gets bigger and more elaborate."

"Then comes pumpkin time and they don't waste a second slicing it up."

He shrugged. "So what are you going to do back in Partridgeville?"

"Fade. Decline. Some people do it gracefully; I rushed into it. I just wanted to get it over with. I've had absolutely no remorse about becoming a harridan. It suits me. I feel comfortable with it."

He stopped and stared at her in the mirror. "Why don't you act again? I mean, like, you're amazing. Out here, it's all angles and how the camera treats you. But what you do, that's another language. It's, like, important. Why stop?"

She beamed at him mischievously. "Because I was ahead.

And I want fools like you to remember me that way. I mean, I'm doing it for you, staying out of the limelight. How would you like me to come back and destroy all those illusions you have about me? They're very tricky things, illusions. You bring them out on the wrong day, the wrong year, and they just don't look the same. No, I'm content to be a frump, a curmudgeon, and sit on my laurels."

He resumed his snipping, but at a slower pace. "Wald's going east, I hear. Broadway. He said to a friend of a friend of a friend that's he's found this *powerful* play. That was his word, powerful, and he's going to do it on Broadway. Produce it."

Suddenly Coleen began to follow his ministrations, tilting her head to determine his effects.

"You've still got the bones, honey," he said to her.

"Bullshit. I never had bones. What I had was talent. And balls. Which, if you want the truth, is often not enough. You've got to do politics, too."

"You make it sound like why bother. There must be something to it, success, fame, riches; everybody wants it."

"Of course. Because they can't have it. They don't have the strength or the stomach. But if they did, and got it, they'd see it's all crap. Here today and gone tomorrow. Or gone today and here tomorrow."

"Oo-oo-oow." He sounded as if he'd burned himself. "Now you're getting real depressing."

"See what happens when someone lets you do her hair for nothing?"

He put the point of the scissors against his lips and pantomimed thinking. "I honestly think it helps being a ditz. I mean, it gets you through a lot of stuff. Life simply wafts about you, like smoke. Sometimes people buy your act, sometimes not. But whatever, ditzes are cool. They don't count on anything too much. And nobody expects too much; it's not a bad place to be."

"And you don't think I qualify as a ditz?"

He shook his head sternly. "Sorry, no. You've got, like, genius and you're stuck with it. And Nora's doomed to be admired. And Ben's fate is to be serious. Honey, that's like the worst." He looked in the mirror and scowled. "Now, where was I?" He